RIGHT AS RAINE

AN ASTER VALLEY NOVEL

LUCY LENNOX

Cover Art: Natasha Snow Designs

Cover Photo: Wander Aguiar

Editing: One Love Editing

Proofreading: Victoria Rothenberg

Beta Reading: Leslie Copeland, May Archer, Shay Haude.

KEEP IN TOUCH WITH LUCY!

Join Lucy's Lair
Get Lucy's New Release Alerts
Like Lucy on Facebook
Follow Lucy on BookBub
Follow Lucy on Amazon
Follow Lucy on Instagram
Follow Lucy on Pinterest

Other books by Lucy:
Made Marian Series
Forever Wilde Series
Aster Valley Series
Twist of Fate Series with Sloane Kennedy
After Oscar Series with Molly Maddox
Licking Thicket Series with May Archer
Virgin Flyer
Say You'll Be Nine

Visit Lucy's website at www.LucyLennox.com for a comprehensive list of titles, audio samples, freebies, suggested reading order, and more!

AUTHOR NOTE

Thank you to my husband for trying to help me make the football details as accurate as possible. Despite being a Falcons fan for almost twenty years, I don't have a head for the game. I'm sure I've made mistakes, and I promise you they're all mine.

I made up a fictional Houston football team named the Riggers, so let's just pretend the Texans don't exist. M'kay? Thanks.

Thank you to my older sister who is a physical therapist and who consulted with me on some of the injuries described in the novel. In this story you will meet an OT who is sometimes referred to as a PT. I included this in the story because it is a common mistake, but I wanted to clarify that there is a difference between the two. (For more information about the OT in this story, check out the novella *Winter Waites*.)

Finally, thank you for picking up this book. With so many amazing stories out there, I know it's often hard to choose. I hope you find the following story worth your precious reading time. Enjoy!

PROLOGUE

TILLER

"Raine!" Coach V.'s bark was as familiar to me as the sound of the crowd cheering on a Friday night or Saturday afternoon. The problem was, this time the sound was muffled by thousands of gallons of blood rushing through my ears. I could have sworn I felt my heartbeat in my brain.

"I'm fine, Coach," I mumbled. Only, it sounded like "Mah fo" for some reason.

"Like hell you are. Q-bie! Get your ass over here with the med kit and some glucose. Raine's bonked. Again."

I wasn't sure *bonked* was a term used in football, even at the pro level. But then again, I was a rookie. What the hell did I know?

I turned on my side and dry-heaved. Coach Vining squatted down a safe enough distance away to avoid any vomit, but close enough he only needed to hiss for me to hear him. "This ain't peewee league no more. Your coach told me you had a problem forgetting to eat. Remember we had a little conversation about it when I recruited your sorry ass?"

I tried to say, "Yes, Coach," but it came out as more dry-heaves.

"So we had a conversation, you and me. And I told you to get your nutrition in order. Hell, I even suggested you hire a professional meal service or some shit. You remember what you said?"

I coughed and rolled back to my back. The scorching heat of the turf against my sweaty jersey was reassuring. It meant I was alive and still in Houston busting my ass for the Riggers. Playing for the NFL was a dream come true, but right about now I would have given my left nut for a different dream.

"I said I'd handle it, Coach."

"Damned right you did. You said you'd handle it. And here we are only four games into regular season and you've passed out three times already from low blood sugar. What the hell you eating, son?"

He didn't give me time to answer before he continued.

"Whatever it is, it ain't enough. Pro ballers have to eat a minimum of four thousand calories per day. You know this. And if you don't, you're even more of a dumb shit than I already thought. So here's what we're gonna do. One of my boys has some kind of nutrition degree and knows how to cook healthy. You're going to find someone like that who knows what's what and hire them to keep your body fueled like a goddamned pro baller. You got me?"

I thought of his four grown sons. One had played football for Alabama, one for Clemson, one for UT, and the other had wrestled for A&M. They were hard workers, and all had big, muscled bodies. Hell, one of them currently played for the Bengals. If Coach wanted me to consult one of them for nutrition help, I would do it.

"Richie?" I asked, thinking of the wrestler. He probably had the most experience in managing his nutrition, but he was a mean fucker —always spouting off about fairness but only when it cut against him.

"Nah. My youngest. You met Mikey at the WAGs dinner before preseason."

Fuckin' A, I'd forgotten. Coach had a fifth boy. A little runt of a guy with nerdy glasses and dark, messy hair. He was the opposite of a ballplayer. The kid had looked like he'd been plucked out of a riveting lecture on the periodic table to come to the friends-and-family thing.

"Mikey," I said stupidly. "He's a chef?"

Coach shrugged. "Nah. He's a gopher. I only said find someone like him who knows about nutrition and cooking for athletes. Not him, though. He works for Bruce as an errand boy. Someone *like* him. You got me?"

Q-bie had come racing back from the sidelines and was busy sticking me with an IV to push his magic fluid. Within a few moments, I was well enough to sit up.

"I don't need a chef," I muttered. "I need a bodyguard to keep the media away from me."

I was the first out player in the NFL who'd made the starting lineup. Since I'd been out since high school, there'd been no way of putting that Genie back in the box, even if I'd wanted to. Which I hadn't. The Riggers had known I was gay when they'd recruited me, but my stats made me downright irresistible. If they hadn't drafted me, someone else would have. I was a Heisman winner, and that trumped sucking dick any day of the week.

Coach narrowed his eyes at me. "Then get you one of them, too. Just fucking get your shit together, rookie. And remember what I told you about earlier. This ain't the time for any of that crap. No dating. Just football. A lot of us are counting on you. Understand? We need you to stay focused."

The reminder wasn't necessary. Football was everything, and I had no plans to fuck it up with any kind of media attention if I could help it. My goal was to lie low and concentrate on being the best damned wide receiver in the league. As my dad always said, "The rest of it can wait. Football can't. You're only in prime shape for a small window of time. Make it count."

So that was my objective. Avoid any media attention that was unrelated to my skill on the field. Keep my head in the game. Save the dating and relationship stuff for later. My position playing on the starting lineup for the Riggers was still unbelievable to me, and I was going to bust my ass to prove I was worth the time and money this man and the Rigger franchise had chosen to invest in me.

"Yes, sir."

He stood up and wandered off, muttering under his breath about rookie idiots. When he got a few feet away, he turned back. "Might as well have Bryant and D'Angelo come over and eat some healthy shit too when you find someone to cook for you. Those guys don't know their ass from a complex carbohydrate."

With another nod, he turned and strode toward the fumble drill happening on the other side of the field. "Tighten up, Butterfingers!" he yelled to Jamal Johnson, a three-time Super Bowl–winning running back. The man almost never gave up a fumble, so it was kind of funny to see him called Butterfingers in practice.

I closed my eyes and groaned. I'd been an NFL player for only a couple of months and I was already fucking up. Hopefully this Mikey kid could recommend someone. And if he couldn't do that, at least asking him for help would convince Coach I tried.

I'd do just about anything to keep Coach Vining happy and convince my teammates, the fans, and the league that football was my number one priority. My *only* priority.

PROLOGUE
MIKEY

"I got a player needs a chef," Coach—because god forbid we be allowed to call him Dad—said across the dinner table.

My ears perked up for a split second before I remembered my new rule. Never, ever work for another one of my dad's players. Ever.

Coach eyed me as he shoveled in a forkfull of the veggie lasagne I'd made. The man probably hadn't noticed it didn't have meat in it. I'd been sneaking vegetarian meals into my family's dinner rotation for years. The only one who noticed was my mom, who appreciated eating "lighter" from time to time.

"Not you, obviously," he mumbled as he ate. I looked away. "Someone you know. From school maybe."

"I don't know anyone looking for a job right now." Except for myself, of course. I didn't intend to sound so petulant, but it was true. Besides, working for a pro baller was a pain in the ass. Most of them were used to being treated like prima donnas. However, the money had been amazing...

I sighed and sent another silent apology to my bank account for losing our sweet gig with Nelson Evangelista. Even though I currently had a temporary job as a stand-in personal assistant for the owner of the Riggers while he looked for someone more permanent, I'd never again have as sweet a deal as I had living and working with Nelson.

"Be a team player, son," he said with his mouth full.

"I'm not one of your players," I reminded him for the millionth time.

"He needs a professional. Someone who knows nutrition. The man needs to learn how to fuel his body. Surely you know someone."

I took a long swallow of ice water. "His manager should be able to help him find a personal chef."

Coach shoveled in another bite as my mom made a sound of interest. Then he continued as if I hadn't said anything. "The kid keeps passing out. He's not eating enough, or he's eating junk. Hell, I have no idea. But it's clear no one ever taught him how to eat like a performance athlete."

I cringed at the idea of any young, healthy pro athlete trying to fuel their body with crap. Poor kid.

I'd had to move home after Nelson had cut me loose. He'd decided to give his new girlfriend the job of being his live-in personal assistant. I wondered how that was going. If Miss Gulf Coast could navigate her way around an Excel spreadsheet, I'd eat my shoe.

Not really. But I'd eat trans fats, and that was pretty much the same thing.

"I'd volunteer to help him out, but I'm not interested in working for another player," I said, lying through my teeth. In fact, I'd loved living in Nelson's multimillion-dollar home with its amazing gourmet kitchen. That kitchen had been a dream come true for a wannabe chef like me. And having my own suite of rooms far away from Nelson's own living space had been amazing—far better than any kind of apartment I could have afforded.

Until I'd moved my shit into his bedroom. But that was a subject for another time. And by "another time," I meant never.

Although, I couldn't deny how nice it had been not to pay rent for those two years. I'd socked money away like crazy, saving for the cafe I wanted to open one day. Now that I remembered the feeling, I was almost tempted to find out more about becoming a full-time personal chef. But how much money would make it worth dealing one-on-one with another spoiled, entitled ballplayer? At least it would be an opportunity to actually work in my field instead of doing these PA gigs.

"Nobody's asking you," my father growled at me with a pointed stare. "You working for Nelson was clearly a recipe for fucking disaster."

It turns out, you can be a grown-ass adult and still be cowed by your parents. My jaw clenched against the words begging to spew out. Words about parenting ultimatums needing to die a quick death before the child in question turned twenty-four fucking years old. I fought against the desire to go to work for his player just to prove my father wrong.

"Who is it?" I asked instead, knowing I was tipping my hand. It had to be a rookie if he was having trouble keeping up with the demands of his job. And rookies were total assholes.

"Raine. Wide receiver from University of Colorado."

My stomach swooped. Tiller Raine. Tiller Raine who'd won the Heisman. Who'd been on the cover of magazines. Who'd made my father strut around like a jackass for months bragging about his first-round draft pick. Who was currently, albeit secretly, saved into my Favorites photo album in a screenshot from an ad for Under Armour. In the ad he was wearing nothing but compression shorts with a giant, NFL-sized bulge in the middle.

But I'd cropped his face out of the photo because his expression said he knew exactly how fucking beautiful he was. Cocky asshole. I'd met him once at a cookout thing my father had forced me to. Raine had looked right through me like I'd been a hologram. If I couldn't do anything for him, I didn't matter to him. It was behavior I'd seen time and time again over the years from my brothers' jock friends and my dad's jock players, including Nelson Evangelista.

"Extra no," I said firmly.

Mom reached over and squeezed my hand. "But honey, he's so good-looking. And he's *gay*."

The last part was whispered because even after my being out for over a decade, my family still had a hard time with it in some ways. I'd actually been impressed with my dad recruiting an out player— even now, no one knew about Nelson—until I'd heard him brag about Raine's stats to one of his other coaches. Coach had sounded prouder of Tiller Raine than he'd even been of my brothers, who'd all been successful athletes themselves.

Hell, even my brother Jake played pro ball for the Bengals. But he was no Tiller Raine.

My father blustered. "Don't matter if the man's gay, Loretta. Ain't nothing happening between these two. Mikey will stay away from Tiller Raine. I only wanted you to help find him a goddamned personal chef! Forget I said anything. Jesus."

"His sexuality has nothing to do with anything anyway," I said peevishly. "Even if I did take the job, it's not like I'm going to sleep with my boss for god's sake." The "again" was left unspoken since my mom presumably didn't know about my stupid slipup with Nelson.

"Damned right you're not," Coach said in his most blistering voice, the scary-as-fuck one that made grown men cry.

I tried not to roll my eyes and remind him I'd said it first. "It doesn't matter. I'm not doing it."

Coach banged his fist on the table. "*No one asked you to!*"

"Good," I said, trying not to cry at the lost money. It couldn't be worth dealing with a cocky rookie like Raine. "Then there's no issue."

My mom frowned. "Didn't he buy Dougie Crenshaw's house?"

I thought of the kicker who'd retired and moved to Florida last year. He was a total sweetheart. He'd been on the team for years and years. Hell, the man had practically been around during my entire childhood. I'd been to his house a million times. I fucking *loved* his house. And my mom got to the most important part before I could even put it into words.

"Yes," she said, answering her own question. "The one with that big commercial kitchen. Dougie's wife, Kate, liked to throw parties, and she had a catering team come in all the time. Remember?"

"Are you sure Raine bought Dougie's house?" I asked, imagining cooking in that incredible facility. There was a giant picture window with a view of a lake on the golf course with a little bridge over it and fountains in the water. Not only that, but there was a comfortable sitting area in the kitchen that I'd always snuck away to during the Crenshaw's parties. I'd curl up in one of the overstuffed chairs and watch the caterers bustle around with trays of canapés while the chef worked his magic at the stove and barked orders to his sous chefs.

"I'm sure," Coach said around another bite of food. "Had to pick him up on the way to practice the other day because his car wouldn't start."

I pictured all the rookie players and their hundred-thousand-dollar sports cars and jacked-up SUVs. "His car wouldn't start?"

He scoffed. "Good ole boy refuses to replace the pickup his granddad gave him when he was in high school. I'm surprised that piece of shit can pass inspection, much less start on a regular basis. I told him he'd better at least buy some kind of backup for the days his junker throws fits."

My mother started talking about her Tesla and how he should get one of those for the drive to and from practice. I tuned them out as I scrolled through the mental list of friends I had who might be interested in and capable of this job.

I still came up empty.

"What if, until he finds someone, I use his kitchen while he's at work and leave the food for when he gets home," I said. "I wouldn't even need to see him."

As the idea fleshed out in my head, I continued thinking out loud. "In fact, if I used that kitchen, I could offer a healthy meal service to all of your players and deliver them to the practice facility. Maybe I could turn it into a catering side business."

Mom's face lit up. "Honey, what a wonderful idea."

Coach still looked annoyed. "No. Besides, you already have a job. Bruce counts on you."

He was right. And I actually liked Bruce. Working for him was easy, and running errands meant getting out of the office and into the

Houston sunshine. I hated the heat but craved the sun. Being stuck in a dark office was my biggest fear, and I couldn't even imagine sitting at a desk all day.

Being Bruce Lester's temporary yes-man was the perfect way to keep money coming in while I found the right permanent job. Ultimately, my dream was to open a cafe, but I still needed both more cooking and some small-business management experience before I would feel confident going out on my own.

"By the way," I said, happy to change the subject, "Bruce asked me to arrange for lunch for the management meeting tomorrow. Will you be there? If not, I can bring some food to your office. It's nothing fancy. I'm making grilled chicken and the pasta salad you like."

Coach nodded and said he'd be in the meeting. Mom smiled at the news and offered to help. "I'm happy to be your co-pilot, dear. We can get started prepping after dinner."

I returned her smile. My mother was well-meaning but flighty. I'd tried to teach her the phrase *sous chef* many times, but it never stuck. "That would be great. Maybe we can make some extra to take next door since Mrs. Nibert is still recovering from her knee surgery."

Mom tittered happily at my offer and began regaling us with neighborhood gossip. For once, the topic of conversation around the table was no longer about Coach's cocky players, the Riggers, or football in general.

The following day was jam-packed. I got up early to finish prepping and packing the lunches and made it to the practice facility just in time to help Bruce's secretary, Greta, handle a group of unexpected VIP visitors who wanted a last-minute tour. After showing them around and returning to serve lunch, I thought things would slow down enough for me to catch my breath.

But then Bruce called me into his office after the meeting, and I caught sight of Tiller Raine.

No gay man on earth could catch his breath when faced with this guy.

"Mikey, have you met our newest wide receiver yet? This is Tiller Raine. Tiller, Michael Vining, Coach V.'s youngest boy."

I stared at the wide receiver like I'd never seen a famous pro football player before, which was pretty funny considering I'd been around them practically my whole life and usually didn't give a shit one way or the other.

But this guy? I gulped. This guy was freaking gorgeous. Like... melt your feet to the floor and make you beg beautiful. His body was muscled perfection, and his messy golden-brown hair made me immediately wonder what he looked like freshly fucked.

I swallowed again, wondering if I needed a saliva gland checkup since mine seemed to be malfunctioning.

"H-hi?" I managed to say.

Tiller nodded and held out his hand for a shake. His reaction was all business, and his face was impossible to read. "Nice to meet you."

I reached for his giant paw hesitantly. Wide receivers were known for big hands and strong grips. But when Tiller's hand clasped mine, it was gentle and kind. I stared down at our joined hands and wondered how much these hands were insured for. Incidentally, I wondered how much I'd have to pay him to keep his gentle, warm hand in mine.

I jerked my hand back and hid it behind my back. "Can... can I help you with something, Mr. Lester?"

Bruce raised his eyebrows at my formal language. He'd known me since I was a preteen, and I'd called him by his first name since I graduated high school. "Mikey, you okay?"

No. No, I was not. I shook my head to clear it from the ridiculous baller-induced brain fog and focused back on my boss. "Yes, sir. *Bruce.* How can I help?"

"Markus Harris reached out to me in hopes of getting some help finding a personal chef for Tiller, here. I remembered this was an area of expertise for you, so I hoped you might be able to help us."

It wasn't until that moment, I realized there was another man in the room. Markus Harris was a well-known sports agent who represented several of the Riggers, so I'd come across him several times in the past few years.

He didn't like me for some reason, which meant I avoided him like the plague. I was disappointed to realize Tiller was one of his clients.

I nodded at Markus, cleared my throat, and looked back at Bruce. "I spoke to Coach about it last night. I can't think of anyone who would be a good fit. I'm sorry. You might—"

Just as I was preparing to suggest he reach out to the department at UT to inquire about recent grads looking for work, he held up a hand to stop me.

"You misunderstand," Bruce said with a kind smile. "I was hoping you might help him directly. Greta has found a permanent PA for me, so I thought this would be a great way for you to stay employed while you're continuing your job search. You can cook for Tiller through the season and start any new position afterward. That way he gets help learning how to manage his diet, and you have the freedom to continue your search without feeling rushed. What do you say?"

Every square inch of my body began to sweat at once.

"Oh." I could have really used some of that saliva right about now. My throat clicked as I tried to swallow again. "Oh."

Out of the corner of my eye, I saw Tiller's full mouth turn down briefly. I closed my eyes and tried not to notice him. Reason number one, this would never work.

"It's just that..." I began. I didn't have anything else to say, really, but I'd never been one to abide awkward silence.

Markus eyed me from his spot on a nearby chair. "Didn't you work for Nelson Evangelista?"

"Yes, but—"

"Then you already know the demands of a professional ballplayer's career and schedule," he interjected. "You're familiar with the demands of confidentiality. In fact, I assume you already have an NDA on file with the league as you are Coach Vining's son."

"Of course, but—"

His smile was sharklike. "Then it's settled. The sooner Tiller can get this sorted out, the better. You can move into the apartment over the garage and start tomorrow."

My heart thundered as I remembered my dad's fist banging on the table last night. "I don't think Coach would—"

Bruce offered me another familial smile. "Don't you worry about Coach. I'll handle him. Besides, it was his idea Tiller get a personal chef in the first place."

I snuck a glance at Tiller, who was standing next to me looking as shell-shocked as I was.

"But..." I tried again.

Markus let out an impatient sigh. "Whatever Evangelista was paying you, we'll double it and include room and board if you're willing to use the apartment. Especially if you also agree to take on some PA duties. So long as you're using his kitchen, you may as well manage the household as well."

Suddenly, the vision of my own little cafe became a little clearer. Nelson had paid me an outrageous sum to be his personal assistant. Even if I only spent the next six months working at twice the rate, I'd save up a ton of money and get the hell out of my parents' house.

"And the garage apartment is completely separate?" I asked, clarifying that this would not exactly be a live-in situation like before.

Tiller nodded. "I'm not looking for live-in help, but you're welcome to the apartment. There is a back entrance to the kitchen, so you can use it without coming into the rest of the house."

He said it in a way that implied I was somehow interested in getting all up in his personal business. "I know the house," I snapped. "I've been there many times."

Tiller's eyes widened in surprise. "Good, then you won't need my help getting settled," he gritted out.

As if, I wanted to hiss. Instead, I turned back to Bruce. "And it's just for the rest of the season?"

Markus was the one who answered. "Definitely. In the meantime,

I'll look for someone more permanent for Mr. Raine during the off-season so you can be on your merry way."

I didn't bother looking at him. "Fine."

Bruce chuckled lightly under his breath. "Mikey, you're your father's son. Fiery and forthright. Can't hide your real feelings to save your life. Carry on." He gestured me out the door with a flap of his hand.

When I stepped back out into the open space by Greta's desk, I let out a deep breath and put my hands on my knees as if I'd survived running through a maze full of creepy-crawlies.

"Everything alright, dear?" Greta asked with a knowing smile.

"A little heads-up would have been appreciated," I muttered.

Her eyes sparkled above her reading glasses. "Aw, where's the fun in that?"

"You hired a PA?"

She nodded. "You remember April Samina from the travel department?"

I pictured the young, energetic woman and knew right away Greta had made the perfect choice. "Fine," I said with a dramatic huff. "I know when I'm outshined and outmatched."

"It's always good to maintain your dignity as you depart the field, darling," she said with a sniff. "Even after a historic loss."

"I want my pasta salad back," I told her with a laugh, standing up straight and trying to stretch the tension out of my body. I'd brought her an extra tub of it to take home for her husband.

She grinned. "Too late. I ate the whole thing, even Reggie's portion."

I snorted and began to twist at the waist, but I ran right into a delicious-cologne-smelling beast.

"Oh, fuck," I blurted, windmilling my arms in an effort not to keel over.

Strong hands grabbed my sides and held me upright. I glanced up into Tiller Raine's stormy-gray eyes and tried not to get a stupid crush on a cocky rookie football player which meant I jumped back with a choking grunt sound and almost fell over again.

The edge of Tiller's mouth turned up the barest amount. I glared at him. "I'm fine, thanks," I snapped before reminding myself this person was now my boss.

Tiller's nostrils flared. "Listen, Mikey. You don't need to like this," he said in a low voice. "And I don't need to like this. But we both have a job to do, so let's just focus on the job. Got it?"

For some reason, that hurt. I wanted to be allowed to dislike him for no reason, but the same didn't apply to him disliking me.

"It's Michael, actually," I corrected, even though absolutely zero people used my full name outside of doctors and government offices. "And yeah, focus on the job. Fine."

How many times could I possibly use that word in one day?"

"Fine," he repeated with a nod.

"Yeah. *Fine*."

We stared at each other for a few beats before Tiller seemed to snap out of it and reached into his pocket for his keys. He pulled one off the key ring, and I tried not to notice the ancient worn leather fob that looked like it belonged in some kind of museum. My dad had mentioned Tiller's old truck. I didn't want to notice endearing things about my new boss. Therein lay madness.

"Key to the apartment," he said gruffly, handing it over. "I'll get a copy of the house key made and bring it over to you after practice."

I noted his use of the word *practice* instead of calling it as *work* like the old-timers did. *Rookie*. "Thanks," I managed before remembering what I'd been hired for. "Any allergies, picky eating, or health issues I need to know for your diet?"

He shook his head. "Whatever is fine."

Great. *Fine*. I'm sure I could narrow down the choices from about ten thousand options. No problem. "So... I'll just... throw together anything?"

Markus had joined us at this point and decided to weigh in with a big annoying clap on Tiller's shoulder. "He's a pretty laid-back guy. It's what makes him such a team player. Isn't it, Raine?"

Team player or annoyingly unhelpful?

The great Tiller Raine gave us a sum total of one word in

response. "Sure." Which suited me just fine. This time I'd made myself a promise. No sleeping with jackass ballplayers. No sleeping with players of any kind, in fact. And absolutely no sleeping with my boss.

1

TILLER - FIVE YEARS LATER

"Did you take your fish oil supplement?" Mikey asked. I'd learned early on that, despite his hopeful claims the day I hired him, the man didn't actually answer to Mike or Michael.

"Yes, dear," I muttered, shoving shit into my duffle. I was running late to practice, and for some reason I couldn't get the bag to close.

"Don't call me that. You do know I've already packed your stuff, right? That's why the bag won't close. You packed stuff on top of what I'd already packed."

I glanced up at him. Mikey stood leaning against the doorjamb to my bedroom. He wore faded plaid pajama pants and an oversized Riggers T-shirt he'd most likely stolen from my ridiculously large stash if he hadn't gotten it from Coach. I remembered the first year he'd worked for me when we'd been diligent about ignoring each other for the most part. He hadn't come in my personal area of the house, and I hadn't gone anywhere near his garage apartment. But it didn't take me too long to realize he actually *had* come into my personal space since he was the one who did the laundry.

I hadn't intended for him to do the laundry. That fact needs to be clear. I'd hired a housekeeper to handle cleaning and laundry, but

Mikey had quickly made the executive decision that the housekeeper needed to go.

"She took pictures of your underwear and put them on Instagram," he'd told me when I'd finally noticed and confronted him about her disappearance. "So I fired her."

"You can't fire her. She works for me," I'd said. Stupidly. "Get her back."

"Mhm. Okay. Sure."

I'd never seen her again.

After yanking out the duplicate gear and tossing it onto the unmade bed, I zipped the bag closed and headed his way. "Antone, Peevy, and Colin are coming for dinner. That okay?"

I passed by him and tried not to inhale. A sleepy Mikey was the best kind of Mikey, and I had no business even knowing that, much less enjoying it. It had only taken a year and one crazy playoff season for Mikey to stop worrying about showing up perfectly pressed and dressed to prepare breakfast, and honestly, I'd been relieved. It was easier for me to think of him as a generous roommate who happened to fix me breakfast than an employee who dressed to impress.

"Colin is not okay," he said as he followed me down the hall and into the kitchen. "He looks at me funny."

I whipped around and almost knocked into him. "What? Funny like how?" If any of my teammates even *thought* about messing with my... Mikey, they were going to have words with me.

He sighed. His hair was so adorably messy, I wanted to put my fingers in it. I'd been having these inappropriate thoughts more and more lately, and it made my teeth ache. "Fine, I kind of... hooked up with him, okay? And he's upset because I won't do it again."

I stared at him. The sun streamed into the kitchen from the huge windows, and every stainless steel surface gleamed in its usual pristine state. The only thing on the large island besides the usual giant pottery bowl full of fresh fruit and Mikey's personal recipe notebook on its custom stand was a single place setting with a steaming casserole dish on a trivet right next to it and the familiar thermos with my protein smoothie in it. I knew from experience there would be a large soft-sided cooler bag in the fridge with my snacks and lunch already packed and ready.

Mikey was an amazing chef. I was spoiled as hell, and everyone on the team envied me. Thanks to his knowledge and talent, I ate like a king and my body was fueled to perfection. Over the past five years, I'd packed on lean muscle, and I now felt better than I had at sixteen. Who knew nutrition made such a difference? Everyone but me, apparently.

"You slept with Colin Saris?" My voice might have squeaked a little at the end.

"I didn't sleep with him. We just kind of... did some other things. Don't tell anyone, though. He's not out."

"No shit he's not out," I snapped. "The man has a different woman in his bed every damned night. How the hell did *you* end up there?"

I wasn't sure why the idea of my assistant slash chef sleeping with one of my teammates upset me so much, but it did. It really, really did.

"Long story," he said with the flap of a hand. "Anyway, I'll steer clear tonight. Maybe Sam wants to come over and watch a movie with me."

I pictured Sam Rigby, Mikey's unlikely best friend from high school, the gruff motorcycle guy who I'd never really been able to pin down. Sam was gay or bi, so why hadn't the two of them gotten together? Maybe they had. Maybe they had a history together I didn't know about. I reached for my chest and rubbed it.

"Who says I don't want to watch a movie with you and Sam?" Hopefully I didn't sound as whiney as I felt.

"Stop whining. Of course you can watch a movie with us. You just have to kick out your teammates before we start it."

Now I was whining for sure. "They never leave. They come here and eat all our food and never fucking leave."

The truth was, that was my fault. I'd worked very hard to fill my house with teammates as much as possible to keep from winding up alone with Mikey. Ever since the day Bruce had made the original arrangement, I'd known Mikey Vining would be a dangerous temptation.

But he was hella off-limits. Like... *seriously* off-limits. Lion enclosure at the zoo off-limits.

"And you can't complain about our movie selection like you did last time," he continued as if I'd never said anything.

"You picked *The Shining*," I reminded him. "And I had nightmares for months. Anyway, don't change the subject. You and Colin? He's gay? Since when?"

"He's probably bi since you yourself pointed out all the Rigger chicks he's slept with. And I know for a fact he's slept with Ira Whatsit—that ball boy or whatever you call them. That's how I found out about his big dick. Ira said it wasn't to be missed. He lied."

Against my will, I pictured my teammate in the shower. He wasn't exactly a porn star, but the man had assets. I wasn't about to debate it with my assistant, though. That would be crossing a line. I grunted instead.

Mikey continued. "It doesn't matter. I shouldn't have hooked up with him in the first place. My dad would fucking kill me if he found out."

I thought about Coach Vining discovering his slutty running back had fucked his baby boy. It wouldn't be Mikey who'd get killed in that scenario.

"Well, I can't uninvite him. Just stick near me or Sam and we'll run interference." I made a mental note to text Sam on my way to practice. He worked days as a contractor and some nights as a bartender, so calling him this early in the morning was a no-go. Ever since Mikey's appendix had ruptured the second year he worked for me, Sam and I had become close enough friends to bypass Mikey from time to time, especially if it was related to protecting Mikey.

Mikey narrowed his eyes at me. "I can handle myself."

It wasn't the first time over the years he'd made the same statement. And he'd been right exactly zero percent of the times he'd made such a claim.

"Remember Jack?" I asked, ticking them off on my fingers. "Or Lonny, or Ben, or Marco?"

He gave me the evil eye and nodded at the casserole dish. "Eat your slop before you're late."

I pulled the top off the casserole dish and saw my absolute favorite breakfast dish. My heart did a little flip. "You made me egg surprise?"

"It's called crustless sunrise veggie quiche."

"No it isn't. I named it when you first came up with is. You can't fancify it just because you feel like it." I dished out a huge portion, and Mikey slapped my hand away when I reached in for another half portion to add to it.

"I can and I will. One day I'm going to publish my cookbook, and it's not going to be called egg fucking surprise. You'll puke if you eat that much before practice. Why do you think I bought smaller plates?"

I glanced at the plate with a frown. "These are our same plates."

"Pfft. Sure they are. Same plates. Stop being a pig."

I squinted at the plate and turned it around on the place mat. The colorful design looked exactly like it had since I'd bought them my rookie year. "The decorator said they were from an art gallery downtown. One of a kind."

"Well, your decorator's art gallery must source from the same place as Crate and Barrel. What do you want me to say?"

I shoved the food into my mouth and groaned. Like clockwork, as soon as I'd downed half my portion, Mikey reached back to pour me a coffee from the carafe on the counter. I was sure he was already on his second, or even third, cup himself, but he didn't allow me to have coffee on an empty stomach, and I sure as hell wasn't allowed more than one cup.

"What are you doing today?" I asked, taking my first sip and savoring it.

"I'm delivering muffins to Kiki's, two lasagnes to D'Angelo's house, and a cold couscous salad to Hilltop Cafe."

"The one with the feta?"

He nodded and took another sip of his coffee. "They're putting it with their veggie panini on the daily lunch special, I think. I had to make four giant trays after it sold out last time."

"Did you save me some?" It was a stupid question, and his facial expression confirmed it.

"It's in your lunchbox along with grilled salmon, a big salad with eggs on it—shut up, I don't want to hear it—an apple, some almonds, and your lunch smoothie."

"I hate eggs in my salad," I muttered under my breath anyway.

"Cry into your giant piles of money," he shot back. It was one of his favorite expressions, and it kind of made me laugh every time he said it. Not that I'd tell him that.

"I can't. Last time I did that, I tried wiping my eyes and my Super Bowl ring gave me a black eye."

Mikey snickered, and that's all I needed to hear to know I was going to have a great day.

And I did. It was the day after that when everything went to hell.

2

MIKEY

I wasn't a big football fan despite growing up immersed in it. Or maybe because of growing up immersed in it. But I still went to every home game out of habit. Maybe I'd stopped for a little while during the Nelson Evangelista years since he had a habit of making illegal hits that turned my stomach, but as soon as I'd started working for Tiller, suddenly I was interested again.

Whatever.

Anyway, on this particular Sunday, I was grateful for it. Sam had come with me, and we were sitting in my dad's box with my mom and brothers when it happened. It was late in the third quarter, and the Riggers were up by fourteen over the Raiders. Tiller had made several incredible catches, two of which had resulted in touchdown runs, and one had been a TD reception in the end zone. He was on fire as usual. His reputation as a focused professional had certainly made my father proud over the past few years, especially after his role in helping bring home the Super Bowl win last year. He'd begun using Tiller as the example, even though Tiller had no work-life balance whatsoever.

Other than swimming and reading thrillers and mystery novels in the sun by his pool, he didn't seem to have much of a hobby. I knew at one point growing up he'd been an avid snowboarder, but once he'd been recruited to play college ball, he'd had to promise to give up any and all other dangerous sports. Now that he was a multimillion-dollar NFL player, there wasn't a chance in hell his contract would let him on the slopes.

I hadn't even seen him bring home a man in the five years I'd lived there. Well, he'd brought home teammates, and I'd met his family when they'd come to visit from Denver or we'd traveled to them. But I'd never heard about his love life or even a sex life to speak of. I'd asked Colin about it the night we'd hooked up.

"He pays for it on road trips," he'd said with a laugh. "Gets rent boys up in his hotel room and goes at it all night to work off the stress. Coach finds out, it'll be his ass."

I'd felt sick to my stomach then. At least until I'd begun to question whether or not Colin had been telling the truth. It didn't matter either way. It was none of my business, but I wondered why a man so built and beautiful and talented would ever have to pay someone to sleep with him.

Sam grabbed my arm. "Fuck, double coverage."

My eyes snapped to number twenty-three in the white uniform with navy and orange accents as he tried his hardest to lose the two magnets attached to his ass.

The ball came sailing his way just as he juked left and found a spot. He snatched the ball out of the air and turned.

Right into a Mack truck.

The linebacker had been braced and waiting. Tiller had hit him shoulder-first so hard, his helmet bounced when his head hit the ground.

I gasped and clawed at Sam's arm. "No. No, fuck."

Mom patted my shoulder. "He's okay, honey. He's taken worse hits than that before."

How the hell did she stay so calm? I'd often wondered if maybe she was medicated. How else could she have watched my brothers all get the shit beat out of them on the field and mat without having to be admitted into some kind of program for chronic anxiety?

"He's not okay," I said quietly enough that only Sam could hear.

"No," he agreed in his usual gruff way. Sam wasn't an easy person to read at the best of times, and when he was worried about someone he cared about, it was even worse.

I stood up and went forward, grabbing a pair of nearby binoculars and trying to focus them on the still player on the field with my hands shaking as much as they were.

"Get up, get up," I muttered. "Get your ass up, Raine."

The medical professionals rushed out and helped him up to thunderous applause.

"See, honey? Right as Raine."

I'd heard that phrase about a million times too many over the last several years. The man was known for shaking off hard hits, it was true. But when he came home to me, I saw the real-life aftereffects of it. He'd never, ever been "right as Raine" after one of those hits. He'd been bruised and bloodied, weakened by pain. Even after tending to him with ice packs, ice baths, and even massage in some cases, I'd had to watch him move gingerly and return to work way too soon.

"I'm going down there," I said as soon as they started helping him off the field. He was cradling his right arm against his body, and if he had an injury like that, it could mean the end of the season for him. The Riggers had won the Super Bowl last season, so they were expected to return to defend their title this year. They wouldn't have nearly as good a chance without Tiller.

Sam nodded and stayed where he was. He wasn't all that great with emotion, and he probably expected I was going to lose my cool pretty rapidly. I, too, wasn't all that great with emotion. Instead of bottling it up and smashing it down, I poured it out and frothed at the mouth with it. It was part of what made me special. Or so I'd been told. It was also part of what made me damp during Super Bowl commercials.

My feet flew as I made my way down to the locker room and medical bay. It didn't matter what kind of security pass I had when everyone who worked at the stadium knew I was Coach Vining's son. Several of the guards had known me since I was young, and the assistant coaches had all gotten lectures from me behind the scenes about helping keep junk food out of my dad's hands after his cholesterol and blood pressure results had come in too high.

"Mikey, what's shakin'?" Krystal asked from the hallway outside the medical offices. She was one of the physical therapists on staff.

"Where's Raine?"

She opened the door next to her and pointed. "Second bay on the right. Dislocated shoulder went back in already. Hopefully nothing more than a deep hematoma from impact other than that."

I made my way toward the bay, ignoring a man I didn't know telling me this area was off-limits to fans. Finally, I saw Dr. Bindi come out of the bay and stopped short. "Michael. Good to see you."

"How is he?"

He held up a finger and ducked back into the bay where I heard him ask Tiller if I could come in. I didn't wait for a response. I hustled in there and started snapping.

"Why the fuck did Maple Leaf throw that pass to you when you were in double coverage and that giant fucking side of beef was standing there waiting to take you out?"

My eyes roamed over every inch of his body, taking in the sweaty, matted hair, the tired and pained eyes, and the missing jersey. Other than holding a very painful arm against his front, he seemed okay. My body began to shake violently as the adrenaline crash dropped. I didn't like to think about why I cared so damned much.

He let go of his hurt arm and reached out a hand to me. "Come here."

I took it and stepped closer, still examining every inch of him I could.

Tiller eyed Dr. Bindi. "Can you give us a minute? And look out for my agent—he's probably going to come storming in any minute, too."

As soon as we were alone, Tiller pulled me close and gave me a tight side hug. The move surprised me. We'd never hugged before or shown any other kind of physical affection other than the odd slap to the back of his head when he annoyed me or him ruffling my hair because he knew it drove me crazy.

I didn't mind the sweat at all. In fact, I might have liked it a little too much.

It was the fact he was shaking too that I minded. A lot.

"Fuck," he said gruffly into my neck. Even his voice was shaking. "You're a sight for sore eyes."

"Are you okay?" His voice wasn't the only one shaking. "I thought maybe you'd lost consciousness. I couldn't breathe."

"I think I was just stunned for a minute. My mind kept going toward the goal when my body had been laid flat out."

"Concussion protocol?" I asked, pulling out of the hug so I could look at his face.

He nodded. "They're going to put me in the tube regardless, but they're pretty sure there's nothing like that. They're more worried about my arm. I can't really... I can't really move it."

I grabbed a nearby towel and began to wipe the sweat off his face and push his hair out of his eyes. "You need a haircut," I murmured.

His voice was rough with pain. "You like it shaggy like this."

I caught his eye at the unexpected observation. "Is that why you canceled the haircut appointment with Ricki?"

He blushed and looked down. "How mad is your dad going to be?"

I felt my nostrils flare. "Well, I hope he skins Maple Leaf alive. He deserves it."

Tiller winced out a slight smile. "His name is Mopellei. Or you can call him Derek."

"I'm not calling him shit. Stupid Canadian asshole. Does he even have any other play than send the ball to Raine and hope Raine saves everyone's fucking bacon? Jesus. Shake it up a little. Doesn't he realize that's why you're in double or triple coverage to begin with? Fuck."

"You sound like your dad right now." Tiller tugged on the hem of the Raine jersey I wore. "When did you get this?"

Oh god, he was going to be insufferable. "I spilled beer on my Saris jersey and this is all they had on the clearance rack at the concession shop."

Thunderclouds darkened his face. "I will find every Saris jersey in my house and burn them in your favorite oven."

I laughed. It felt good to laugh. Whatever his injury was, we'd get through it the way we always did. "Mess with my ovens and see how many eggs I can fit on one salad. I dare you."

Dr. Bindi came back in with another doctor. "You remember Dr. Sullivan. She's the soft-tissue specialist. We're going to take you for some tests to assess the damage to the shoulder and arm. You'll need the brain scan, too, just to rule out the concussion. I'm afraid the rest of your evening will be taken up with tests. Is there anyone you want us to call to keep you company?"

Tiller pointed his thumb at me. "Already here. Let's get this party started. And if you can find me some pain pills, I'd be much obliged."

I blinked at him. Tiller hated taking medicine. He didn't like giving up control or forgetting what people said. It was one reason he never got drunk either. If he was asking for pain meds, he was way worse off than he was letting on.

I brushed the towel over his forehead again and then down his sweaty chest. "Close your eyes and listen to my voice. I'm going to tell you the story of what Wally did when he got recruited to play for Notre Dame."

"He didn't play for Notre Dame," Tiller corrected.

"No. No, he did not. He ended up playing for Clemson. That's what makes this a good story. Even my dad doesn't know this one. I'm not sure Wally realizes anyone knows this story. It involves the Notre Dame coach's daughter and some seriously poor decision-making on my brother's part."

He tried to laugh but winced. "Oh god. Tell me everything. I love a good Wally story."

Over the next six hours of waiting and testing, I told him every Wally story I could think of and a few about Richie. When they finally gave him serious IV pain meds, he was able to relax enough to slip into sleep. I used that time to wipe him down, at least the parts of his body not covered by the hospital gown they'd changed him into. I didn't want him caked in game sweat for the rest of the night, but I didn't want to cause him any pain either.

Do not look at his body. He's only this perfect because that's his job. You've met enough of these assholes by now to know they're not for you. Especially this one. Do your job.

I tried not to remember what it was like over five years ago when my father had walked in on Nelson humping me into the sofa in my parents' family room or the helpless nausea I'd felt when I'd learned of Nelson's trade to Seattle only ten days later. There were a million reasons I shouldn't think of Tiller as anything other than my boss, but my father's reaction was definitely the biggest, meanest one.

When Tiller was finally cleaned up as well as could be, I settled into a chair next to his bed in the little curtained off area where they'd stashed us between tests. I pulled out my phone and left Sam a voicemail update before texting Tiller's mom.

Me: *No concussion. Severe bruising to deltoid, biceps, and right pec. Dislocated shoulder. Possible radial nerve damage to non-dominant arm. Couple weeks in a sling.*

Jill: *Well, shit.*

I laughed.

Me: *That about covers it. He's gonna be pissed when he sobers up.*

Jill: *How you gonna keep him still? Want me to come?*

I thought about Tiller's mom. Jillian Raine was a successful midwife in Denver. When she took unexpected time off, it inevitably disappointed several of her pregnant patients. She usually planned her vacations at least a year in advance to avoid disruptions.

Me: *I think we'll be okay. My plan is to get him hooked on Law & Order SVU. There are like four hundred episodes.*

Jill: *He loves that stuff. Has he done NCIS and Leverage? Hawaii Five-O?*

I looked over at her son. He always looked vulnerable in a hospital gown. I hated it—hated seeing him less than a hundred percent. Mostly because I knew *he* hated it more than anything. His work was his life, whether that was a good thing or not.

Me: *If all else fails, I can always put on Drag Race. The man can't pass* *through a room where it's playing without getting sucked in against his will.*

Jill: *You're evil. I love it.*

I shot a quick pic of Tiller in bed now that he had a little line of drool hanging out of his mouth and sent it to Jill. She responded with a laughing emoji.

Jill: *Thank you for being there. I love you both.*

Me: *Love you too. Tell Moose the same.*

Honestly, I was surprised Tiller's dad hadn't already been lighting up my phone with concern over Tiller's injury status. I liked the man fine, but sometimes I wondered what Moose would do if Tiller could no longer play the game.

I sent my mom and dad an update although I was sure Coach was probably well aware of the situation. Within minutes, he responded.

Coach: *Mikey? What are you doing at the hospital?*

Me: *Tiller's still here for tests.*

Coach: *What does that have to do with you?*

I felt my blood go cold. Ever since Tiller had offered to make my "one season only" gig permanent, my dad had been very vocal against it. He'd even gone so far as to get me a different job by sending me over to another player's house under false pretenses. A straight, *married* player's house.

I'd tried explaining that Tiller and I were not in an inappropriate relationship of any kind, but Coach seemed to think two gay men in the same proximity couldn't keep their dicks in their pants.

After five years of valiant effort, I could now confirm we could, in fact, keep our dicks in our pants.

Regrettably.

Coach: *I'll be there in five. You can leave now.*

I didn't respond.

"Baby?"

I looked over to see Tiller blink awake. He looked dazed and confused, which explained the endearment. Over the past few years, he'd slipped and called me baby when he'd been very tired, hurt, or sad. I'd tried not to think too much about why he did it or why it socked me square in the gut when he did.

"Yeah?" I reached out and took his good hand in mine. "How you doing?"

"Wanna go home."

"I know. Why don't I go find someone and ask how much longer?"

"You have your car?"

I smirked at him. "Actually, I have your car. The SUV."

The corner of his mouth quirked up. "You love that thing."

"If you're going to leave an eighty-thousand-dollar vehicle in the garage, then hell yeah I'm gonna use it."

"My truck," he slurred. "Granddad."

I squeezed his hand. "I know."

He turned his head on the pillow and locked eyes with me. "Wanna go home with my... Mikey."

Oh hell. No. No, no, *no*. I was not going to get soft and smushy for Tiller Raine. My boss. My dad's star wide receiver. No.

I cleared my throat and stood up, dropping his hand like a hot potato. "I'll go check on your status. Hang tight."

When I found a nurse, she paged the doc and got the go-ahead for us to get the hell out of there. I helped Tiller change into the warm-up suit and running shoes I'd had the foresight to grab from the locker room before leaving the stadium.

Just when I was finishing pulling his shirt on and getting his arm back into the sling as gently as I could, my dad and Tiller's agent came racing in.

"Shit," Markus said the minute he saw the sling.

"Fuck," Coach groaned, raking a hand through his thinning hair. "Fucking Mopellei. I'm gonna kill him."

Tiller narrowed his eyes at my dad despite his hazy pain medicine fog. "You called the play, Coach."

I stepped back and tried to disappear into the corner of the room. If he was going to challenge my father's coaching, I was going to do my best to become one with the beige vinyl wallpaper.

Markus, in his efforts to be the consummate mediator, held his hands out in a calming gesture. "That's unproductive. Why don't we talk about what it's going to take to get you back in the game? Where are the doctors?"

After consulting with the doctors and learning that Tiller was out for at least four weeks, the mood in the room dropped a thousand degrees and the tension rocketed up.

"What are you still doing here?" my father snapped at me.

I opened my mouth to respond, but Tiller beat me to it. "He's my ride."

Coach's nostrils flared. "What, did you just abandon your boyfriend midgame?"

So... I may or may not have told my dad a little white lie. No harm, no foul, right?

Tiller's eyes snapped to mine. As far as he knew, I hadn't dated anyone. Ever. We simply didn't discuss our love lives with each other. I assumed it was one of the reasons he'd reacted so strongly when I'd mentioned hooking up with his teammate.

"Um. He's... he had to leave," I said lamely.

"Who?" Tiller asked. "I thought you brought Sam."

Coach looked at Tiller in confusion. "Yes. Sam."

Tiller's eyes widened in surprise, and I saw that shit was going to get out of control very quickly if I didn't do something. Fast.

I cleared my throat and looked at Tiller as casually as I could. "Remember when you told that fan about your eyebrow—"

He didn't even let me finish because he knew exactly what I was going to say. Tiller was asked all the time about a scar in his eyebrow. When he'd told the story of tripping over a crack in the sidewalk while eating an ice cream cone, the fans were always so disappointed. So he'd decided to start telling people he'd gotten a late hit in a game in college. It wasn't true, but it was simply more believable.

Like me telling my dad I was dating Sam so he would stop worrying about me hooking up with Tiller.

Tiller nodded. "Oh, right. Sam. Sorry. It's the meds. They're messing with my head."

Markus was pecking away at his phone. He finally glanced up at me. "I'm shooting you an email with the contact information for the rehab manager to coordinate getting Raine back out on the field. Let me know if you get any pushback and we'll find someone else."

I glared at him. "He's not even—"

My dad cut me off. "He'll be fine by tomorrow to start. Tell them to contact Krystal once they're ready to transition him back to the team therapists."

"But he—" I began. Tiller shot me a look of warning, and I clamped my lips together. It was none of my business. I was simply the PA. I was supposed to do as I was told.

I'd never been very good at that.

After a few more minutes, Coach and Markus blew back out of the hospital room like they'd never been there.

Tiller looked over at me. "Sam?"

"Don't ask," I said on a sigh. "I needed my parents off my back."

"So... you're not...?"

"No! God, no. Me and Sam? No. He's a nice guy. Sexy as hell, but—"

Tiller's nostrils flared. "No need to elaborate."

"You don't find him attractive?" I asked. Even though I knew Sam would never go there, I'd always wondered about Tiller.

Tiller shook his head. "First of all, he's too damned quiet. Can't ever tell what the man's thinking. Secondly, he needs someone he can fuss over, someone to take care of. That's not me. Third, he's probably a top, and I probably am, too."

I tried not to whimper with the confirmation Tiller liked to top. It had to be the meds that were loosening his tongue, because we'd never talked about our sexual preferences before. It was part of the boss/employee line we both tried never to cross.

"Well, too bad," I said, shaking off my mental imagery of being topped by Tiller Raine. *Hard.* I cleared my throat. "I plan on fussing over you and taking care of you, so you'll need to get on board."

His lips turned into a slurry grin. "I like being babied by you, though. That's different."

"Well... good. Um..."

"What about you?" Tiller asked.

"What about me?"

He narrowed his eyes. "You and Sam."

I shook my head more violently than necessary. "Nope. I love him. I do. But you remember how he was when I had my appendix out. He's awful in an emergency, and I attract emergencies like you attract cheerleaders." I bit my teeth together. Hadn't meant to say that last part.

"There has to be another reason."

I busied myself straightening up the two items on his side table. "He kissed me once, and it was just... meh."

The silence was enough to make me look up. He was glaring at me like I'd said something offensive.

I threw up my hands. "What?"

"You and Sam. Kissing. *Mpfh.*"

The look in his eyes turned heated, and it made my stomach all squirrelly. "Oh, hey. Let's get you out of here." I bolted for the hallway, praying I could find a nurse or anyone who would release us from this oddball conversation and let us end this crazy day.

Thankfully, my dad had already greased the wheels and the nurses' station was already processing his discharge.

When we finally got home, it was well after midnight. "Bed," he murmured.

"Food first," I said.

"Not hungry." Tiller leaned heavily against me as I guided him into the house from the garage with an arm around his waist. He was a little unsteady from the pain meds they'd given him.

"Too bad. I'll make something easy and quick. Sit here in the comfy chair." I maneuvered him to the overstuffed chair in the sitting area of the kitchen before moving to the big Sub-Zero fridge.

"This is your chair."

"Actually, it's yours. I just use it."

He shook his head and closed his eyes. "Nah. It's yours. Can't imagine anyone else sitting in it. I love coming home and seeing you curled up here. Makes me happy."

"Stop being so sweet. Go back to being whatever stupid nickname your teammates use. Raine of fire? Raine down hell? Raine it in? Purple Raine?"

He snorted but didn't open his eyes. "Purple Raine. Nice one. No sweet Raine?"

I shook my head emphatically even though he couldn't see it. "Never. Not possible."

"What're you making me?"

I flicked on the gas stove and filled the pot from the built-in faucet over the range. "Protein spaghetti with garlic marinara."

He didn't say anything for a few moments. "I think food is how you love people."

God *dammit*.

I bit the hell out of my lip before responding. "Nah. It's just how I make my living."

Tiller snorted. "I got a bridge to sell you."

I got busy making enough spaghetti for both of us and then doubled it to make leftovers since it was another one of Tiller's favorites.

If feeding people was my love language, Tiller was the most beloved human on earth. And I was in big fucking trouble.

Because I wanted him. I wanted him so fucking badly.

3

TILLER

"I will not watch one more episode of this bullshit," I grumbled. "Benson should know by now to steel her heart against this shit. And if Peter doesn't stop lecturing her like a child..."

Sam groaned.

"Where's Mikey?" I asked, trying to haul my ass out of the recliner with only one good hand. "He promised we could get sushi tonight if I made it through five more episodes."

Sam laughed. "Not sure it counts if you bitch about it the whole time."

"Mike!" I called out.

"He's not going to answer you if you yell for him like that. You know how much he hates being summoned with a raised voice. Don't you think he had enough of that growing up?"

He played the guilt card. Jerk. It was bad enough I'd had to spend the afternoon trying hard not to picture the two of them kissing, but he'd also assisted me so much over the past couple of weeks, I couldn't help but remember what a nice guy he was. And he was protective as hell of Mikey which I had to appreciate.

I shuffled into the kitchen from the theater room and found

Mikey sitting at the island scribbling in a notebook. His dark-framed glasses had slipped down his nose, and his eyebrows were furrowed in concentration.

"What're you working on?" I asked, going to the fridge to get out the pitcher of lemonade.

He stood up and pushed me toward a chair. "Sit. I'll get it."

"I'm not an invalid, you know," I said with annoyance. "I can pour it with one hand."

"Yes. Yes, you can. And you can spill it like you did the jelly beans you must have had someone sneak in behind my back. We're going to be stepping on those fuckers for weeks."

"Never mind that. Can we please have sushi?"

He slid a menu over to me. "Take this in and ask Sam what he wants. His boyfriend is going to pick it up on his way over."

"Boyfriend? Sam? Who? Not you." Why did I sound like a Dr. Seuss book all of a sudden?

Mikey craned his neck to make sure Sam was still safely locked away in the theater room. "He's been seeing someone a couple of weeks. We don't like him," he whispered. "He's high-maintenance and a total dick."

I looked down the hall again before turning to Mikey and matching his whisper. "Why is he with him? And why is he coming to our house if we don't like him?"

Mikey shot me a look. "Because we like Sam, and Sam likes Rico."

"Rico?" I asked way too loudly. Mikey waved his hands through the air as he shushed me. "Rico Moreno? The guy who cleans our fucking pool? Sam's dating the pool boy?"

Mikey rolled his eyes. "Apparently he gives good head. Drop it. Let the poor guy get past his dry spell before encouraging him to brush the guy off."

"How do you know about his dry spell and how good the pool boy sucks dick?"

Suddenly I imagined Mikey and Rico out behind the pool maintenance shed with Rico on his knees for Mike.

"Don't go there, Raine," Mikey warned.

"Sorry," I muttered. "I just..."

"You're bored. And you're turning your own life into a telenovela. I get it."

I reached for an apple and bit into it. "I think we should fly to Florida for the game."

"Don't be ridiculous. Coach already told you you're not welcome. Maybe if you weren't a controlling bastard who can't stop trying to wave his injured arm around while yelling at poor Brent Little, he wouldn't have taken such a strong stand. It took four days for you to get your voice back after that, and you're lucky you didn't damage your shoulder again with all that wild gesturing."

"His feet were stuck in molasses," I countered. "He finally gets to start against the Denver Broncos and he can't even get off the starting block."

"You're not the coach," he tried reminding me.

"Mpfh." I took another bite out of the apple. "Fine. We'll throw a game-watching party here instead."

Mikey handed me a glass of icy-cold lemonade. It tasted amazing. After growing up in Colorado, I still hadn't gotten used to Houston "winters." Heat in early December was just plain wrong.

"All of your friends are going to be in Florida. It would just be the three of us, and Sam probably has to work. Tell me what you want for sushi and I'll put in the order."

He ripped a sheet out of his notebook and passed it to me with his pen. While I jotted down the stuff I wanted, he disappeared down the hall toward his bedroom. I took the menu and paper to Sam. When I got back to the kitchen with our orders, Mikey had a folder sitting by my seat at the island.

"Pick one of these. We're spending Christmas in Colorado."

I blinked up at him. "We're what?"

"Your mom and dad want to see you." He didn't look up at me as his fingers flew over the meal-ordering app on his phone.

"Too bad. I don't want to see them. Do you have any idea how many times my father has asked me why I haven't just sucked it up and gotten back to work?"

Mikey looked up, his soft brown eyes twinkling with knowing humor. "That's why we're not staying with them. We're going to rent one of these cabins and hole up for the rest of the month."

My heart started racing. "A month? Are you serious? I'm not leaving for a month during the season. I can't. I'm the Rigger's starting wide receiver."

"You can and you will. And right now, Brent Little is the Rigger's starting wide receiver."

The reality of his words hit me in the gut. I *hated* letting Coach down. If I could have sold my soul for a working arm, I would have.

Clearly Mikey was being ridiculous. "I still have to go to the games."

His eyes bored through me again. "You've been banned until your arm is better."

I sputtered. "Not true. That was one game. One. And... and it's just taking me some time to get used to sitting the bench, that's all. I'll be fine for the game against Jacksonville."

He shook his head and nudged the folder closer to me. "Nope. Coach said to get you the hell out of town and out of his face before your shoulder is, and I quote, not the only injured part of your anatomy. So pick one."

I firmed my jaw and tried returning his laser stare. "I will not."

Mikey laughed and stepped closer to me, leaning in until our noses were almost touching. "You will. You and I both know what Coach says goes, and you and I also both know I run your schedule. Where I tell you to be, you go. And I'm telling you to go to the mountains."

Mikey stepped back and pointed to the folder. "You'll get to see snow. You'll get some peace and quiet. Hell, maybe you can even get some reading in. There's a new John Meadows novel out, and I asked your friend Julian to send me a list of the ones he's read recently. Besides, all the places I picked have a gym, a sauna, and a hot tub. You can keep in shape while we're there. We can even call in a trainer if you want. Coach gave me someone to call in Denver for a physical therapy referral."

I grumbled and opened the folder. He kind of had me at the mention of snow. Other than away games in colder locations and the odd short visit to my parents after the season ended, I hadn't seen snow in years. I would love a chance to walk in the woods, hear the familiar crunch under my boots, and feel the crisp bite of cold air on my face.

"You're going with me, right?" I asked, thinking a few weeks away with just my... Mikey would be pretty nice. "What about your catering clients?"

For the first time in our conversation, he avoided meeting my eyes. "It's not a problem."

I reached out and grabbed his chin, forcing the eye contact. "How so?"

Mikey swallowed. I tried not to fixate on the movement in his throat, but the creamy skin was too tempting to look away from. "I'm... kind of... done? With the catering thing, I mean."

I tilted my head as the words tried to make sense. "What do you mean, done? Why?"

He bit his bottom lip and shrugged. "I kind of got a book deal."

I damned near fell off my stool. "You *what*? A book deal? For a cookbook?"

Mikey's grin was sudden and overwhelming. I wasn't sure why he was suddenly affecting me this way, but when he smiled full-on, it made me feel like I'd just scored the winning touchdown in the Super Bowl.

"I pitched the idea to an agent a few months back, and she liked it. She took the idea to a few publishing friends of hers—editors, I guess —and they all wanted it. The idea sold in an auction? I don't really understand how that all works, but it was for a lot of money, so..."

My selfish ass was more distracted by the fact he hadn't told me he was doing any of this than the fact he'd just announced very exciting news. "Wow, Mikey. That's incredible. Why didn't you tell me you'd pitched it?"

His cheeks turned pink, and his eyelashes flitted a little in a combo deal of Mike's nervous tells. "Um, I assumed it wasn't going to go anywhere."

He was oblivious to his own talent. I reached out with my good hand and clasped one of his.

"That's fantastic! Wait... so, when you said one day when you publish a cookbook... you already knew this was happening."

"Well, not really. I didn't have the offer yet. And, honestly, it hasn't really sunk in. I still feel like it's all a dream."

I put my hand on his shoulder and squeezed. It was the closest I was allowed to come to the giant, crushing hug I really wanted to give him. Early on, my agent had warned me against anything inappropriate with "staff," and since Mikey was my only real staff anymore, that meant no sneaky physical touches that could be misconstrued. Markus didn't have to worry. Coach V. would kick my ass and then beat me some more if I even thought about touching his baby boy. No, I couldn't touch Mikey, despite how much I may have wanted to.

But I could look my fill. And I did. All the fucking time. Mikey happened to love swimming and lying out in the sun. I took every opportunity to do the same whenever he spent time by the pool.

"Anyway," he continued, as if I wasn't picturing his smooth abdomen bisected by a dark happy trail leading down into his swim trunks. "It sold as a 'Chef to the NFL Stars' kinda deal, so I was going to talk to you about it before signing the final papers to make sure you were okay with it. I don't have to mention your name or anything. I can always use my dad and brothers as my example, but it's still public knowledge I work for you."

I kept my hand on Mike's shoulder and ran a thumb up the side of his neck. When I realized what I was doing, I jerked my hand away and stepped back.

"You can use anything you want of mine, including my name. It's going to be amazing. I'm so excited for you. What do you need from me to make it happen?"

Suddenly, I was hit with a horrific thought.

"You're not quitting."

I didn't even have the balls to form it as a question.

Mikey's eyes widened. "No. Jesus, no. That is... not unless you want me to?"

I shook my head emphatically, unable to form the simple word around the temporary rock of fear lodged in my throat.

He grinned again. "Good. That's settled. No, I just let go of my catering clients for now so I could focus on the book without letting any of your stuff go. Before each recipe, there will be some text explaining the science behind why the recipe is ideal for top-performing athletes and how it can be adapted for mixed audiences or nonathletes. I'll use my catering time to write instead."

"That sounds great," I said sincerely. "Your dad must be proud."

Mikey's face darkened. "I haven't told him yet."

"Why not?"

He sighed. "He's not going to be supportive. He's going to tell me I shouldn't give proprietary or helpful information of any kind to his competitors. He seems to think part of the reason the team has been in better shape these days is because, and I quote, 'Those bozos are spending so much time at Raine's house they must be picking up a thing or two about nutrition.'"

It was true, but I decided not to say that out loud. I valued my nuts too much.

"No offense," I said, "but you didn't invent nutrition. Any other team can get—and already has—nutritionists on staff. So that's bull-shit. I hope you know that."

Mikey moved back over to the other side of the island to get the lemonade pitcher out of the fridge again. "I know that. It's why I didn't let fear of his reaction stop me from pursuing my dream. But I still don't want to tell him until the project is further along."

"Understood. It's your business, and you're an adult."

Mikey poured more lemonade into my cup before delivering the killing blow. "So I was kind of looking forward to getting away to focus on writing and tinkering with some of the recipes. If we stay here..."

He didn't have to say it. Our house had become a revolving door of friends and family over the years. Most of the time it was great. We both thrived having people around, but if you wanted to be alone, our house wasn't the place to do it.

"Okay," I said. "If Coach said it's okay, *and* if I can get the games on TV, we'll go."

He looked at me with an expression that said, "What kind of fool do you take me for?"

"Tiller, every cabin I picked has Wi-Fi, a big-screen TV, and satellite service. We're not going to Siberia."

I flipped through the options and stopped when I saw the one with the nicest gourmet kitchen. It also happened to be farthest from Denver. Win-win. "This one," I said, pulling the printout from the folder and handing it to him. "And book yourself in first class next to me. Don't make me upgrade you at the gate like every other fucking time. It annoys the crap out of me, and you know it."

"Fine. We leave tomorrow. This time pack more than just sweats."

"That was one time, asshole," I muttered. "And you had nicer clothes for me in your bag anyway, so it wasn't a problem."

He laughed and pulled a bottle of white wine out of the fridge for him and Sam. "I'll need to borrow one of your winter coats. I don't own one."

I stared at him with my mouth dropped open until Mikey started laughing. "Kidding. God, you're gullible. I had to buy a thick down parka two years ago when we went to Minnesota for that charity exposition thing. I don't expect you to remember since you were so busy bitching about the game. The game *for charity*."

"Tom Billing's an ass," I grumbled. "Ever since I accidentally spilled coffee on him during that interview a million years ago, he refuses to throw the ball to me. Ever. Remember that pro bowl game where he literally threw it at the coach instead of me? Prima donna."

Mikey shot me a look. "You deliberately removed the coffee cup lid and tipped the drink onto his shoes."

I opened my mouth to disagree, but he continued before I could get a word out.

"While saying, 'Maybe if someone lit your feet on fire, you would actually leave the pocket for once.'"

I narrowed my eyes at him. "Was I wrong?"

His face softened into a laugh. "Not really. But you probably ruined a thousand-dollar pair of shoes."

"As if he's paid for a pair of Nikes in his entire life," I scoffed. "Please."

"He called me the other day. Did I tell you?"

I stared at him. "Tom Billing called you?"

Mikey looked offended. "He likes my muffins."

I imagined the handsy quarterback setting his sights on Mikey. The man was straight as far as I knew, but Mikey was sexy enough to tempt anyone who had even a teaspoon of bi-curious in him.

I picked at my fingernail and sniffed. "I'm sure he does."

Mikey's grin was adorable. He had this little tiny half dimple next to the left side of his lips. I'd always kind of wanted to kiss it. Just a little bit.

"The protein ones with sneaky veggies," he continued, as if I hadn't said anything. "He wanted the recipe after his housekeeper tried recreating it with no luck."

"You're not giving it to him, I hope." I took a sip of my lemonade and watched him over the rim of my cup.

"I will if he lets me call them the Tom Billing Power-Up Muffins in the cookbook."

Before I had a chance to ask him if we could stop talking about Tom Billing, Sam came in.

"Rico's on his way. You have any wine?"

Mikey nodded and waggled the bottle he'd already pulled out. Then he turned and pulled one of the bottles of ice water out of the fridge he always had ready for me.

"Here, switch to this for dinner. You're behind on your water intake."

Sam met my eyes behind Mikey's back and mimicked his lecture. Mikey didn't even turn around before calling him on it. "Cut it out, asshole. Do you have any idea how much I get paid to tell this princess when to drink his water?"

"Too much," Sam said. "I drink plenty of water without having to pay a single person."

I shot him the bird and tried not to show how hurt I was at the reminder Mikey was here because he worked for me.

He was my employee. That's all this was.

4

MIKEY

So maybe going away had been my idea, not Coach's. But when I'd casually mentioned sending Tiller to Colorado in front of my dad, he'd blown out a giant exhale of relief. "Yes, please. Get him the fuck off my bench and send him home," Coach had said. "Moose'll set him straight."

I didn't mention I was going too and we weren't actually staying with Tiller's parents. If he found out Tiller and I were going to a secluded mountain cabin alone, he would assume we were sleeping together and blow a gasket. So I let him believe Tiller was going to Jill and Moose's place for the holiday and I was visiting a friend from college in Steamboat Springs, Colorado.

I felt like a sneaky teenager which made me feel like an ass whose father had way too strong of an influence over him. Even though I was pushing thirty, my father remained the single most influential person in my life. How pathetic was that?

When we got to the check-in counter at the airport, I split off to go to the regular people's line while Tiller headed for the first-class one. It took him a second to realize I was no longer behind him, but when he did, he hissed at me loudly enough for everyone to hear. "Get over here, you moron."

I dutifully followed, knowing from years of experience how this was going to play out.

"I can't fucking believe you did this again," he snapped under his breath.

"You cuss like my dad," I muttered. "And you know how I feel about spending your money."

When it was our turn at the counter, Mr. NFL Superstar turned on his charm and laid down his celebrity card. "Hi..." He squinted at the woman's name tag. "Nessa. How are you this morning?"

She blushed right on cue and fluttered her fake eyelashes. "I'm doing great, thanks! How can I help you today, Mr. Raine?"

He put his hand on top of my head and turned me to face Nessa. "My assistant here made a mistake when he booked our reservations, and I need to upgrade him to first class to sit with me, please. We have some work to do, and I don't want to waste our time in the air."

It was bullshit, of course. He just preferred sitting next to someone who wouldn't pester him about his job, the team, stats, and insider information. When I was his seatmate, he had a buffer between him and the oftentimes rabid Rigger fandom. It didn't hurt that I was so much smaller than he was and he wouldn't have any issues fitting his giant shoulders and legs into the space between our seats. First-class seats were big, but not NFLer big.

She clicked on her keyboard and sighed, huffed, and scraped her upper lip with her bottom teeth before finally letting out an *ah-ha* noise. "Got it. Gimme just one... there. I'll print these new boarding passes out for you and get your bags checked in."

When Tiller tried handing over his credit card, she blushed again and pushed his hand away, her own hand lingering on his. I turned around so I could roll my eyes without being rude to her face. The businessman behind us in line caught my eye.

"Is that Tiller Raine?" he whispered.

I shook my head. "Bobby Simplethorn. You probably know him from that hemorrhoid commercial."

The man looked at me in total confusion. "What?"

I sang a little jingle. "*Nothing softens bottom thorns quite like*

Simplethorn... No? You don't know it? Huh. Bobby here is the CEO. That miracle cream is his baby. I can introduce you if you want?"

The man winced. "Uh, no. That's okay. Thanks, though."

I shrugged. "Suit yourself."

When I turned back to face the lady at the counter, I found both her and Tiller staring at me. Nessa turned to look at Tiller with a raised brow.

"No," he said before she could ask. "The closest I've come to hemorrhoids is dealing with this pain in my ass." He thumbed at me over his shoulder. "And now I'm regretting the seat change."

Nessa looked confused, so I leaned forward and plucked the boarding passes out of her hand before she had a chance to change her mind. I'd already mentally ordered my first free drink and wasn't about to give up the chance at an in-flight buzz courtesy of Tiller Raine's largesse. Or, Nessa's largesse as the case may have been.

"Thank you so much, Nessa. Have a wonderful day."

I turned to head toward the TSA area when I heard Nessa call out, "Have a safe flight! You too, Mr. Raine. Good luck against the Jaguars on Sunday!"

There was a familiar beat of silence in which time seemed suspended. I'd often referred to this moment as similar in feel to putting on a pair of powerful, noise-canceling headphones. It was almost like the air around us formed a vacuum for a moment, sucking in and pressing against us before rushing out like the tide and grabbing up every fucking Rigger fan within a ten-mile radius.

Sure enough, after the beat of silence, it was mayhem. Fans came out of the woodwork, including airport employees, a nearby pilot, three families, and untold numbers of business men and women. Everyone was friendly and patient, but no one more so than Tiller Raine, who thrived in situations like this one.

He was a natural around his fans. You'd never know that they intimidated the hell out of him. He was always worried about disappointing them. One of the first things he'd said to me when I'd started accompanying him in public was to always treat the fans with respect no matter how they acted. At first, I thought it was the same old "the customer is always right" mentality everyone had in sales. Don't piss off a season ticket holder. My father had said it in front of me tons of times over the years. It took me a little while to realize how different that was from Tiller's motivation.

"Without them, I wouldn't be living my dream," he'd told me one night after I'd almost lost my temper at a fan who wouldn't get out of Tiller's face. We'd been at the grocery store late at night to satisfy someone's frozen greek yogurt bar craving (hint, it wasn't mine), and the man in line behind us had practically demanded an inside scoop on the upcoming game. Tiller had said it so calmly, and then he'd laughed when I'd gawped at him.

But once I'd calmed down, I'd realized he was right. And knowing how much he cared about his fans, his job, and the team had given me a newfound respect for him. Before that, I'd seen players come and go from the Riggers without seeming to care about much more than their team paycheck and endorsements. They mostly indulged fan's requests for pictures, hugs, and autographs when asked, but I'd only ever met a couple of players before Tiller who'd truly embraced the fans as the reason for their success.

So I stood there in the airport terminal and held Tiller's leather backpack while he laughed and chatted and signed autographs until a security guard came to escort us to the gate. Tiller thought it was generous VIP treatment, but I thought it was more likely TSA's need to clear the area near the security checkpoint.

Po-tay-toe, po-tah-toe.

"That was fun," Tiller said as we walked through a corridor to a single security checkpoint. Two women who looked vaguely familiar in a "were you on *Real Housewives*" kind of way went through ahead of us. The security escort brought us to the gate and handed us over to the gate agents, who promptly tittered with excitement and hustled us onto the plane to introduce Tiller to the pilot, who was a big fan. I tossed a polite smile and nod at the tall, good-looking man in uniform and found my seat. By the time Tiller had done his thing with Captain Tall & Sexy, I was settled with everything just so.

It wasn't until Tiller came and booted me out of the window seat that the flight attendant finally noticed me.

"I'll have a vodka cranberry, please," I said politely. "And he'll have a bottle of water."

Tiller leaned across me to smile at the flight attendant. "Actually, Lisa, I'd love a coffee, please. Cream and sugar. Thanks."

I tried not to sound like his mother, but I failed. "He'll also have a bottle of water," I repeated.

Her eyes flicked between us before nodding and assuring us it would only take a moment. I sat back and exhaled. Traveling with Tiller was always a production. Any minute they'd start general boarding and the Train of Stares and Whispers would begin.

"Sorry," he muttered so low only I could hear it.

The apology surprised me. I turned to him and asked what he was apologizing for.

"I know you hate all of this. The fans and stuff." His cheeks were a little ruddy, and his eyes wouldn't meet mine.

I put a hand on his arm. "I love that they love you. And I love how kind and attentive you are to them. It's just..." I stopped to think through how I really felt. "I hate that you can't have a normal life sometimes."

Tiller's eyes widened. "I love this life. Are you kidding? Everywhere I go people tell me how good I am at my job."

"Not always," I reminded him carefully, trying not to think about the time a guy walked right up and sucker punched him while accusing him of single-handedly losing a game that week. I'd scrambled on top of the asshole like a rabid spider monkey and tried scratching his eyes out in retaliation. Maybe it hadn't been pretty, but it was the only tool in my personal assault toolkit.

Tiller's face softened to an expression of warm affection that made me squirm in my seat. He grinned. "No, not always. But when the haters attack, I have you."

"Mpfh." I turned back around to receive our drinks. "Thanks," I murmured to the flight attendant.

When general boarding began, I tried to remind myself he *liked* the attention. It was something he'd told me many times before, but I had a hard time believing him. Maybe it was because every time my father had been approached in public, he'd griped about it later in private. When I was in elementary school, Coach had worked at SMU in Dallas, so when he'd moved up to coach for the Riggers, most of Texas's football fans already knew exactly who he was. He'd been a local celebrity in Texas my whole life. There'd never been a time I could remember when he wasn't approached in public to talk about the game. I'd gotten so used to the invasiveness of it, the fact it took my dad's attention away from our family, that I had a hard time believing Tiller could see it as a good thing.

But I watched him respond with smiles and nods, thoughtful responses to questions, and humble gratitude for compliments. The man was fucking gorgeous, and watching him respond with enthusiastic kindness... well, it did stuff to me.

Dirty stuff.

I cleared my throat and pretended to check my email on my phone. Out of the corner of my eye, I could see Tiller's thick, muscular thighs stretching the faded denim of his favorite pair of jeans. I knew from doing our laundry that there was a thin, threadbare spot in the crotch of those jeans, and... not gonna lie... I'd spent some time trying to figure out if I could spot any of his colorful boxer briefs through the loose threads.

The man probably thought I was a perv.

I was a perv.

A high-pitched shriek made me jump. I glanced up to see a teenage boy frozen in shock next to me. He stared at Tiller for a beat before breathlessly asking, "Are you Tiller Raine? *The* Tiller Raine?"

The kid had smudged eyeliner around wide eyes, and his cheeks were rapidly turning red as he stared at my boss. Under his half-zipped hoodie, I saw a Riggers T-shirt I recognized as one of the ones shot out of the fan cannon at home games. Lucky bastard.

"Sure am." Tiller reached out his hand to shake. I tried not to notice the familiar scent of our laundry detergent on his sleeve. For some reason, it smelled ten times better on his body than mine.

"Omigod," the boy wheezed as he took Tiller's hand. "You have no idea... you..."

An older woman put her hands on his shoulders and leaned forward to smile at Tiller. "You've made a big difference in our house. Thanks to you, Barrett came out to his team last year like it was no big deal."

I felt more than saw Tiller's entire body language change. It wasn't the first time someone had said something similar, but every time it happened was just as special and important to Tiller as the first had been. I felt the familiar lump form in my throat.

"Kick-ass, man," Tiller said gruffly. "It takes guts to do that. Big guts. Proud of you."

I reached into my wallet and pulled out a card to hand to Tiller. Tiller shot me a thankful smile before handing my card to Barrett. "This is Mike, my right-hand man, and here's his card. Shoot him an email and we'll hook you up with some signed merch when we get home in a few weeks, alright?"

Barrett noticed me for the first time and blushed even more. "Is he... are you two...?" It was clear what he was asking, and it also wasn't the first time we'd gotten this particular question either.

"No," I said quickly. "I'm his assistant and personal chef. My job is to make sure he eats more avocado and broccoli and less Snickers bars and cheese dip. Some days are harder than others."

Tiller elbowed me in the side. "He's a strict mofo... er, guy," he said, blinking up at Barrett's mom and mouthing an apology.

She nudged the kid forward and smiled again. "I'm married to an actual offshore rigger. I promise you don't know words I haven't heard after Barrett's dad comes home from the rigs. Thank you so much. You made our day."

As Barrett moved away grudgingly, he called out, "Our week! Our year!"

Tiller grinned as he sat back in his seat. "That was cool. And his dad is an actual rigger. What're the chances?"

In Houston? Fairly high, but I didn't say it.

He continued. "Can you imagine a football player at your high school growing up having the balls to wear eye makeup and be out?"

"You were out in high school," I reminded him before taking a sip of my drink. Oh god, that was amazing. I took more of a gulp the second time around.

"I was. Mostly because my dad told me you couldn't be out and play professional ball. I realized early on that if I didn't come out while I was a nobody, I'd for damned sure never be able to come out when I was somebody. So I ripped off the Band-Aid. It didn't hurt that I was dating the hottest guy in school at the time. The bragging rights were worth it."

I rolled my eyes and continued making love to my cocktail. "Must be nice to be you."

His eyebrows crinkled. "I thought you were out in high school, too?"

I sighed and put down my glass. "Not by choice. And I didn't date anyone because I had four older brothers who all played varsity ball and were four times the size of normal high school kids, remember? If anyone had gotten the urge to do anything other than run the other way when they saw me, my brothers would have pounded their gay asses into the ground."

His confusion turned to anger. "Your brothers are homophobes?"

I realized my mistake and tried to correct it. "Wait. No. Not at all. Well... actually, yes, they were. Before I came out. But when I came out, they were suddenly the most uninformed group of dude-bros to ever try to be supportive. They were protective as hell. No one was good enough for their baby Mikey, and they didn't make a secret of the fact that anyone who messed with me messed with all the Vining boys. You wanted to get the shit beat out of you by two defensive backs, a running back, and the best varsity wrestler in the state? Then you could think about looking at Mikey V. And by the way, the *V* very quickly came to stand for something besides 'Vining' if you catch my drift."

Tiller barked out a laugh that made everyone's head turn. I

scooted down in my seat and waved my hand in the air for another drink.

After the flight attendant nodded and smiled at me, I felt a warm breath against my ear. "When did you finally get that sorted out, Mikey?"

I shivered and quickly cleared my throat before lying my ass off. "First week freshman year in college. Gang bang in the dorm next to mine."

If I'd been expecting shocked silence, I was disappointed.

He barked out another laugh of pure disbelief. "Liar."

He was right, but not for the reason he thought.

Technically, the *V still* stood for virgin, but I'd be damned if I'd ever tell that to Mr. Popular Superstar, who, one had to assume, was about as far away from being a virgin as I was from catching a Super Bowl–winning touchdown pass. I may have slept with a few men along the way, including Nelson Evangelista, but I'd never given up my ass to anyone.

I was a control freak, and I'd never been with anyone I trusted enough for that. Why the hell hadn't I seen that as a red flag with Nelson? I'd let him do damned near everything else to me, including deny me in front of his family, the team, and even his closest friends. When I'd asked him why he wouldn't claim me even in front of the close friends and teammates who'd known he was gay, he'd told me I wouldn't understand the difference between the team's "tolerance" of a gay player and their acceptance of a player who actually brought a man around and flaunted his sexuality in their face.

I hadn't believed him at the time. My father had done his best to accept me after I'd come out, and he'd been the first coach to draft and start an out player in the NFL. Yes, he'd freaked out when he'd found me with Nelson, but that had been a fraternization problem, not a gay problem.

Right?

Sometimes I wondered if I was being deliberately obtuse. I closed my eyes and tried not to think too closely about it since it didn't matter anymore. Nelson and I had been broken up for five years, and

Tiller was my boss. I'd had a little lapse in judgment hooking up with Colin Saris, but that was history.

What I needed was to find a normal man to go out with. Someone who was as far away from professional football as you could get.

Maybe I'd meet my very own mountain man in Colorado and have a vacation fling. I decided to spend the rest of the flight daydreaming about it.

Only, the mountain man who showed up in my daydream looked surprisingly like the star wide receiver for the Houston Riggers. *Dammit.*

5

TILLER

Not gonna lie, I loved traveling with Mikey. He was so organized, I didn't have my usual worries about what I'd forgotten, whether I was going to be late, or where I was supposed to be. He took care of all of that. Even if I had to forgo my favorite airport snacks, it was still worth it to have his company beside me.

I also credited traveling together with bringing us closer together as friends in the early days of his employment. The first season he worked for me, he didn't travel with me at all. He was simply my personal chef at home. When I traveled, he packed me a giant cooler bag with enough snacks and supplemental protein meals to get me through the days I was gone. It wasn't until the following spring, after I'd made the permanent job offer and realized he was also doing the work of my PA and my housekeeper, that I first asked him to travel with me.

I'd been heading to Hawaii with several of the guys for a month of fun in the sun after a tough season in which we'd lost during the playoffs. We'd booked a big rental house with everything you could ever want, including a chef. But at the last minute, the chef had canceled for personal reasons, leaving us in the lurch. We'd gotten together and made Mikey an offer: come cook for us and we'd all pay an exorbitant fee for his time and travel.

After that... well, I'd become closer to an NFL diva than I'd ever thought I would. Spending a month in Hawaii without deviating from my newly healthy eating plan was kick-ass. I felt strong and clearheaded for the first time in my life, and I didn't want to lose it by eating heavy shit or too much takeout. So I started bringing him on the road if I was going to be gone longer than two or three nights. I'd taken a shit ton of flak for it at first, but once the team caught wind of how good his cooking was and how quickly my stats had improved with his nutrition help, the team got on board and started asking if they could pay him to make enough for them, too.

It had scared me at first. I thought he'd end up making so much money that he'd stop wanting to wash my dirty clothes and make breakfast smoothies for one. But he hadn't. In five years, he'd never once implied he wanted a change.

Until now.

I couldn't stop thinking about the cookbook offer he'd told me about. While I was excited for him—of course I was—I wasn't going to lie. It scared me. It was the first time I'd allowed myself to see his bigger dreams.

And I wanted him to have dreams. I wanted all of his fucking dreams to come true, and I would do whatever it took to help. But god... I didn't want to lose him either. I'd gotten so used to his company. His announcement about the cookbook project had been a mini wake-up call. Was he hoping to move on to bigger and better things? If he did, would I still see him? He was Coach V.'s son, but I didn't remember seeing much of him around the team before he came to work for me. Would he go back to being a once-a-year family member after moving on?

I must have made a noise in my throat because Mikey leaned over and asked if I was okay. I shifted uneasily in the wide leather seat and looked out at the puffy clouds.

"Yeah, 'course." I struggled to open my water bottle with one arm

in a sling until Mikey grabbed it and twisted the top off. I could feel
the power of his stare on the side of my face.

"Liar," he said softly. "What are you thinking about?"

"Remember that trip to LA when the hotel receptionist thought
we were a couple and put us in a king room together?"

Mikey snorted. "And you told me you were fine on the sofa except
it was a love seat half your size? Yeah, I remember."

Mikey had insisted I share the bed, and then he'd made a big
production over creating a pillow divider down the middle until I'd
finally agreed. It hadn't mattered. I'd still woken up with his warm
body curled against me like a heat-seeking missile. I'd lain awake for
two hours just soaking in the incredible feeling of holding him in my
arms while he slept.

I cleared my throat. "And we stayed up talking half the night," I
reminded him without looking over at him.

He was quiet for a beat before speaking. "You told me about the
time your sister got lost on a trip to the Grand Canyon and your dad
cried in front of you."

I nodded. "And you told me about your Scout leader teaching you
how to make table-side guacamole." I didn't mention that he'd also
told me how much he'd always felt like a disappointment to his
own dad.

Mikey laughed. "Game-changer. I'd never had avocado before, if
you can believe it. Watching him mash all of those ingredients
together sparked something in me, I guess. After that, I started
making all kinds of dips. My brothers thought it was the best thing
ever. They didn't realize they'd suddenly become my taste testers."

I let the subject lighten up from where my memories had gone.
"What the hell kind of Scout leader teaches the kids to make guac?"

"Oh, he was super gay. Hated camping. Thankfully, there were
two leaders and the other one did all the butch stuff. But Mr.
Meadows taught us how to keep the campsite tidy, how to sing camp-
fire songs in two-part harmony, and how to convince someone else to
take the scales off the fresh catch. I loved that guy."

I lifted an eyebrow at him.

"Not like that," he said, smacking the back of his hand against my chest above my sling. "He was a hundred and ten years old. At least to my prepubescent self."

We continued sharing childhood stories until he cut in with a reminder about seeing my parents. "I told them we'd contact them once we got settled and let them know when they can come out to see you."

I bit back a sigh and looked out the window again. I loved my parents, but sometimes seeing them felt like a command performance, and my dad especially would pepper me with tons of questions about why I was in Colorado instead of with my team.

"Not right away, okay?" I asked.

"Of course. Whatever you want."

I knew Mikey wouldn't let me get away with ignoring them forever. He would do what he always did which was manage my parents' expectations with my reluctance and find that sweet, delicate middle ground that would check all the boxes and leave everyone feeling like their needs had been met. He was good at that. So very good at it.

"You should be a hostage negotiator," I muttered.

"False equivalency, I think," he said with a smile in his voice. "Anyway, what the hell are you going to do with yourself in the cabin besides read your new books and sneak in forbidden workouts?"

He knew me well.

"Good question. Probably pester you while you're cooking. Eat lots of your food. Sit in the hot tub and stare off into space."

"Maybe you should start thinking about what you want to do when you retire," Mikey suggested casually.

Too casually.

I turned to look at him. "I'm twenty-seven."

He shrugged. "Sometimes retirement hits you out of the blue in the NFL. Everyone knows that."

Of course, he meant retirement by injury, and I was sure it was on his mind after yet another injury. "Can we not talk about it, please?"

It wasn't the first time he'd brought it up. I knew he was trying to gently nudge me to think about the future, but it was harder than he could possibly know. When you'd been called a football star your entire life and every decision made about your future had revolved around the game, it wasn't easy to suddenly think about something else.

"I just want you to realize there's more to life than football. There's more to *you* than football. I think you've spent a lot of time ignoring those other parts of you."

"Football is who I am," I said in a quiet hiss.

"You're right," he replied calmly. "But it's not the only thing you are."

"How can you say that?"

He turned to me and reached for my wrist, turning my arm so he could trace the tattoo on the inside of my wrist. The touch brought goose bumps up on my skin.

The tattoo was a simple profile of the mountains with GPS coordinates underneath.

"It took me about an hour of boredom in the hospital while you were asleep before I decided to google the coordinates," he said. "It's the Golden Peak Superpipe in Vail."

I nodded. "Yep."

"Which is for snowboarders," Mikey continued. "And it reminded me of the pictures of you in your bedroom at your parents' house. You snowboarded in high school. Won some kind of medal for it and everything."

What else was there to do but nod again? "You already know this. We've talked about it before."

Mikey studied my face for a minute. "Does that mean this a subject you want me to drop? Because you're acting like you do whenever I mention the phrase 'cauliflower pizza crust.'"

I shifted in my seat so I could face him better. "No, it's not that. It's just... it's a moot point, you know? I can't snowboard anymore, so there's no point in thinking about it or talking about it."

Even my college coach had forbidden me from the laundry list of other sports and dangerous activities that could put my football career in jeopardy. I hadn't laced up my snowboard boots since the winter of my senior year in high school.

"You're not going to play professional football forever, you know. That's my point. What do you want to fill your life with after you're released? Maybe you'll want to move back to Colorado so you can ski and snowboard again."

I loved the mountains, and I missed the snow. Badly. I also missed summer in Colorado with the long days and huge blue skies. Sunshine on my back and cool evening breezes through the aspen trees. Everything about my home state called to me, and as long as I'd lived in Texas, I'd felt the loss of it deep in my bones.

But I also loved football, and it was true what I'd said before. I barely knew who I was outside of it.

"Maybe," I admitted, trying to think of other things I liked that I rarely had time for. "I like to plant things. My mom always made the most colorful flower baskets in the summer and hung them on the front porch. She also has baskets along the back deck railing that we used to plant."

"She still does," he said. "At least, they were overflowing with color the last time we were there in May."

"I always loved the flower baskets everywhere in Vail during the summer, too. Maybe after I retire, I can go work in the plant department at Home Depot."

Mikey snickered. "I'd love to see your reaction the first time you got that paycheck."

"Depending on when I retire, I won't need the paycheck. But I can't imagine not working in some capacity. I'd go stir-crazy."

The plane jolted and had a sudden drop in altitude. Mikey gripped my arm the way he always did during turbulence. "We're okay," I murmured softly as the plane steadied again.

"What about coaching?" he asked as if it hadn't happened.

I shrugged. "I'm not great with kids."

His brown eyes flashed at me. "Bullshit."

"Fine, but I don't have enough patience for teaching, and I'm not sure I'd know how to pull back from pro level at this point. I'd probably send kids to the ER left and right after running them too hard or having too high expectations."

"I can see that." We sat in silence for a little while. "You're good with people, Tiller. They listen to you. What you say makes a difference to them. You could always be a motivational speaker. Remember the talk you gave at that camp?"

I remembered. The year after I'd joined the Riggers, the team captain had spearheaded a fundraiser for a camp for LGBTQ youth. It had been the team's way of accepting me and showing they stood firmly on my side as an out player. I'd been asked to give a talk to the kids the following summer about what it was like to live authentically, how to handle bullies, and any other issues relevant to being LGBTQ in sports, the public eye, or life in general.

After puking several times with nerves, I'd gone out there and given it my best. And I'd loved it. I'd loved seeing the kids collectively lean forward with interest, relax back into their seats with relief, or even tear up with the realization they weren't alone. I'd felt for once that my words and actions could make an impactful difference in someone's life.

"Yeah," I said, noticing a roughness in my voice I hadn't expected. "Yeah, that was good."

I spent the rest of the flight thinking about the future. It was something I hadn't done much of before, and I realized somewhere along the way, I'd stopped daydreaming. After being drafted into the NFL, I'd felt like my dreams had come true, and there'd no longer been any point in daydreaming about more. But now Mikey was throwing images at me that made me wonder if it was time to start daydreaming again. Daydreaming about a different kind of future.

The swoosh of fresh powder under my board as I sailed through frigid air up the side of the pipe. The scent of fresh soil being turned with a trowel while colorful pots of flowers sat nearby waiting to be planted. The feeling of fullness in my chest as I looked out across a group of LGBTQ youth looking for connection and reassurance.

I glanced over at Mikey, who seemed to be dozing more than reading. His book was about to slip to the floor, so I reached over and took it out of his hands gently before tucking it beside him in the seat. After a few more minutes, he began to list sideways toward the aisle. I grabbed his arm and pulled him my way until his head rested on my shoulder.

His hands wrapped around my arm like a hug as he settled against me. I smelled his signature scent that was a combination of soap, deodorant, coffee, and some kind of baking spice like vanilla which I'd never been able to figure out. He didn't bake much since I wasn't allowed to eat that kind of treat often. I often wondered if it was his shampoo or something instead of actual kitchen vanilla.

As my head slipped back into the dreamworld of my post-retirement future, I wondered where Mikey would be while I was busy pursuing new paths. Would he be on some kind of whirlwind talk-show tour touting his newest best-selling cookbook? Would he be living in a chateau in Europe cooking for a wealthy family? Hell, he'd probably own his own restaurant. If he continued to focus on healthy eating for athletes, maybe he'd move to Los Angeles and open a cafe or catering business there.

I ground my back teeth together wholly unsure whether I'd ever want a life of post-retirement leisure if it meant saying goodbye to Michael Vining.

6

MIKEY

I was still rubbing sleep out of my eyes when Tiller ushered me into the passenger seat of the big SUV I'd rented. The leather was cold against the fabric of my jeans, and I shivered inside the big puffy coat I'd hastily pulled on the minute my suitcase had come spinning off the carousel. Tiller chuckled and closed the door, trapping some of his exhalation vapor inside with me.

It was cold as balls.

I was a Texas boy born and raised, but I actually liked visiting places that had a true winter season. Every time we'd visited Tiller's parents in Denver, I'd parked myself in front of their real wood fireplace and toasted my socked feet on the stone hearth until I couldn't stand the heat anymore. I relished the chance to truly enjoy a hot chocolate without sweating my ass off.

"You got an address?" Tiller asked, hopping in the driver's seat and slamming his door closed.

I pulled up the Waze app and clicked on the address I'd already preprogrammed. The smooth voice began navigating Tiller out of the area. We drove out of the airport I'd always thought looked like a giant white caterpillar and began making our way toward the city of Denver.

"You sure you don't want to stop by your parents' place?" I teased.

"Funny man. Remind me to get you a Comedy Central Standup Special for your birthday," he grunted.

The heat finally kicked in enough for me to pull off my coat. I noticed Tiller hadn't even put his on yet which was either a testament to his killer metabolism or his Colorado blood. Either way, he pretty much slayed the black sweater and faded blue jeans he had on. The arms of the sweater were pushed up, revealing a corded forearm still tanned from all the time spent outside in the long Texas fall. When my eyes traveled down his arm to his big hand on the wheel, I suddenly realized he was driving one-handed.

That jolted me wide-awake.

"You're driving with a clipped wing!" I yelped. "Pull over and let me drive. Jesus, Tiller."

"I'm fine."

"You're in a sling, for god's sake." My heart hammered in my chest. "Why didn't you let me drive?"

He glanced over at me with a smirk. "Uh, because you were still drooling in your sleep at the rental desk?"

I didn't remember going to a rental desk, so maybe he had a point. "Fine, then pull over at a coffee shop and we'll kill two birds."

Tiller shook his head. "I've been driving these roads for a million years. This is my hometown, remember?"

I stopped arguing but only because I knew he'd want to stop soon enough for coffee himself. Now that I'd made the suggestion, he wouldn't be able to stop thinking about it. Sure enough, when we got to the far side of Denver, he pulled off the interstate and found a Starbucks. I pretended not to hear him order himself a sugar- and cream-filled monstrosity before he rattled off my skinny chai latte order like he'd done it a million times. When he added a slice of pumpkin bread and a blueberry scone, I decided to forgive him for almost killing us with the one-armed driving stunt.

We switched places and got back on the road. It took us almost three hours to get to Aster Valley, Colorado, but the time passed quickly with talk of what Tiller still needed to get his friends and family for Christmas, what we wanted to get for Sam—who was next to impossible to buy for since he didn't like owning more than would fit in the saddlebags on his motorcycle—and whether or not Tiller's teammates had started planning their big end-of-season trip yet.

When we crested the final mountain pass, a small, snow-covered town appeared in the valley below. Lights twinkled from shops and houses in the shadows between the peaks on either side while the top of the mountain to the east still shone with the last traces of the warm glow of sunset on snow. I felt like we'd found a little hidden gem nestled in a secret spot deep in the Rockies.

"Have you ever been here before?" I asked.

Tiller shook his head. "Never even heard of it, I don't think. Wait... Aster Valley... didn't there used to be a ski resort here?"

I let out a soft snort. "You're asking the wrong Texan."

He pulled out his phone and did a search. I was surprised he still had enough cell signal to get any results.

"Here it is. Yeah, in the early 2000s, Olympian team member and two-time world champion in downhill and Super-G, suffered a career-ending injury due to a hazard on the slope. The resort was sued into bankruptcy by his insurance carrier, and the slopes were shut down." He read silently for another minute. "Damn. Looks like it must have done a number on this town. Can you imagine losing that income and those jobs? A town this small? I mean... it couldn't have been that big of a ski destination if I'd barely heard of it, but still."

"The nearest decent airport is Yampa Valley. It's still like an hour away," I added. I'd looked into flying closer to Aster Valley, but ultimately decided it didn't make sense since the flight times would put us at the cabin later than if we flew into Denver and drove.

Tiller shrugged. "Maybe it struggled competing with Steamboat. Which is weird because usually a smaller ski resort only thirty minutes away from a bigger one does well with the overflow. I wonder why no one bought it and reopened it."

We made up a few stories about what had happened to Aster Valley in the twenty years since the accident, including haunted slopes and ornery old town leadership, so by the time we reached the quaint little main drag, we were suspiciously surprised by how benign it seemed.

"This is goddamned adorable," Tiller said. "Look at that yarn shop. And an honest-to-goodness diner. They're all decorated for Christmas."

He was right. While Aster Valley definitely looked half-asleep, it was charming as hell. Several storefronts were empty, but the ones that weren't seemed to be well-kept with pride. Holiday lights and holly sprigs circled the streetlight poles, and there was a big banner across the street announcing the Aster Valley Holiday Fest the following weekend. A few pedestrians bundled up in coats and hats made their way along the wide sidewalk with paper shopping bags dangling from mittened hands.

"We've arrived on a Hallmark movie set," I said a little breathlessly.

"Well, maybe the low-budget version," Tiller said, pointing to a darkened old theater with an empty marquee. Several key letters were missing from the sign, so it read "Valley eater" instead of what I presumed to have been The Aster Valley Theater at one time.

I flapped my hand in the air. "Imagine how cute that would be if someone bought it and fixed it up! It could be one of those bougie dinner-and-wine theaters."

Tiller reached over and yanked my collar up. I shot him a confused look.

"You're just cute when you get passionate about things," he teased.

I slapped his hand away and kept rolling slowly through the town, trying to take in all of the quaint shops and loads of potential. "Robert Redford needs to come here and inject some money into this place."

We quickly left the main area of town and wound our way up the mountainside until pulling through a wooden archway with faded letters carved into it.

"The Rockley Lodge?" Tiller asked, his voice laced with curiosity. "Sounds bigger than a little rental cabin in the woods."

I navigated the narrow snow-edged lane between the trees to a clearing. "It's a little more than a cabin," I admitted before catching sight of it.

It was a giant, log-hewn structure that looked like something out of an architectural magazine. The lodge was crafted with an artistic mix of wood and stone and boasted a huge, welcoming front porch lit up with actual gas lanterns hanging from iron pegs.

"Holy fuck," Tiller said. "We made a wrong turn."

"No. We definitely rented from the Rockleys. Or, rather, the company that manages the Rockley Estate. I think the rental guy on the phone told me the owners passed away, so maybe it's being managed by a company now. I didn't pay much attention after he offered me a big discount for the month."

I pulled around the circular drive, noticing it had been neatly snow blown or shoveled or something. Whatever it was snow-dwellers did to remove the snow from their driveway. The place was well-kept despite being about ten times bigger than the two of us needed.

"Too bad everyone else is stuck in Houston or we could have a kick-ass house party," Tiller said, opening the door and letting in the arctic air.

I reached back for my puffy coat and scrambled into it, zipping it up to my chin before hopping out of the rapidly cooling SUV.

"It has a ton of bedrooms. I think it used to be a big family lodge," I said, coming around to the other side of the vehicle and standing next to him as we stared up and out at the many-leveled wings of the lodge. "Don't worry. They said the bedroom wings are all closed off for people who don't need them. The master and housekeeper's rooms should be open for us."

He turned to face me with a frown. "Housekeeper?"

"Me."

"No. I know. I just... you're not the housekeeper. You're a guest."

I moved toward the front door and pulled my phone out to find the security code for the keypad. "I'm their guest, but I'm your housekeeper. It's fine. I'm sure the housekeeper's room in this place is nicer than most people's regular bedroom."

"You're not my housekeeper!" His voice carried through the frigid night. "You're my... my..."

I waited him out so I could hear the way he always seemed to finish this sentence when it came up.

"My Mikey," he finished weakly.

I fucking loved hearing him say that. "Be that as it may, your Mikey is just fine. If not, I know from experience I can fit in a king bed with you." I winked at him before turning back to tackle the lock. I ignored the slight hitch of breath he took when I'd winked at him.

Being alone with him like this was oddly electrifying.

The lodge was just as stunning on the inside as it was on the outside. The decor was chunky leather and wood softened with colorful textiles and some stunning framed photographs of—what I assumed were—local flora and fauna as well as landscapes from the area.

A giant stone fireplace had pride of place in the cozy sitting room attached to the large kitchen, and I could picture spending nights curled up on the overstuffed armchair in front of the fire while Tiller watched football on the flat-screen TV from the long sofa. The kitchen itself was to die for. It had everything I could ever want and had already been stocked by arrangement with a grocery delivery company.

I was in heaven.

"It'll do," Tiller said with a tease in his voice. I shot him the bird without looking away from the commercial-sized mixer on a stand at the end of a pristine stainless-steel countertop.

"My precious..." I murmured, running my hands over the controls.

"I'm going to take a shower, then try out the hot tub. You want to join me?" Tiller walked over to the fridge and reached in for a bottle of water while I imagined joining him in a hot shower and helping soap up his broad shoulders and rounded muscles. "Mike?"

The image of soapy bubbles sliding between his firm ass cheeks and down his hairy, muscled legs was making me feel a little—

"Mike!"

I jumped and snapped my head up, grateful beyond measure that there was a counter between us to hide my inappropriate boss-boner. "What?"

"Hot tub. Meet me there in ten, okay? I think you could use it. You seem a little out of it."

"Oh, uh..." I pictured him in swim trunks sliding down into the hot water as the snow settled in the hills around us and the closest person was probably at least a mile away. "Uh-huh. Yeah. Sure."

When he left the room, I scrambled to the housekeeper's quarters behind the kitchen and was not surprised to find a well-appointed suite complete with a mini kitchenette, a sitting area, and a giant, luxurious bathroom. I stripped down in record time and made it into the shower in time to grasp my dick for a quick stroke.

"Motherfucker," I said with a gasp. It felt so good to touch myself while continuing the mental imagery of Tiller in the shower somewhere else in the house. I knew it was inappropriate to jerk off to thoughts of my boss, but I also knew that my brain was Las Vegas. What happened in there, stayed in there. I could use whatever it took to get off, and no one else would ever be the wiser.

I pictured him leaning over slightly to place his hands on the tiled wall. His ass cheeks would separate just enough to give me a peek at his hole, dusky and covered in a little bit of hair. I groaned when I pictured sliding to my knees and tasting him, sticking out my tongue and teasing him until he had to bite his fist to keep from screaming.

"*Nghhh!*" My orgasm slammed into me, taking the breath from my lungs so quickly, I inhaled some of the shower spray and began to sputter and cough.

Classy, Mike.

When I finally recovered enough to finish washing myself, I felt an odd combination of raw and relaxed. I dried off and threw on my swim trunks before wrapping a dry, fluffy towel around my shoulders and heading to the fridge for an extra-large glass of wine to take with me to the hot tub. I may or may not have thrown back a glass of wine first as a "sample" before committing to a healthy second pour.

Tiller was already in the water with his head thrown back and eyes closed. I dashed across the frozen tundra and had just enough dexterity to set my wineglass down before dumping myself unceremoniously into the hot water with a squeak and a splash followed by relieved sigh.

Tiller opened one eye and peered at me. "That was an entrance."

I reached for my drink and took a healthy swallow. "It's cold as fuck out here."

"Mmm."

"If this was my lodge, I'd put underfloor heating from the door to the hot tub. Maybe some of those gas heater things, too." I continued imagining how fun it would be to own a place like this. I could turn it into a bed-and-breakfast and have people to cook for every day.

Once I settled my ass into an ass divot built in to the plastic frame of the hot tub, I looked around. The moon was half-full and hung low over a nearby peak, illuminating snow-brushed evergreen trees on the mountainside below. The only ambient noise was the churn of the water in the hot tub and the periodic creaks of branches or something in the nearby woods.

"God, it's peaceful here," I said, stating the obvious. "Why haven't we come out here in winter before now?"

The unspoken words plonked heavily between us.

Football season.

"I just mean, it's really nice," I said lamely. "I like it. It's so different from the view at home. Not that I don't love the view from the kitchen. You know how much I enjoy looking out at the... golfers."

Why was I suddenly babbling like a fool? I hated golf. I hated the fact we lived on a golf course. The only redeeming quality was the view of the lake and the frequent, joyful moments of watching golfers shank their balls into the drink right outside our window.

"You hate the golfers," he reminded me. "You once said, and I quote, 'Golf isn't much different than glorified fly swatting.'"

I took a sip of the crisp chardonnay. "I stand by my assessment," I said with a sniff.

"You also said baseball was more interesting to watch than golf."

"True story, bro." I took another sip and overshot my mouth. Cool liquid slid down my chin and chest.

Smooth.

"And then," Tiller continued, "you said boiling water was more interesting to watch than baseball."

The wine went to my head faster than I expected, and I remembered we were at altitude. "Boiling water has more action and unpredictability than someone hitting anything with a stick," I said in agreement. "And I'm glad you recognize that."

His low chuckle did things to my own low things. Damn the man. I'd rubbed one out for a reason. It was supposed to have allowed me to come out here and share this hot tub with Mr. Sexy Pro Baller without getting a boner.

Epic fail.

"Makes me wonder what you think of football," he said deceptively casually.

"I love football," I said truthfully. "When you're playing it."

Red alert. Warning. Warning.

My words settled around us like mini depth charges waiting to detonate and blow all kinds of peaceful shit apart.

"I didn't mean to say that out loud," I admitted in a whisper. "Can we..."

He interrupted me. "You mean that?"

I made a little growling sound in my throat. "What happens in Vegas was supposed to stay in Vegas," I reminded my stupid, fucked-up brain and mouth.

"We're not in Vegas," Tiller said with a grin.

No. No we sure as hell weren't. We were half-naked together in a hot tub a mile away from the nearest anyone. And the buzz of white wine was making me stupid while the buzz of his sex appeal was making me hard as fuck.

"Tennis!" I blurted. "Now there's a game. All that back-and-forth. All those... fuzzy... balls."

I sighed. So much for a change of subject.

Tiller turned and gave me a knowing grin. "Isn't that just another example of someone hitting something with a stick?"

I thrust my wineglass at him. "You should have some of this."

His eyes widened in surprise. "Me? Drink alcohol during the season? Are you high? My... Mikey... would kill me if he found out."

I sighed and closed my eyes, leaning my head back and trying to find my Zen again. "Your Mikey is fallible, you know," I muttered.

Tiller was quiet for a moment. Gentle water movement noises were the only thing breaking the silence between us until he spoke.

"Nah. My Mikey is perfect."

Woah.

His Mikey was drunk. And so unbelievably happy. For the moment. It was enough.

7

TILLER

Mikey was adorable on his worst day, but when he was shirtless and tipsy? Jesus fucking Christ. The man was irresistible. As he sloshed wine down his front and began to giggle every time he mispronounced a word, I found myself staring at him like a creeper and grinning at him like a loon.

I was besotted, and honestly, I'd been obsessed with him for a while now. If he weren't the coach's son, I'd have had a hard time resisting him.

Hell, who was I kidding? I still had a hard time resisting him. It was impossible. I wanted to taste the wine on his lips, move my mouth down to test the shape of his throat, nip on the edge of his ear, and discover exactly what spots made him gasp.

I wanted to pull him onto my lap and knead his rounded ass cheeks with my hands. He was wildly expressive when he told a story, so I could only imagine how expressive and reactive he'd be in bed.

My jaw clenched against a groan as I felt my dick fill with interest. *Down, boy. This man is not for you. Pick someone else.*

I sighed and closed my eyes again. It had been over three years since I'd even been touched sexually by another man. Surely my desperation for Mikey was the result of this killer dry spell. Not that I wouldn't be attracted to him regardless. I definitely would be and had been. The man was the sexiest human being I'd ever met. But this itchy, grasping sense of *need* was unlike anything I'd ever experienced before. It clawed at me like I could barely hold back the desire to pounce on him and make him mine. The way I wanted him was animalistic. Confusing. Downright obsessive and possessive.

"When was the last time you had sex?" Mikey's voice shocked me out of my mental spiral. I almost wondered if he'd read my mind.

I glanced at him. "Are you asking me about my love life?"

He grinned. "Nah. Just your sex life. Totally separate thing."

His eyes were glassy from the wine and the altitude, as well as the long day of traveling. His lips were wet from his last sip, and his cheeks were pink from the heat of the water and the cold night air. I wondered if I'd ever seen him look so beautiful.

"Long time ago," I admitted.

"Rent boy?"

I gaped at him. "What?"

He blushed and looked away. "Never mind. Sorry. It's none of my business. Inappropriate. *Very* inappropriate. Jesus, Mike."

I reached out and touched his shoulder to get him to turn back to me. "Are you asking if I sleep with sex workers?"

He set his jaw. "There's nothing wrong with sex workers."

"Are you a sex worker?" God, he was so confusing. Sometimes I thought he talked himself around in circles in his head until stuff popped out all mixed up from his mental blender.

"Me?" he squeaked. "No one would pay me for sex."

I laughed. "That's patently false. Hundreds—no, thousands—of men would pay to watch you do a simple slow striptease."

His wide brown eyes blinked at me slowly. "Wha?"

I laughed again. "You have no idea, do you?"

Mikey shook his head. "It's just that... I heard a rumor about you..."

Laughter time was over. I remembered the game in Green Bay a year ago when I'd made a joke about being so hard up I was willing to pay for company to come suck me off in my hotel room. It had turned into a big joke on the team. The only way Mikey could have heard about it was from a teammate.

"Saris," I growled. "Fucking asshole."

"Not gonna argue with that," Mikey said.

"What did he say to you?"

"That you paid for it on the road. I knew better than to believe him, but..."

"But what?"

When he didn't answer, I reached out to tilt his chin back toward me. "But what?" I asked more softly.

"I never see you with anyone," he said, looking sheepish. "I just... I don't understand. You're so... um... *you,* and I just thought you'd have..." He seemed to struggle with his thoughts.

"Complete a thought, Mikey," I urged gently.

"You're sexy as fuck, and I thought you'd have a revolving door of men in your bed, okay? You happy now?" He threw up his hands, splashing both of us with warm water.

I was. I totally was.

"Three years and four months," I said. Mikey blinked at me with spiky lashes.

"Huh?"

"You heard me. I got a drunken blow job on the road during preseason from an old college teammate. He approached me in a hotel bar and told me he'd always envied my being out. Said he'd fantasized about sucking me off for years." I shrugged. "So I let him."

That wasn't the whole truth. The whole truth was that we'd played the Seattle Seahawks in that preseason game, and Nelson Evangelista had found a way to tell me he'd fucked Mikey V. for almost a year behind Coach's back. I must have given him the reaction he'd been looking for because he'd spent the rest of the game taunting me with details about Mike's tight ass, his hunger for cock, and his willingness to be humiliated in the bedroom. He told me over and over again I should tap that.

It was one of the rare times I'd gotten drunk in the past decade, and as soon as I'd run into Trae, I'd let him do whatever he wanted.

Thankfully, that hadn't included bringing him back to my room for anything more. He'd sucked me, I'd finished him off with my hand, and we'd gone our separate ways when we'd left the lobby men's room.

I'd never asked Mikey about Nelson. I'd known, of course, that Mikey had worked for Nelson, *lived* with Nelson, before coming to work for me. But I'd decided to believe the part about them sleeping together was all made up. For three years, I'd shoved down the thoughts of the giant linebacker and my... Mikey whenever they'd reared their ugly heads.

But now I couldn't stand not knowing.

"You and Evangelista?" My voice was rough, and it got Mikey's attention. His eyes widened comically.

"Who told you that?"

Now it was my turn to look away. I didn't want to see the truth in his eyes. "Never mind," I said, standing up and reaching for my towel. "Sorry I asked. That was inappropriate."

Mikey swallowed but didn't correct me, didn't tell me it was okay that I'd asked a personal question. Instead, he let me go.

It was for the best. We didn't *do* personal questions. It was one of the unspoken rules between us that kept our relationship platonic. Safe.

I walked through the frigid air and into the house, trying hard not to crush my back teeth to a fine powder. After stopping by the kitchen for my requisite couple of bottles of water, I made my way to the master suite. The king-sized bed mocked me from its place in the center of the room.

The second hot shower was quicker than the first, just enough soap and water to get the hot tub chemicals off my skin. I followed it with a thorough tooth-brushing before pulling on my flannel pajama bottoms and a soft T-shirt and sliding into bed.

Alone.

In the morning, I found Mikey adorably sleep-tousled and flustered, trying to figure out the fancy coffee machine in the kitchen.

"Morning," I said, deciding to pretend like our awkward conversation the night before had never happened.

"Nnfh," he grumbled. "Fucking espresso machine. Why didn't I bring my french press? If this was my bed-and-breakfast, we'd have a french press. What kind of gourmet kitchen doesn't have a french press?"

I could totally see him running a bed-and-breakfast. He'd be amazing at it. I walked up and nudged him out of the way so I could take over. "The kind that has a state-of-the-art, twenty-thousand-dollar Mastrena espresso machine made by Swiss manufacturer Thermoplan instead."

He stared at me. "And you know that, how?"

"Because it's almost exclusive to Starbucks, and I worked there in college."

It was clear Mikey had never heard this part of the Tiller Raine story. I chuckled as I began to make us both lattes with the beans Mikey had clearly brought from home. He was a snob about his coffee beans to the point he had separate expensive ones for him and cheap-ass shit for me.

"I thought you were spoon-fed filet mignon as a student athlete," he said. "No job needed with a full ride."

"Yeah, well, the full ride didn't pay for the new transmission I needed on my truck or the North Face parka I wanted to replace my stupid wool peacoat with."

The sound of the machine's burr grinder was familiar, and I moved through the process of preparing the coffee from muscle memory. When I finally moved to pull the milk from the fridge, I almost accidentally knocked into Mikey.

"Whoa, did you fall asleep on me?" I asked, grabbing his upper arm to keep him from slamming against the counter. The movement in my bad shoulder made me wince, but I bit it back so Mikey wouldn't notice.

He shook his head. "I... I just assumed you'd never had to work for anything."

I let out a loud bark of laughter. "Are you fucking kidding? You don't think I work hard in my job for the Riggers?"

He looked up at me in surprise. "What? No. I mean, yes, of course you do. You work your ass off."

"Damned right." I poured the milk into the little pitcher. "And I worked my ass off in high school and college with part-time jobs until sophomore year at Boulder when the coach told me to fish or cut bait."

"That sucks," Mikey muttered.

I shrugged. "Not really. After I quit Starbucks, I spent more time on conditioning and stuff. Probably wouldn't have done as well if I hadn't been able to focus on football."

Mikey made another grumbled sound of disagreement but didn't say anything. It was rare for me to witness his pre-coffee moments in the morning, but it was always entertaining when I did.

I handed him the first latte. "Here you go, sleepyhead."

He took it over to the overstuffed chair by the dark fireplace and plopped down in it, pulling his knees up to his chest and inhaling the steam from his mug. "Praise the lord."

When I finished prepping my own cup, I took it over to the sofa and set it down on a table before moving to start the fire. Thankfully, someone had already laid it out, so all I had to do was open the flue and light the newspaper under the kindling.

We sat in companionable silence for a little while as the flames caught and the wood started to burn. Once Mikey had enough caffeine in his system to function, he began to speak. His eyes remained on the fire.

"We dated for over a year," he said softly. "He wasn't out. Obviously. But some of his close friends knew. About him, I mean. Not about me."

I realized he was talking about Evangelista, and I wasn't quite sure I was prepared to hear it. He continued despite my silence.

"It was so stupid. I just... I was lonely, I guess. And I..." His voice trailed off. I glanced over at him and saw him staring into the fire with flared nostrils.

"You...?" I nudged.

"I wanted to be wanted. I was tired of being alone. I'm not really a hookup guy."

I thought about his hookup with Colin Saris but kept my mouth firmly closed. It wasn't my place to judge. Besides, there was nothing wrong with hooking up. For god's sake, I'd do anything for a hookup these days. It simply wasn't easy when you were a recognizable public figure and there were people hoping to sell your story to the highest bidder.

"You don't have to explain yourself to me," I told him. "You deserve to be wanted and loved."

He snorted softly. "He didn't love me. I'm not sure Nelson is capable of loving someone besides himself."

I'd never played with Evangelista. He'd been traded to Seattle right before I was drafted, but I'd heard all about him, and I'd had plenty of chances to watch him on the other side of the field when we'd played against his team. He was a typical cocky bastard, a dime a dozen in this business. Mikey's assessment didn't surprise me. But imagining the two of them in a relationship did.

"That was five years ago," I said. "What about since then?"

For the first time, he looked over at me and met my eyes. "Since then I've had you to keep me busy."

Heavy silence descended for a beat while I tried to figure out what he meant by that. Suddenly, he grinned and shifted in his seat, stretching an arm up over his head. "And my right hand. Anyway, let's go out for breakfast at that little diner we saw. I feel like playing hooky today."

I sat there frozen with a rapidly filling dick, imagining Mikey V. stroking himself under my roof—down the hall from where I was doing the same thing half the time. Even though he'd originally moved into the apartment over my garage, two years into his employment, we'd discovered black mold in the walls. He'd temporarily relocated into one of the guest rooms down the hall from my bedroom and had never left. We'd never talked about it, but it was pretty clear we both preferred being under the same roof. Neither of us enjoyed being alone all that much. It was one of the reasons we encouraged Sam and some of our other friends to stay over whenever they were hanging out with us late at night.

Lately, though, I'd begun to recognize part of the reason we encouraged others to stay over was to keep us from having too much time alone together. Because now that it was just the two of us, I couldn't stop thinking of crossing the line with him, of touching him, of tasting him, of fucking his sweet ass deep into the mattress in the bedroom or even taking him on his hands and knees right here in front of the blazing fire.

I clenched my teeth together and tried to imagine anything that might kill my erection.

Coach Vining finding out you want to bone his baby boy.

Done.

I stood up and swallowed the last of my lukewarm latte. "Give me five minutes to get dressed and we'll go."

8

MIKEY

The drive into the little town of Aster Valley was completely different in daylight. The atmosphere was still charming, but this time we could clearly make out the abandoned ski slopes leading straight down to the main part of town. It turned out that our Rockley Lodge had originally been a ski-in/ski-out location perched right on the edge of one of the main runs. The abandoned lift stood silent and still in the clear mountain air, and the sun cast shortening shadows through the fir trees at the edges of the open trails.

"Hell, we could have taken a sled into town," Tiller muttered as he pulled into a parking space in front of the Mustache Diner. "Who knew how close we were as the crow flies?"

I hauled myself out of the large SUV. "But then we would have had to climb back up with a stomach full of waffles," I added. "Which basically means you would have had to pull me on the sled."

When we entered the old-fashioned diner, there wasn't a hint of recognition on anyone's faces. Maybe it was the fleece beanie Tiller had on or the scarf wrapped around his neck, but it was surprisingly refreshing.

"Sit anywhere, hon," a man around fifty with salt-and-pepper hair and scruff said from a nearby booth he was busy wiping down.

We hustled away from the drafty doors and found a red vinyl booth in the back. The old Formica table was in tip-top shape, and it was clear whoever ran the place took good care of it. Laminated menus sat tucked behind the caddy of condiments against the wall at one end of the table. I grabbed two and handed one to Tiller. "You can have a cheat meal if you want. I'll make up for it at lunch and dinner."

"Yes, mother," he murmured under his breath. His lips were curved up in an indulgent smile as he perused the menu, so I didn't worry too much about it.

"What do you want to do today?" I asked.

Tiller set the menu down and looked up. "You always ask me that when there's something you want to do."

He was right. "I want to walk up and down Main Street and check out the shops. One of the reasons this place made my short list is because there's an actual spice merchant here, if you can believe it. They do a ton of online business, but they have a storefront in Aster Valley, too. It's called—"

The older man with a giant salt-and-pepper mustache appeared with his little order notepad at the ready. "The Honeyed Lemon. Four doors down and across the street," he said, pointing his pencil eraser in the direction of the Valley Eater we'd seen the night before. "Best damned smoked paprika you'll ever taste. Truman makes it himself. People come for miles around for the stuff, and I think I heard it's the secret ingredient in the BBQ sauce used by the Partridge Pit chain. Definitely swing by and get a sample to take home. Now, where y'all from?"

I blinked at him. "Um, Houston? And you?"

He grinned. "Mobile, Alabama, but I've been in Aster Valley for a hundred years now. Name's Pim. What can I get ya?"

Tiller opened his mouth to order coffee, but I got there first. "He'll have an ice water and small orange juice. I'll have a coffee, please."

Tiller's mouth snapped closed, and his eyebrows furrowed. I was impervious to his glare by now, so I didn't mind.

"Y'all sound like Bill and me. He's always ordering for me. As if he knows what I want all the time."

A man's voice came from behind the half wall to the kitchen. "Because I do."

The look of affection on Pim's face as he swatted his hand in the direction of the kitchen made my heart clench. I wanted that one day.

"Hang tight and I'll be right back with those drinks," he said before bustling away.

I met Tiller's eyes. "Family," I said, referring to the diner being managed by a gay couple. Tiller nodded.

"That's a nice surprise. Wonder how long they've run the place."

The bell over the door jangled and a cute teenage boy came rushing in with cheeks pink from the cold and shaggy dirty-blond hair every which way from the wind. "Sorry I'm late! Tutoring ran over." He tossed his backpack behind the counter and grabbed a half apron and an order pad before leaning in to kiss Pim on the cheek. "Did you remember to take your pills?"

He brushed the kid off. "Stop nagging me, son. Of course I remembered. The drill sergeant in there wouldn't let me forget," he said, nodding at the kitchen.

"Dad," the teen called toward the kitchen. "Mrs. Winnovich said to tell you guys happy anniversary tomorrow. Then she made me listen to the story of the wedding again. You owe me half an hour of my life back."

Tiller and I watched the little family scene play out as we realized this was most likely Pim and Bill's son. He was either in late high school or early college. He wore a letterman's jacked with the name Solomon embroidered on it.

After washing his hands in the sink behind the counter, the young man came over to our table. "Hi, I'm Solo. Have you ordered breakfast yet?"

We gave him our orders and then watched as he teased his dads while he helped Pim serve the rest of the customers in the diner. Most of them appeared to be regulars, but it was clear some were tourists like us.

When he came by with a pot of coffee to offer me a refill, he asked if we were staying in town long enough to visit the winter festival.

"We didn't know about it," Tiller said. "What's it like?"

Solo's face lit up. "So fun. There's a parade, a craft market, and probably my favorite is the ice-carving competition." He went on to tell us more about the festival and how people from all over Colorado came for the weekend. "It's kind of our thing. You should definitely stay for it."

Tiller assured him we were here through Christmas. Pim overheard and came over to let us know if we had any questions about spending the holidays in Aster Valley to swing on by and ask away.

We left the diner with full bellies and a plan to come back later in the week to try the Thursday lunch special since the diner was only open for breakfast and lunch. I had such warm fuzzy feelings about the sweet diner family, I had an odd desire to bake something for them for their anniversary.

"You should make your holiday spice muffins," Tiller said before moving to the outside of the sidewalk. I noticed he did that often as if there was ever going to be some kind of traffic danger in little Aster Valley, Colorado.

"You have a sweet tooth? After a meal like that?"

He glanced at me from the corner of his eye and grinned. "Not for me. For the couple in the diner. I know you. You want to cook for everyone you meet, especially the nice ones."

His knowledge of how my mind worked made me feel warm inside, but I tried to fight the feeling. It wouldn't be a good idea to get all schmoopy for a man like Tiller Raine.

The spice shop was down the street to the left, so we made our way through the crisp, clear morning until we found it. It was a quaint corner shop with large windows surrounded by wintergreen garland sprigged with twigs and clusters of berries. A brightly lit Christmas tree filled one picture window, and as we got closer, I noticed the ornaments were little sample bottles of spices.

"When was the last time you went to a small-town holiday festival?" Tiller asked. "I mean... I think Boulder does a fall festival, but I was always too busy with football to pay much attention. And I know Aurora does a Punkin Chunkin. I went one time in high school."

"We have rodeos in Texas. Does that count?" I teased.

Tiller held the door to the shop for me, and I entered into a warm and cozy space filled with the savory scents of exotic spices. Glass jars lined glossy-painted shelves along each wall, and large wooden casks formed tables here and there with special displays on them. A nerdy little twink in an honest-to-god bow tie stood behind the counter running long, slender fingers down a handwritten notepad while he typed something into an iPad with his other hand.

"I want him," I whispered to Tiller without thinking. "He's the cutest thing ever."

"Mpfh. He could be your twin. That's creepy."

His words took me aback. "What? No. What?"

Tiller's low chuckle warmed me even more than the cozy atmosphere of the shop. "You're oblivious. And is everyone in this town gay?"

Please let everyone in this town be gay.

The young man looked up from his work and startled as if he hadn't heard us come in. "Oh. Sorry. Can I help you find something, or are you happy to browse? I'm Truman Sweet, by the way. The, ah... shop owner?"

He blinked rapidly as he took in Tiller's height.

"You're really tall," he blurted. "Oh god. Sorry. That's..."

Rude? I thought. Adorable? Endearing?

"It's fine," Tiller said with a smile. "And true."

Tiller was six foot four which wasn't all that tall compared to some of the other guys on his team, but with his broad shoulders, he looked even taller than he was.

"I'll bet everyone asks you if you play basketball," the shopkeeper said with a blush.

I nudged Tiller and pointed to a bottle of the smoked paprika Pim had mentioned. It was just out of my reach on a higher shelf.

Tiller chuckled again and reached for it before handing it to me. "Not usually. But it comes in handy when I have to grab things for this guy." He thumbed over his shoulder at me. "He's five seven on a good day."

I punched him on the shoulder before turning to grab a basket by the door. Even though we'd only been in the store for ten seconds, I could tell I was going to want to try tons of things in there.

Tiller wandered over to the counter to continue chatting with Truman while I browsed. The left side of the store was mostly spices. Some were being sold under the Honeyed Lemon brand, and some were obviously imported.

"Oh, shit," I breathed, reaching for a packet in front of me. "You have amchur powder."

Truman leaned to the side so he could see me around Tiller's wide shoulders. "Oh! Yes, and if you like that, you should try the anardana, too. Get the one from Hotz, it has a more nuanced flavor than mine. I haven't been able to get it quite right yet."

As I filled my basket with little bits and pieces of interest, I listened with one ear to Tiller's polite questions about Aster Valley. Truman was soft-spoken but seemed to be a native Aster Vallian. Or whatever they were called.

"Nina Humphrey, down at the Crooked Bar Ranch, does horse-drawn sleigh rides if that's something you might like," Truman said, wringing his hands. "And then there's... um... well, there's a little ice-skating rink set up behind the Sip and Save, but it's not really big enough to do much actual skating on. You're better off going to the ice arena in Steamboat, honestly."

"I'm not much for ice-skating," Tiller admitted. "But the sleigh ride sounds nice. What about the ski lift? Does that still run at all?"

Truman's jaw set, and his hands almost turned white from how tightly they gripped each other. "The ski slopes are shut down."

"No, I know. I read about it," Tiller said, without noticing Truman's reaction. "I was wondering if the lift ran for like... seeing the views from up there or taking hikes down the mountain or anything."

Truman shook his head. "Afraid not. Not for a long time now."

Tiller apparently wasn't done with his interrogation. "Have any of the development companies thought about starting it back up again? Is that something the residents would even want?"

Truman opened his mouth to respond but then closed it. He tilted his head in thought. "Well... I don't know. At first it was like the place was cursed or something. No one would even consider it. But it's been almost twenty years now..." He glanced up at Tiller. "Wow, wouldn't that be great? Put the old history behind us and move forward again? I guess if... if it meant jobs and stuff, the residents would probably be all for it. But it would depend on the developer and the kind of people it brought to town."

Tiller nodded and turned to me. "Find anything good?"

When he saw my full basket, he laughed and reached out his hand to take it from me. My stomach did a little swoop every time that smile was directed at me, and I had to force myself to pay attention to what he was saying. "Go grab another one, and Truman can start ringing these up."

When I got up to the counter with the rest of my selections, I asked Truman about where he sourced his spices. He blushed again and blinked rapidly at me. "I mean... I grow them? In a greenhouse? Most of them, anyway."

"How do you manage that while you have the shop, too?" I asked. "Do you have a partner?"

"Oh, goodness no. Not... a partner, like that. The shop is closed Monday through Wednesday during the planting and harvesting weeks, and then I bring work here for some of the processing and packaging," he said, stretching his arm out toward a long wooden worktable that spanned almost the entire width of the back of the shop. There were mortars and pestles on a shelf behind the table and hanging scales at either end of the table as well. Empty glass jars and packaging supplies took up some of the lower shelves. "And I ship all online orders from here. If I have a big supplier order and need time at home to work on it, my friend Chaya comes in to help. And I've asked Solo from the diner for help a few times, too. He's very responsible. Pim and Bill use the same point-of-sale system I do, so it's easy for him to mind the shop."

Once he got on a roll talking, he seemed to loosen up a little. When Tiller tried to pay, I pushed him out of the way with my hip and forced my card at Truman with a smile. "I'm sure we'll be back before we leave. You have an incredible store here."

His eyes widened. "Oh, well, thank you so much. Are you... Oh, I'm being silly. Of course you're a cook. I only mean... like... what do you enjoy making?"

Before I could answer, Tiller stepped forward again. "He's an amazing chef. He makes this lentil soup I can't get enough of."

I leaned in and stage-whispered, "It's kaali daal."

Truman laughed behind a hand. "Did you..." He rifled through the paper shopping bag where he'd been stashing my items after ringing them up. "Oh good. You grabbed the asafetida. You have to tell me what you think. You should be able to get the lentils at the supermarket around the corner."

When we finally waved goodbye to the kind shop owner and made our way back onto the street, I was excited to get back to the house and start cooking. I had a million ideas and no clue which one to start with.

"What are you hungry for?" I asked Tiller.

He patted his stomach with his good hand. "Uh, a five-mile run to burn off these pancakes?"

So that's what we did. Rather, that's what he did. I, on the other hand, set out all of my new goodies and began sketching out ideas for new recipes with them. I got a few things started and then browsed online for tips about staging food for photographs. Since I was a complete noob going into this cookbook project, I hadn't realized the chefs had to help develop photo concepts for the book.

And I knew about as much about photo styling as I did about the various species of boa constrictors.

"What're you working on?" Tiller asked on one of his passes through the kitchen for more ice water and a banana.

"Watching YouTube videos on food photography."

He stepped up behind me until I could feel the damp warmth coming off his sweaty skin. "You want to take pictures?"

"Definitely not," I said with a sigh. "But apparently I need to at least have a say in how I want these dishes presented in photos. I'm not sure yet who's doing the styling and photography, but I don't want to sound like a yard full of crickets when they ask me what my vision is."

"Why don't you hire an expert?"

Sweet little multimillionaire and his innocent view of the world.

"Uh, because it costs thousands of dollars and I don't have an NFL contract?" I closed the laptop and reached for my bottle of water. I'd already noticed how dry the air was here, and I'd been trying my best to stay hydrated. All I needed was to have Tiller accuse me of not practicing what I preached.

He was silent for a minute before shrugging. "I do. I can pay for it."

I turned to face him, almost in slow motion. It was one thing for him to buy me breakfast with his millions of dollars. Often, he paid for things like that when we were together because it was easier to get one check and the impact on his wallet was infinitesimal. I used to fight him on it all the time until finally realizing it made him feel good to take little burdens off me like that.

But this? This was personal. This was like offering to buy me a car.

"Um, no. But thank you for offering," I said, trying not to lend any additional meaning to his casual offer than a friend trying to help another friend out.

"Wait," he said, taking a seat at the kitchen island and pulling the laptop open again in front of him. "Hear me out."

"No, thanks," I singsonged, moving over to check on the bread dough I'd left to rise. I didn't usually make bread, but this was a high-protein, vegan loaf that would allow families to continue making sandwiches for people who didn't like the idea of using lettuce leaves or thin wraps. People like Tiller before I finally got him onto the seven-grain wraps he swore by now.

"Don't be stubborn. Listen to me." Tiller's voice had turned serious, so I stopped and met his eyes. "Let me do this for you."

Well, hell. How weird would it be for me to rip off my clothes and attack him right here on the kitchen island?

I spoke around the thick lump in my throat. "I can't."

"Mikey..."

No. Hell no. If he started using that affectionate tone with me, all bets would be off.

My clothes begged to be tossed aside. My dick begged to press up against him with a groan of hard need. Apparently, I was a "kind offerings" slut. What was up with that?

"I..." My voice sounded breathless and weird. I cleared my throat. "I appreciate your help. I do. But this is something I need to do myself."

He met my eyes for a moment before nodding firmly. "Then I'll help in other ways. Free ways. How about that?"

I nodded, refusing to think of the kind of *free ways* I might enjoy. "I'd like that. Thank you."

Tiller's grin was the one that could be used in war to subdue angry villagers. Or the one that could be used in a club to attract horny twinks into wanting to climb the man like a tree.

He hasn't had sex in three years.

My stomach wobbled again. What if... what if I could take care of that for him? Just... a quick suck or jerk. Or hump. Or sixty-nine... Would that be so bad? We were a thousand miles away from everyone we knew. No one would ever find out if we hooked up on vacation.

I let myself fall into the daydream as I began punching down the bread dough. Of course, I wouldn't actually do it, come on to my boss, but a boy could dream, right?

It was nice being here alone with him and kind of pretending to be a couple. Clearly we weren't actually pretending to be a couple, but everyone in town had made assumptions, and... well, it was kind of nice. I liked the idea that it wasn't so unbelievable a man like Tiller Raine would pick a little nobody of a guy like me. That wasn't to say I thought I was a nobody. But to the rest of the world, I was.

Tiller finished eating his banana—something I refused to watch him do because I was a professional, dammit—and walked over to my side of the island to throw the peel away. After chucking it in the trash can, he came even closer to me.

I watched him like a hawk out of the corner of my eye until he lifted his good hand and rubbed his thumb across my jaw.

Blood flooded my dick as I sucked in a breath of surprise.

"Little bit of flour dust," he said in a low, deep voice that made my toes curl in their thick, fluffy socks.

Do not come in your pants.

"Oh," I said instead.

He exhaled and stepped back, leaving his warm banana breath in my personal space. "Kinda cute," he said over his shoulder as he walked away.

As soon as he was gone, I threw the dough back under a tea towel and hotfooted it back to my room for yet another masturbation session.

At this rate, December was going to be a very long month.

9

TILLER

I couldn't sleep. Mikey and I had stayed up late playing Scrabble on a deluxe spinning board we'd found in the cabinet under the TV. The man had some Scrabble chops, but I'd still beat the pants off him.

Every time I scored high on a short word, he made the most adorable miffed sound in his throat and squirmed in his seat as he struggled to come up with a plan to do better on his next turn. Needless to say, by the time we'd gone our separate ways to bed, I'd been turned on and frustrated as hell. Instead of tugging one out, I'd forced myself into a cold shower and tossed and turned for another hour.

But now I was too annoyed with myself to stay in bed and try to sleep any longer. There was no point. I threw the covers back and got up. After grabbing a string cheese and my water bottle out of the fridge, I made sure the door to the back hallway was closed before I turned on the TV so I wouldn't accidentally wake him.

I flipped through my movie account that Mikey had set up for us before deciding on an old heist movie. *The Italian Job* was one of my favorites, and I settled into the familiar opening scene after stoking the fire back to life in the fireplace.

The sofa was soft and comfortable under the afghan Mikey had been using earlier, and I could smell a faint trace of his familiar Mikey-vanilla scent on it whenever I shifted.

About halfway through the movie, I heard the creak of a door opening. I turned around to catch him shuffling out of the back hallway with a deep red quilt wrapped around his shoulders. His hair went every which way from his pillow, and his eye squinted against the light from the TV.

"Did I wake you?" I asked softly.

"No. I shouldn't have had the hot chocolate before bed. The caffeine." He grabbed his water bottle out of the fridge and came over to curl up in the chair he'd been sitting in earlier. "*The Italian Job*?"

"Mm-hm. You want me to change it to something else?"

The edge of his lip curved up. "Hell no. I love this one."

I clicked Play again and settled back into the sofa cushions. Somehow, without really stopping to think about it, we watched three more heist movies, one after the other. When one finished and we took a bathroom and snack break, we talked about our favorite parts and what we would have done differently. It turned out, Mikey was as much of a heist fanatic as I was.

"Do you have a 'go bag' packed?" he asked, looking over his sexy glasses as he cut up a pineapple and tossed it together with some raspberries and blueberries.

"Not exactly," I said hesitantly. "But I know exactly what would go in it."

"Ah-ha!" he said with a laugh, pointing at me over the kitchen island with the sharp knife. "Tell me."

I began to list the contents of my imaginary backpack, including fake identities, untraceable phones, cash in small bills.

"Multiple currencies?" he asked with a twinkle in his eye.

"Dollars—US and Canadian—euros, and pesos. The UK has too many CCTVs, so there's no point in having pounds."

We laughed over some of my more outlandish ideas before settling back in to start the next one. I munched happily on the fruit bowl he'd fixed while he snuck bites from something he had stashed in his pajama pocket.

"What do you have there, little sneak?"

"Muffing," he muttered around a full mouth.

"Is it chocolate muffing?" I teased.

"Moe."

I stood up and walked over before crouching down to get in his face. "I think it is. And I think I deserve to share your secret chocolate stash."

He clamped his lips closed and shook his head while shooting me innocent puppy eyes.

I reached under the blanket and into the pocket of his pajama pants. Mikey stiffened, and I suddenly realized what I was doing. Instead of yanking my hand away, I met his eyes and reached in deeper.

Time seemed to stand still while I searched his pocket. I came out with a small zip-top bag of colorful gourmet jelly beans. My fucking favorite. The baggie had a sticker from Honeyed Lemon on it.

"You little harlot," I said in a low voice, shaking the baggie in front of him like I was a cop who'd found a bag of smack. "Sneaking around with your fancy little stash and not sharing any with me."

His cheeks were the same shade as the cotton candy beans. "You can't have them. You're on a strict—"

I cut him off with a grin. "Don't you dare. These are four calories per bean, and I can burn off this entire bag with a simple beatdown of one small personal chef."

We locked eyes for a second before we both moved. I snatched the bag out of his reach as he lurched up to try and grab it back. He ended up climbing my body to get at the candy in my hands while I held it as high as I could with my good arm. As eager as he was to get the jelly beans from me, he was also conscientious of my injury. We grappled for a few moments before I faked a gasp of pain.

Mikey lurched back and fell onto the overstuffed chair with wide, worried eyes. "Fuck! Did I hurt you?"

I stepped back, ripped open the bag, and began pouring colorful sugary beans into my mouth. "Suckah," I said between mouthfuls.

"You cheater!" He lunged for me again, and we both went down. I tried making it onto the sofa so we didn't hit the hard floor, but then the little minx had his fingertips in my ribs, and I could barely breathe through the laughter.

"Gonna choke," I warned, trying not to inhale the jelly beans.

"That's what you get for being a cheaty cheater, you asshole!"

I tossed the empty bag over my shoulder and wrapped my good arm firmly around his back before flipping him onto his back. One of my knees jammed into the crease of the sofa while I used my other leg for leverage to stay on top of him. Mikey squealed and laughed, gasping for breath and struggling beneath me. He was so much smaller than I was, but his body was full of energy and light.

I'd always loved spending time with him. Simply being in his presence tended to both lift my mood and help me relax, but this... this was next-level. Feeling his body squirm under mine was waking up every blood cell and body part I possessed, and when I felt myself hardening, I knew I needed to stop this before it went too far.

"Fuck," I breathed, suddenly coming up against the intersection of stop and don't-ever-fucking-stop. But I couldn't stop. At least... at least, I didn't *want* to stop. I met his eyes. "I want you so fucking much."

There. I'd said it.

The desire in his eyes was unmistakable. Time slowed again as the fire cracked and popped in the background.

"Then take me," he said so softly, I wasn't sure it was real. I stared into his eyes for another few seconds before lowering my face slowly. I wanted him to have plenty of time to resist, to move out from under me or slap me or... give me any indication he didn't want this.

But his brown eyes only turned more melty, and the tip of his tongue came out to wet his bottom lip.

"You're so fucking beautiful," I whispered. "Tell me to stop."

His hands came up to slide along the sides of my neck and pull me closer. "Impossible."

When my lips landed on his, I felt like I could breathe again. He tasted like sweet strawberry candy, and I would never be able to get enough of it.

I groaned against his mouth and tightened my arm around his slender body. He felt incredible in my arms, underneath me, against all the parts of my body that had dreamed about pressing into him like this.

The kiss started out light and teasing, a few hesitant brushes of lips and swipes of the tongue before Mikey suddenly lurched up to deepen it. His fingers tightened on the back of my neck, and his hips arched up into me. As soon as I felt his hard cock press into my stomach, all bets were off. His need was like a powder keg blasting my self-control to ash.

I ground down against his leg while licking into his mouth hungrily. The little whimper sound that came out of his throat only threw more fuel on the fire.

"Fuck." I groaned and then hauled in a breath. "Fuck, I want you so fucking badly."

I shifted until I had a knee pressed between his legs. The hand I had wrapped around his back had moved down into the back of his pajama pants, and I cursed the sling that kept my other arm immobile between us.

The soft skin of his bare ass beneath my fingers made my dick even harder. I squeezed and grunted into his mouth like a damned animal. The soft sounds of his panting and the leg he brought up to wrap around the back of my thighs reassured me he was on board with everything that was happening.

My mind spun with the reality that I was finally, *finally* kissing and touching Michael Vining. I tried not to think about what this meant—whether or not it was a one-off thing—but I couldn't help but think about how it was already the single hottest hookup I'd ever had, and we weren't even naked yet.

Mikey's hands moved under my shirt and around to my stomach. I felt the muscles contract in response, and my dick jerked in desperation. *Please touch me.*

He muttered something against my mouth that sounded like *big fucking dick*, but since my brain cells had left the building, it was purely a guess.

And then his cool fingers were on the hot skin under my pajama pants. I sucked in a breath as they inched closer to my straining cock.

"Please," I croaked. This time it was out loud because I needed it so badly. If he didn't touch me soon, I was going to cry like a baby.

I tried to distract myself by sneaking a finger down the cleft of his ass cheeks. As soon as I brushed the edge of his hole with a fingertip, his hand wrapped around my dick and I cried out his name.

His voice was shaky and breathless as he thrust his hard cock into my side. "Gonna come if you touch me like that again."

"Come. Want you to come," I murmured between kisses to the tender skin behind his ear. I licked and bit at his earlobe as I tried not to thrust too hard into his grip.

"Your arm," he said hesitantly.

"Fuck my arm," I growled. "Hate my arm."

He managed a chuckle between gasping breaths. I yanked my hand out of his pants long enough to suck my middle finger into my mouth to get it nice and wet. When I slid it back down between his cheeks, his strokes on my dick became irregular. He was on the edge, just like he'd said.

I slid the tip of my finger inside him and listened to the garbled sound of need escape his throat.

"That's it," I urged. "Give it to me. Come in your pants like you're about to make me do."

It was dirty and raw—both of us humping and begging and gasping—but I didn't have a single desire for it to be any different. It felt real and perfect and somehow inevitable.

"Tiller!" He thrust his cock into my side and threw his head back with a cry. His hand reflexively tightened around my dick when he came, and between that and seeing his face as he orgasmed, it was enough to finish me off.

I pumped into his grip and pressed my face into his damp, hot neck. As I gradually came down from the high, I realized one of

Mikey's hands was rubbing lazy shapes on my bare back where my shirt was rucked up, and his other hand had loosened its hold on my dick.

I pressed kisses into the side of his neck and down along the ridge of his collarbone. At some point, I must have stretched out the neck of his T-shirt because it was wide enough now for me to see the pale freckles leading to one shoulder. A few wisps of chest hair peeked out from the shadows, and I could smell the soap on his skin from the shower he must have taken earlier. It mixed with his own body scent in a way that drove me wild.

Hell, everything about Mikey drove me wild.

"You okay?" I asked, almost too scared to listen for the answer.

I nuzzled his cheek and felt his smile before he spoke. "Mm-hm. You?"

After letting out a sigh of relief, I propped myself up so I wouldn't squash him. "More than. That was hot."

He flushed a deeper pink and nodded. "No kidding. I've wanted to do that for a long time."

I realized we were both in the awkward position of being one-armed. He had a handful of jizz while I had one arm in a sling. I sat up and reached for the kitchen towel I'd been using as a napkin with the fruit bowl earlier. When I handed it to him, he smiled and cleaned off his hand before squirming to get the rest of the way out from under me.

"Gonna need to, ah, change my pajamas," he said without looking at me. This awkward shyness around me was new, and while I found it a little endearing, I didn't want him to ever be uncomfortable.

"Can I... I mean... we could... take a quick shower? Together?"

Mikey's eyes widened as he looked over at me. He was probably wondering how someone so dorky could possibly whack the dork meter even higher. "Yeah. Yeah, that's... yeah."

It turned out, this dork was in good company. I grinned at him. "So... that's a yeah, then?"

He swatted me with the nasty dish towel and then took off

running toward the back hallway. "Last one in is a cocky pro baller!" he yelled over his shoulder.

I took my time standing up and shimmying the sticky pants off my junk. Mikey was wrong.

The last one in was the luckiest man on the goddamned planet.

10

MIKEY

I knew I wasn't dreaming because I stubbed my toe on the bathroom doorjamb hard enough to make me feel like puking.

"Arghh!" I yelped, doubling over to look at the damage.

Tiller came up behind me muttering, "What the hell?"

He led me over to the toilet and closed the lid before sitting me down and squatting to inspect my foot. The toe I'd caught on the edge of the frame was red. Watching Tiller's giant, capable hand on my foot made me swoon a little. There were moments that hit me every once in a while, reminding me that I worked for a celebrity. These same hands had been featured in ad campaigns, interviews, and countless discussions on sports talk shows.

And now they were tending to my boo-boo.

"I'm fine," I said reflexively, trying to pull my foot out of his grip. He held on and continued to gently press here and there to test the digit.

"I've never chased someone away enough to literally endanger their well-being," he teased.

"So, I'm your first?"

He glanced up at me with a grin. "Guess so. Lucky you."

No shit.

I reached out and ran a hand through his hair. I'd always wanted to touch it, but now I felt like maybe I could actually get away with it. The wavy locks slipped through my fingers, and Tiller made a sound of pleasure. I moved my hand down to stroke his cheek.

"You are an ugly SOB," I murmured affectionately.

His face crinkled with a chuckle. "And you're obviously going to survive this horrific injury. Get your ass up and get naked."

Tiller stood and turned toward the big tiled shower, reaching for the dials and spinning them to start the spray. I watched the muscles of his butt move through his pajama pants and couldn't believe I was actually going to be able to see his bare ass up close and in person.

I shook my head to rid it of the bucketloads of desire I had for him. This was *such* a bad idea. Being completely naked with him would make me want more. Lots more.

"What are we doing?" I blurted. "This can't... we can't..."

Tiller's startled expression turned my way. "I was just... going to take a shower? I thought you..."

"No, I know. Yeah. But..." I stopped and threw my hands out. "You're... and I'm..."

I didn't want to say the words *boss* and *employee* because I didn't want to make Tiller feel like he'd done anything wrong. He hadn't. I'd wanted everything we'd done together. But at the same time, I didn't want to fuck up his career either. And he had no idea what hooking up with me could do to his position with the Riggers.

His face relaxed a little. "Stop thinking right now and get your clothes off." When I didn't move, he frowned. "Unless you don't want to. I didn't mean to imply—"

"I want to! Jesus, of course I want to. It's just such a fucking bad idea. Right?"

Tiller shrugged and reached for the strap to his sling to start removing it from his bad arm. "Probably. But I'd really like to rub against your naked body right now, so I don't want to overthink it and fuck up my chances."

Once he got the sling off, he reached behind his head and

grabbed a handful of cotton, pulling the shirt off and revealing his multimillion-dollar torso.

I drooled and stared like a fangirl until he started to laugh. "You've seen my chest before."

"Not like this. Not... in a 'you just had your finger in my ass' kind of way. Totally different."

His eyes simmered with heat as he crooked a finger at me. "How many times am I going to have to ask you to take off all your clothes?"

His voice was hypnotic. I stood and walked over to him before reaching out and running a tentative hand across all of those delicious muscles. "Holy mother of god."

Tiller reached for the hem of my sleep shirt and yanked it up. When it hindered my ability to fondle his pecs, I finally helped him get it off me. He must have known I was self-conscious around his incredible body, because he treated me like I was the sexiest man alive.

"You make me hard every day," he said in a low voice. "Did you know that? I come into the kitchen sometimes and just stare at your ass. Sometimes you wear those blue shorts that pull between your cheeks when you lean over, and I want to kneel down on the ground right there and fucking stick my face in your ass."

I stared at him and gulped. This couldn't possibly be happening. "Ngh."

He smiled and continued while he pulled at the tie on my sleep pants. "I'd eat your ass right there in our kitchen. Pull those shorts down and stick my tongue inside you."

I choked on my tongue a little and made a snorting, gasping sound at the same time. Tiller just took it in stride. He moved around behind me and ran his hands along my bare skin.

"I want to lick every inch of you," he murmured against the back of my ear. "Taste your cock, eat your ass, kiss your mouth until I can't breathe anymore."

I started panting, unable to take a deep breath without feeling like I was going to faint dead away from hard need.

"Would you like that?"

"Mm-hm. Yeah. Yep. Yes. That. Like that." I cleared my throat to speak more clearly. "I would like that. Please. Yes, please."

Tiller's huge hands spanned my stomach, and I couldn't help but stare down at the stark contrast between his tan hands and my winter-pale belly. His fingers moved down into the nest of hair at the base of my dick, and my hard-on jumped up to meet it. I leaned back against him, noticing the thick ridge of his cock was still covered in soft flannel.

"All that talk of naked and you're still dressed," I said, arching back into him to feel more of it against my lower back.

I felt him shimmy out of the pants until his cock pressed bare and hot against my skin. "Oh fuck." I kind of wanted him to put it inside me, but I sure as hell wasn't going to ask him for anal when I'd never done it before. It was a bell that wouldn't be able to be unrung as soon as either one of us finally wised up and decided how stupid this was.

"Want to fuck you into the nearest flat surface," he mumbled in a rough voice. "Pound this sweet ass and listen to you beg for it harder."

"Jesus fuck," I breathed. "I never pegged you for a dirty talker."

His deep chuckle was familiar and warm. "Don't like it?"

"Are you kidding? I'm going to come untouched right now if you keep at it. And I already came once tonight." Well, twice, but I wasn't about to tell him about the masturbation session earlier.

His hands continued to explore as heat started floating out of the shower enclosure. I was in no hurry to speed things along. If he wanted to waste every ounce of snowmelt in Colorado, that was fine by me. Apparently my libido was the opposite of an environmentalist.

"Your body is perfect," he continued, running his hands up the inside of my thighs until he cupped my balls in one hand and stroked me with the other.

"Your shoulder," I warned half-heartedly. Was there something less than half-heartedly? If so, that was how weak my warning was.

"It's fine. Turn around."

When I spun to face him, I had a hard time meeting his eyes. This was really happening. I was naked with my boss. I was bare-assed with the highest-paid receiver in NFL history. I was getting ready to give a blow job to one of my dad's players.

Again.

Nerves swooped in my stomach until Tiller reached for my chin with the side of his index finger. Twin divots of worry crinkled his forehead.

"Hey. It's just us here. Talk to me."

I met his eyes then and saw such sweet concern and understanding. I saw the man I'd come to care for as way more than a boss.

"What if this is a mistake?" I didn't want to ruin my chances, but god. I didn't want to fuck things up with him either. "I don't want to lose you. As a friend, I mean. Or... anything."

His hand cupped the side of my face. "Then let's not do this. It's okay if you don't want to. I never wanted to pressure you for—"

I put my hand on his. "No! That's not what I mean. You didn't pressure me at all, and believe me when I tell you I do—very much *do* —want to."

"Then why do you look terrified?" His smile was kind as he ran a thumb along my cheek.

"I don't want to fuck us up. I don't want you to get in trouble. I don't—"

He shut me up with a kiss and then leaned down and grabbed me around the back with his good arm before lifting me up. I automatically straddled his waist and wrapped my arms and legs around him as he moved toward the shower. I had to step down to the wet tiles to help adjust the temperature of the water while the warm steam immediately landed on my skin.

Once the temperature was just right, Tiller nudged me under the spray but never took his hands or lips off me. He grabbed the bar of soap and started running it all over me, paying close attention to my ass and my junk. My dick was hard, and my balls ached. I finally sank down to my knees and looked up at him through wet lashes. "Can I?"

The look on his face was a heady mix of tender and hungry. He grunted his approval and grabbed my hair gently with his good hand as I leaned in to rub my face along his thick erection.

Fuck, it was a nice dick. Thick and ruddy, hard as fuck. I grabbed it at the base and licked around the head, never taking my eyes off his.

My heart hammered with excitement and lust. I'd dreamed about this so many times, and now it was real. I was getting ready to suck Tiller Raine's cock.

I was on my knees for the kindest man I knew, and it was the hottest thing I'd ever done.

"Just like that," he murmured as I began to run my tongue around him and pull him into my mouth. One of my hands clutched the rounded hamstrings on the back of his thigh while the other cupped his sac and rolled his balls. "Oh, god, that's... fuck. Don't stop. Please, baby. Just... oh sweet fuck."

His words only spurred me on. I wanted to do my best for him, to make him crazy with lust until he blew down my throat with a roar. I licked and sucked and pulled until my hair was dripping with shower water and my chin was dripping with spit. Tiller's hands had moved down from my hair to settle on either side of my face, but they didn't control me. They simply held me gently and caressed me, at complete odds with the shaking, barely contained energy I felt in his leg muscles.

"Fuck my face," I managed to say, gasping for breath between swallows.

Tiller's eyes widened, and his fingers tightened a little on my face, but then he was thrusting tentatively into my mouth. I pulled him deeper with my hands on the back of his legs until he was groaning and fucking into me, crying out that he was going to come.

I moved my hands up to his ass and held him tightly to me when I felt him get close. Even if he hadn't admitted to a long dry spell earlier, I already knew his health status since he had to get checked all the time for his job. There was no way I was giving up the opportunity to take his load and make him even crazier.

My eyes burned with tears, and my nose ran. The sensation of his thick cock wedged in my throat suddenly got me closer to my own release. I reached down with one hand and jacked myself off. The minute Tiller noticed, he did exactly what I'd been hoping for.

He screamed his orgasm loud enough to wake the dead which was definitely enough to wake my dick, too. I shot against the shower floor in spurts as I struggled to keep up with his load. With his head thrown back, all of his stomach muscles rippled under the beads of water clinging to his chest hair and happy trail. I ran my hands up the v of his abdomen and reveled at what an incredibly perfect body he had.

While I was still stunned from the experience, he leaned over and snaked his good arm under one of my armpits before pulling me up into a kiss. My legs were weak and wobbly, but he held me tightly.

"Why did I wait five years for this?" He spoke against my cheek as he rubbed his face against mine. "You're so damned hot, so fucking sweet. I can't get enough of you."

My heart still thundered in my chest as I leaned against him and soaked in his words and this feeling. I felt invincible.

And I never wanted it to end.

"Stay with me tonight?" I asked hesitantly. I wasn't sure what this was or what he was expecting. But I was afraid if we went our separate ways to our different bedrooms, the magic spell would be broken and this time-out-of-time experience with him would disappear forever.

His eyes met mine, and I thought I saw some of the same feelings swirling through his eyes. Maybe it was just wishful thinking.

"Yeah," he said. "I'd like that." Then he winked at me. "Or, as my... Mikey says, 'Mm-hm. Yeah. Yep. Yes. I would like that. Please. Yes, please.'"

I pinched his nipple, hard. "Asshole," I muttered.

We finished washing each other as quickly as we could, and then Tiller Raine followed me to my bed and curled his giant body around mine.

I slept like a baby until the doorbell woke us up.

11

TILLER

When the doorbell in my dream continued to ring, I finally somehow realized it was real life breaking through. I blinked an eye open and saw the pale, smooth skin of Mikey's bare shoulder.

Memories from last night flashed through my head, making me hard instantly. I pushed my dick against Mikey's leg without thinking about it. As he groaned and pushed back, I leaned in to kiss his shoulder.

"Stay asleep. Someone's at the door," I said quietly. "I'm going to check."

"Stay here," he mumbled sleepily. "With me."

I kissed his messy hair and moved my lips down to kiss below his ear. "I'm coming right back. Keep my spot warm."

When I got up, though, I quickly realized I didn't have anything to put on. My cum-stained pajama pants were probably still in a puddle on the bathroom floor. I reached for the bath towel I'd discarded after the shower and wrapped it around my waist before moving out to the main part of the house. By now, a loud pounding had taken the place of the doorbell.

"Coming," I called out. "Hold on."

I approached the thick front doors with caution. My agent had put me through media training enough to know never to give strangers a money shot. I was currently standing there in nothing but a towel.

"Who is it?" I asked through the door.

"Stacy Clifton, the listing agent. I'm here for the ten-o'clock showing."

What the hell?

"This is a rental property," I said stupidly.

"I understand. Would you please open the door so I can explain?"

"Give me a minute to get dressed." I raced to the master bedroom, thanking god and whoever else might be listening for not putting windows on either side of the big front doors. I threw on some jeans and a Rigger hoodie before sliding some thick socks on my feet. When I made it back to the front door, I took a deep breath before opening it.

An attractive, smartly dressed woman with an iPad in her arms stood next to an older couple. A silver Mercedes SUV sat parked behind my rental in the circular drive.

"Oh dear lord above," the iPad lady said breathlessly, tucking errant wisps of blond hair behind her ear. "You're Tiller Raine."

I didn't have my usual patience this morning since Mikey was naked in bed waiting for me. I didn't want to miss the opportunity of helping him out with his morning wood.

"May I help you?" I asked.

"Yes, sorry. I'm Stacy... oh, I already said that. And I'm here to show the Civettis this property. I tried getting in touch with your assistant to let him know that we'd booked a showing, but I must have the wrong number."

I blinked against the bright morning light bouncing off all the snow. "I don't understand."

"The property is currently for sale. One of the conditions of the rental is allowing us a few showings when the need arises. Normally, you'd have more notice than this, but Gary and Erica are just passing through and wanted to preview this listing as an investment property."

Her eyes were wide and a tiny bit manic, as if she was trying to send me a message about how important this showing was to her. I didn't imagine many people came through town with the kind of money it would take to buy a property like this, so she probably needed to strike while the iron was hot.

"Sure, ah... come in." I thought of Mikey warm and snuggly in his bed. "Just give me a minute to tell my assistant before bringing them past the kitchen, okay?"

The look of relief on her face was comical. "Yes, of course. No problem. Please give my apologies to Mr. Vining."

I left the door open behind me when I turned to head toward Mikey's room. Stacy immediately began describing the architectural features of the grand entryway, and my ears perked up at her mention of the house's varied history. I kind of wanted to learn more about it. The town had piqued Mike's and my curiosity, and it sounded like Stacy knew some cool stuff about the place.

When I got back to Mikey's room, the bed was empty and the bathroom door was closed. I quickly pulled the bedding up and made my best effort at tidying the mostly tidy room in case Stacy and the Civettis came back here.

Mikey came out of the bathroom a minute later with a fresh pair of pajama pants slung low on his hips. His hair was brushed, and I could smell the familiar mint of toothpaste as I leaned in to kiss him. I wrapped my arms around him, biting back the wince when my shoulder protested.

Time slowed down when I was with him. Nothing else mattered except the taste of him and the smooth expanse of his warm skin under my fingertips.

"Who was it?" he murmured against my lips.

"Mm." I kept kissing him. My head was filled with happy cotton, and my dick was doing its best to drill a nice trench in poor Mikey's stomach.

He pulled back with a laugh and put his hands on my cheeks. They were cool from the water in the sink. "Who was at the door?"

"Oh," I said, trying to shake off the Mikey fog. "Real estate agent.

Apparently the house is for sale and they have a showing this morning. You need to get dressed."

His forehead crinkled in confusion before smoothing over with remembrance. "Shit. Yeah. Sorry. I forgot I agreed to that. But they were supposed to give us advanced notice."

I dropped another kiss on his forehead and stepped back to let him get dressed. "It's fine. Let's go into town and get breakfast again. I want to try the hazelnut crepes."

Mikey gave me the exact reaction I'd baited him into. "Like hell are you having hazelnut crepes. But you can taste mine between bites of your veggie frittata," he said, turning to the dresser to pull out a long-sleeve shirt and some jeans. I watched him like a perv as he stripped down to pull on his boxer briefs, and when I caught sight of his half-hard dick hanging from the tidy nest of dark curls, I dropped to the floor and knee-walked over to him.

"Let me taste."

"I thought I was getting dressed," he said, swatting at me. "I'm not about to let random strangers walk in on Tiller Raine giving some guy head. Get up."

I pouted up at him. "If I can't have the crepes, I want—"

I didn't get a chance to finish. The sound of voices in the hallway came through the closed bedroom door and jolted Mikey and me into action.

"Fuck," Mikey hissed, yanking up his jeans. "Clean the bathroom!"

I went into the bathroom and slid a few of his things into a drawer before wiping down the water spots from the counter with a towel. Why we gave a shit about helping sell this house was beyond me, but I hadn't been raised to be rude.

When I stepped back out of the bathroom, the bedroom door was open and Mikey was chatting pleasantly with the trio in the hallway.

"Oh," Mikey said, eyes fluttering nervously like he'd just been complimented. "Thank you. Those are my holiday spice muffins. You're welcome to try them."

The woman I assumed was Mrs. Civetti looked sheepish. "Are you sure? It's just that they smell divine."

Mr. Civetti laughed. "Poor thing hasn't had breakfast yet. I dragged her out first thing this morning to look at properties without feeding her first. That would be mighty kind of you, sir."

I followed them into the kitchen and watched as Mikey made friends through food. He'd done it so many times before, but it never failed to impress me. As he offered the Civettis and the agent fresh coffee, he explained what made the muffins smell so good and how they were actually healthy, "but you'd never know it."

Once the agent informed the couple who I was, Mikey told them he was my personal chef. Their eyes lit up with interest, and they began asking him a million questions. I loved seeing the interest pointed at him for once. Mikey was incredibly talented and deserved all the recognition in the world.

He talked with his hands and a big smile, answering their questions about how he knew so much about nutrition, interesting things he'd learned in the program at Texas A&M, his work with pro ballplayers and private catering clients, and what got him into cooking in the first place.

I cut in to add that he currently had a cookbook in the works with a publisher and was going to be a household name very soon. It caused a sexy-as-fuck blush on Mikey's face and an excited energy from the older couple.

"Oh gracious, that's amazing," Mrs. Civetti said, turning her eyes on me. "Aren't you the lucky one? This muffin is the best thing I've ever tasted. What are some of your favorite dishes Michael makes back home?"

As I began to brag about my favorite recipes and what a difference Mikey had made to my own health and that of many of my teammates, I saw the heart eyes begin to appear from both Civettis.

"Would you consider a move to Aster Valley?" Mr. Civetti asked Mikey with mischief in his eyes.

Mikey chuckled. "Aster Valley is lovely. I've only been here a couple of days, but I love it so far. I told Tiller I wish I could buy this place and turn it into my own bed-and-breakfast."

I could tell he was joking, answering as if it was a daydream rather than reality, but still, the idea of it made my stomach uneasy.

Mrs. Civetti clapped her hand to her chest and shot hopeful eyes at Mikey. "Oh! That's exactly what we have in mind for this place, but we would need a chef and someone to run it..."

Now my stomach situation turned into an actual wobble. This was bordering on something other than a hypothetical.

"We should get going and let the Civettis get back to their investment assessment," I said carefully. I couldn't decide if I was being an asshole denying Mikey an opportunity or a friend protecting him from getting his hopes up.

"Yes, of course," Mikey said quickly. "We didn't mean to interrupt your viewing. Please take some muffins with you. I'll grab a zip-top bag for you to put them in." He busied himself with the muffins until he had a bag for the Civettis and one for the folks at the diner.

Mr. Civetti held out his card to Mikey. "If you'd like to consider a move to Aster Valley, and you'd like to give serious thought to something like this, give me a call. We aren't sure yet about making this investment since we don't have plans to move here ourselves, but we like to grab opportunities when they seem to line up just right. Meeting you here seems serendipitous."

"Thank you," Mikey said, taking the card. "I really appreciate that. I've always had a dream to run my own restaurant, so I will let you know. It was very nice meeting you."

"Take your time with the viewing," I said. "We're going into town for breakfast."

The agent assured me she would lock up when they were finished. "And I'm happy to shoot you a text when they're done if you'd... like to give me your number?"

I sensed a little puff of air escape Mikey's nose. No one else would have noticed, but I knew him well enough to know he thought the woman was flirting with me. In light of what we'd done together last night, I wondered what he thought of that. Did it make him jealous at all? Possessive? I'd never really understood jealousy in the past, but I'd gotten a swift ass-kicking lesson on it when Nelson Fucking Evangelista had opened his damned mouth in that Seahawks game.

"Why don't you give it to me?" Mikey offered with the same fake friendliness he gave to pushy reporters and Rigger haters we encountered in public. It was kind of cute.

After they exchanged numbers, we headed out the front door and into our rental. Mikey automatically got to drive since I wasn't about to have the "clipped wing" argument with him again.

When he found an open parking space on the street behind the diner, I realized we'd spent the short drive into town talking comfortably like we always did. Nothing was weird or awkward between us after last night.

But.

I wasn't quite sure what that meant. Was the hookup a one-and-done thing? Were we back to the same Tiller and Mikey from before, or had things changed? Were we going to get naked together again?

Lord, please let us get naked together again.

The knocking sound jerked me out of my imagination, and I realized Mikey was standing outside my car door waiting for me with a frown on his face.

"You okay?" he asked when I finally opened the door. "Is it your shoulder? Did we fuck it up?"

He reached out a hand to help me out of the big vehicle, and I continued to keep hold of it after I'd stepped down and closed the door behind me. Mikey looked down at our joined hands and up at my face.

"Are we...? What are we doing exactly?"

I pulled his hand up and pressed a kiss to the back of it. "I want to hold your hand. Is that okay?"

He looked around at the empty street. "Well, I mean... for now because no one is here, but..."

He didn't have to say it. I knew all it would take was one cell phone photo to blow up the sports news. I was out—there was no secret left about that—but a photo of me holding hands with my *coach's* son? No. Absolutely no way that would fly under any media radar.

I pressed the back of his hand to my mouth again and held it there for a few beats before muttering a curse and dropping it. "Sorry," I said with a sigh. "I'm really sorry."

We started walking toward the restaurant side by side. "Tiller," Mikey began, "you know I'm in the same boat, right? I mean, obviously it's not nearly as big a deal if I'm caught with you as you being caught with me, but... my dad..."

He didn't even need to finish. "I know. You're his baby boy. He'd shit a brick."

Mikey searched my face for a minute before nodding absently. "Yeah. That. That's kind of an understatement," he murmured under his breath.

It made me realize that there really wasn't a future for us, not unless I was willing to put him through upending his family and becoming the target of a ruthless media. Anyone I dated publicly would be subject to an insane amount of scrutiny and hate. I was well aware of how many fans I had that enjoyed selectively forgetting about my sexuality. Those same fans would turn on me if I started seeing someone publicly. It was one of the reasons I'd never pursued dating seriously. It wasn't fair to the other man.

Besides, this was the time in my life to focus on football. There'd be plenty of time for romance after I retired. In all honesty, that mantra was getting really old. But I clung to it for dear life because it was one of the only things that had kept me focused enough to become the success I was today.

And it was one of the only reasons I hadn't jumped Michael Vining's bones before last night.

I followed Mikey into the diner in a rapidly declining mood, but I couldn't help but smile when I saw an actual Santa Claus dressed to the nines behind the counter. Whoever it was made the most perfect Santa with a real white beard and everything.

He was eating the hazelnut crepes.

"Don't even think about it," Mikey muttered with a smile in his voice.

"If Santa can have them..." I began.

"Santa is an obvious cardiac risk," he whispered, cutting me off. "You're a pro athlete."

I didn't even actually want the crepes. If I started the day with that much sugar, I'd want to take a nap as soon as we got back to the house which would completely botch my plans to seduce Mikey again. But I loved teasing him, and I wasn't about to miss a chance to hear his prim lectures about macronutrients.

Solo hustled over to us with a pot of coffee. "Who needs the good stuff?"

Both of us raised our hands, and he laughed before quickly turning over our mugs and filling them. "We have a special sweet potato hash this morning with peppers, onions, kale, turkey bacon, and eggs in it. It's really good if you're in a savory mood. We also have a greek yogurt and muesli parfait and... what else? Oh! Brioche french toast with candied walnuts. Not to be missed. It's my dad's surefire way of cheering me up whenever I'm in a bad mood, and it's on special today. You have to try it."

I held out my hand for Mikey to go first.

"I'll have the french toast please." He lifted an eyebrow at me, but I ignored him.

"And I'll try the sweet potato hash. Thanks."

When he moved away to put our orders in, I could see Mikey's wheels turning. "That sweet potato dish sounds good," he murmured, pulling his phone out to make some notes.

"It sounds good because it is good. You make the exact same thing," I reminded him.

He shook his head without looking up at me. "No. You're thinking of the rosemary sweet potatoes I make with the bacon and onions. That's a side dish at dinner."

I took a sip of my doctored coffee and almost groaned in relief. We hadn't gotten much sleep the night before, and I had high hopes for this cup of caffeine. Mikey sipped his absently while he continued tapping notes into his phone. When he finally finished, he slipped it into his pocket and looked up at me sheepishly.

"Sorry. That was rude of me."

I made a dismissive gesture with my hand. "It's fine. I'm still waking up."

I moved my foot across the space beneath the table to rest along the edge of his. His eyes widened a little in surprise, but he pressed his foot back against mine.

"So... that was nice," I began. "The Civettis talking about turning the lodge into a B&B."

Mikey's eyes turned dreamy. "Wouldn't that be perfect? I can totally picture it. It would make the perfect bed-and-breakfast. Well, I mean... if it were mine, I'd probably want it to be a lodge with a fine-dining restaurant attached. I could offer breakfast, no problem, but I think Aster Valley could use a nice dinner restaurant as well. Like a date place. Something fancier than the takeout places around here."

"Mm." I sipped my coffee as I thought about it. "Good point. There really isn't a place like that here, is there? Do you think the town can support it? Maybe with Steamboat so close?"

He shrugged. "If a cozy dinner place gets enough of a good reputation, people will drive to it. Besides, if you market it as a weekend getaway package for anniversaries and other special occasions, you'll get plenty of people coming out from Denver. There are probably tons of couples who don't need skiing but still want a wintery weekend away with a long wine-filled dinner by a cozy fireplace."

I pictured the great room in the lodge that we hadn't used. It had a huge stone fireplace and rich, wide-planked wood flooring. The picture windows along the back wall looked out over the slopes and trees. "You'd make it perfect," I admitted. "The way you describe it makes me think of those old historic homes that have been turned into restaurants in New England."

He nodded. "Exactly. We went to that one place in Connecticut, remember? After the photo shoot thing for one of your sponsors."

I remembered it. Mostly I remembered the golden glow of his skin in the candlelight and the rosy hue to his cheeks after his third glass of wine. The woman who'd hosted us for the visit had spent the entire time flirting with Markus, and it had given Mikey the giggles. I'd stared at him throughout the entire dinner.

"Do you think you'll call them?" I asked, worried about his answer. "The Civettis. They seemed serious about wanting to discuss it with you."

He hid behind another sip of coffee for a few beats. "I mean... it's tempting. I've always wanted to run my own restaurant, and this would be a chance to do it without the financial risk of investing my own money. Honestly, I've been saving for a while, but I'll never have enough to do it the way I really want to. This could be my chance. And I like Aster Valley. I was already daydreaming about turning the lodge into a bed-and-breakfast so... god. Can you imagine?"

"Yes," I admitted. "You would be amazing at it."

He made a shooing gesture with his hands. "Stop talking about it. It's making me nervous. Let's change the subject."

Fine by me. I didn't want to think about him leaving Houston— leaving *me*. Besides, I wanted to get to know him better now that some of our boundary walls seemed to be coming down.

"Tell me about your dad," I said, taking another sip of coffee. "And growing up."

His expression changed to one of confusion. We'd never talked much about our personal stories. "What do you mean?"

I leaned forward and cradled the warm mug in my good hand on the table. "I've met your brothers. Hell, I've played against Jake. They're a bunch of corn-fed bruisers. Then there's you."

He shrugged. "I don't know what happened. Ask my mom. A very quiet and tidy interior decorator named Branson lived next door when Mom got pregnant with me, so you can imagine the jokes my dad and brothers have come up with over the years. I actually even kinda look like the guy. Well, mostly because he wore the same kind of glasses I do. But honestly... it was just a fluke, I guess. One of us was bound to like dessert and dick more than pumping iron and..." He looked around. "Another p-word."

"Did they give you hell about it? When you came out? You said they were protective. That's good, right?"

I hated to think of him being treated as less than or somehow disappointing. I knew Coach V.'s feelings on what made a successful man, and publishing a cookbook probably didn't make the cut. The more I pictured Mikey growing up as the black sheep in his family, the more uncomfortable I felt. I started imagining how I'd handle myself the next time I saw Jake on the field.

"My brothers are pretty cool about it, especially now. They try, at least. The only one who's still weird about me is Eddie."

He was the one I'd only met once. "Remind me where he is now? Galveston? Works with money or something?"

Mikey shook his head. "Houston. He works as a contracts administrator at the port authority. He's the one who played center for UT. He's married to Ashlynn. They met in school. She was a Longhorn cheerleader. It's all very *Friday Night Lights*."

Solo stopped at our table to pour us some ice water before moving down the row of booths with his big water pitcher. The low buzz of conversation from other customers mixed with the clinking of silverware on plates and Pim's periodic shouts into the kitchen to Bill. It was comfortable and warm, and I felt embraced by the newfound familiarity of the place.

"Why is Eddie weird about you? Is it homophobia or something different?"

He shrugged and used his index finger to move his empty sugar packets under the lip of the little plate holding the creamer pitcher. "Partly. He was always friends with the meanest guys, you know? The ones who took great pleasure in intimidating others. I assumed he'd grow out of it eventually, but then he got the job at the port and seemed to connect to the same type of guys at work that he always had at school. Rough, crass macho guys who don't think much of men like me." He inhaled deeply before looking up at me. "He's the one who's always asking me why I dress the way I do, why I pay so much for a simple haircut, and why I can't be 'normal.' He also uses the f-word 'as a joke.' You know the type." His long, slender fingers made finger quotes while he talked, and I wanted to reach across the table and take those fingers into my protective grip, hold him tightly and let him know not everyone felt that way about him.

I wanted to kill his brother Eddie. Men like that were fucking cowards and bullies.

"Doesn't your dad call him out for it?" Coach V. had always been supportive of me being out. He wasn't lovey-dovey about it or anything, but he hadn't blinked about it during the recruitment and draft process. He'd also supposedly made it clear to the rest of the team before I showed up that there would be a zero-tolerance policy for any sexuality-related comments or use of slurs in the locker room.

That wasn't to say he was marching in the next Pride parade. Now that I thought about it, much of what he said could have been lip service in order to keep one of his most expensive players happy. Whatever the reason, it had worked for the most part. But I wasn't naive either. I'd learned early on there was a difference between the team accepting my sexuality on paper and in person.

"Yeah," Mikey said. "He tells him to stop being a jackass. That's it. My dad... well, Coach is Coach."

I could tell he'd been close to telling me more but had remembered just in time that his dad was also my boss. I pressed my foot against his again. "Did you ever hear about the time Antone offered to set me up with his brother-in-law for one of the team barbecues?"

His head snapped up. "Jalen? Dude. That man is hot as hell. I hope you said yes." He seemed to realize what he'd said, and his interest turned to scorn. "I take it back. I don't want to think of you with Jalen Key and his perfect body. Fuck that."

Antone's brother-in-law was an attorney with the body of a professional CrossFitter. He was smart as hell, but he wasn't the least bit humble. About anything.

I took another sip of coffee, trying to savor it since I knew Mikey wouldn't let me have a refill. "I did say yes, but then Coach shot me a look and suggested I save the blind date for another time and place. When I pushed back, he went on to explain it wouldn't be fair to anyone to have a first date take place in such an intimidating situation. I had to agree. It wasn't until later I remembered that Antone and Lacey had brought Jalen to plenty of team parties before."

Mikey's nostrils flared, and annoyance simmered in his eyes. "Yeah. That. That's how Dad is. He's all supportive and shit until it's actually going to affect him and his reputation."

"Has he been that way to you when you've brought guys around?"

Mikey let out a laugh. "It would take an act of god for me to bring a guy around my family. I'd have to be pretty sure he was the one. He'd have to love me like crazy in order to put up with the goon squad and my dad."

Pim appeared with our breakfast plates as the word "love" echoed in my head. Falling in love hadn't really ever been on my radar for this time in my life. This time in my life was about loving football and taking advantage of the opportunity while I could, while my body allowed it. My father had always drilled it into my head that "There'd be time for girls later, son." But hearing the l-word spoken in Mikey's voice did something to me.

I wanted to love and be loved. I wanted my life to be about more than my job. When Mikey talked about relationships and life outside of football, I began to realize how much I was missing. Time was passing, and life was short.

I pressed the side of my foot against his again and started eating.

12

MIKEY

I had a massive crush on my boss. It was fine. Totally fine. This kind of shit happened all the time, right? Like... like when I had a crush on my *last* boss and jumped into bed with him like a dick slut.

Dick slut? Was that even a thing?

"You're frowning again. Need help?" Tiller was stretched out on the sofa by the fireplace in the kitchen watching a game on TV. It had been four days since we'd hooked up the first time. Since then we'd spent every spare minute touching each other and trying to make each other come with our hands, mouths, or dicks. I couldn't stop thinking about it.

I blinked down at the little tomatoes I was chopping. "No. I pretty much know how to chop salad tomatoes," I said with a little too much snark. I was all mixed up inside. Even though we were fucking like bunnies, we hadn't talked about the elephant in the room.

Tiller's eyes widened. "Okayyyy."

"Sorry. It's just..." I let the words trail off as I tried to gather my thoughts. I didn't want to be that guy who made a big deal out of a hookup. But I also didn't want him to think I was a... *dick slut is not a thing...* serial boss-fucker.

Also, hopefully, not a thing.

"Mikey," he said with a concerned tone in his voice. He stood up and came over to me. I put the knife down and wiped my hands on a nearby kitchen towel.

I stood up straight and looked right at him. "I want you to know I don't normally do this."

The teasing glint in his eye made my heart rate tick up.

"That's funny. I've seen you chop tomatoes quite a few times. When you say you don't normally—"

I smacked his chest, grateful he no longer had a sling there. "Shut up, you know what I mean."

He grabbed my smacking hand and pulled it to his chest, pressing it over his heart and damned near making me light-headed. "You don't owe me any explanations. I want you. Full stop. There are no conditions involved. Whoever you are or were or will be... it's all irrelevant to how attracted to you I am and how much I enjoy spending time with you. I know we talked about how impossible it would be to pursue something long-term, but can we just enjoy our time together here in Aster Valley while we have it? I want to be able to touch you and kiss you and stay up late talking to you the way we do at home, but this time I want to be able to hold you while we're doing it."

His words made me feel special which was a rare treat. Tiller always made me feel valued and appreciated, but this was different. "Me too. That sounds really nice."

"And I feel a little giddy getting you all to myself without Sam staying over or teammates dropping by for dinner."

I stepped closer to him, moving one of my legs between his. We'd returned from a long walk in the woods and changed back into lounge pants, so I could feel the curve of his thigh muscle and the rough texture of his leg hair through the thin fabric.

I cupped the side of Tiller's neck with one hand and kept the other on his chest. "One night, when the guys were over watching a replay of that week's game, I got so turned on fantasizing about you, I almost came in my pants right there in the movie room."

Tiller's eyes dilated, and his breathing sped up. "Liar," he breathed. "Tell me more."

"You were so fucking sexy on the screen in your uniform. It was a game against Arizona or someplace hot, and you were pouring sweat. Your skin was tan and slick, and your eyes were fierce through your face mask." I ran a thumb over his eyebrows. "You were glaring at the cornerback covering you, and I kept noticing your eyebrows furrow in frustration."

"Ty Kenner. Dirty fucker," he muttered. "Hasn't met a personal foul he didn't like."

"Anyway," I said with a chuckle, "you were tackled after a good reception and run. When you stood back up, your uniform shirt was caught up under your pads, and I could see your abs. I'm surprised we didn't hear a collective sigh from the stands. Surely it was caught on the Jumbotron."

Tiller's cocky grin was sexy as hell. He moved his hand down from his chest and pulled up his shirt. "These abs?"

I ignored him and his billion-dollar muscles as best I could. "And that's when I remembered I was sitting right next to you on the sofa. I looked over at you in person and then at your image on the screen. I imagined those lickable abs only two feet away from me. And I started getting hard."

His breathing shallowed. "Fuck."

I shifted so my dick barely brushed his. The sound of Tiller's sucked-in breath was my reward. "Then I started to fantasize about what it would be like to wait for you in the tunnel like a groupie. Have you come running off the field in your sweaty uniform and shove me against the cool tunnel wall."

"Oh fuck. Keep going." Tiller pressed our groins together again, making my head spin.

I felt my face heat, thinking about where the fantasy had ultimately gone. "It got kind of dirty after that."

"You're not stopping. Tell me the rest."

"You fucked me face-first into the cement bricks and then told me if I wasn't completely silent you'd let your teammates take a turn with me, too."

I felt his dick jerk against me as he moaned. Clearly, he thought it was as hot as I had. "I'd never fucking share you like that," he growled.

"No," I agreed, feeling breathless. "But god... I looked around the room at all these big strong football players watching the game with us. And I imagined you taking me in front of them and what they'd think. It just... it was a fantasy, you know? And I got so hard sitting there, it literally hurt."

Now Tiller's own face was flushed, and he'd moved a hand down between us to rub against my dick. "How did I not see you hard and aching right next to me? Hm?"

I closed my eyes and concentrated on the feel of his hand taking control of my cock. "I grabbed your sweatshirt and held it on my lap," I admitted. "And then I caught a whiff of your smell on it, and I fucking soaked my boxers with pre—"

He crushed his mouth to mine and kissed me hard. His hand stroked up and down on my dick, and I lifted one leg up around his thigh to give him more room to stroke me.

Things between us were white-hot. I'd fantasized about him plenty, but I'd never in a million years guessed the reality would be even hotter.

"Bed," he said against my lips. "Bed now."

I pulled back from him and double-checked I didn't have any stove or oven burners on yet. Then I grabbed his good hand and yanked him down the back hallway to my bedroom where I made excellent time yanking off my clothes and starting on his.

"Do—" Tiller began, licking his lips. "Do you want me to fuck you? We haven't done that yet, so..."

I jerked to a stop, his shirt hanging from my hand and his pajama bottoms puddled on the floor at his feet. "Um... is that what you want?" I'd never done it before, but I wasn't opposed to having Tiller Raine be my first. Still, the idea intimidated me a little. I wasn't sure I was ready.

He swallowed. "I... I mean, yeah. Ultimately. I'd love to feel you like that. But I..."

We stared at each other for a beat before both speaking at once.

"I've never done it before."

We stared at each other again while the words sank in. "What?" I asked in a supersonic octave known only to bats and very adept canines.

"But you lived with Nelson for two years," Tiller argued. "You're telling me he never—"

"No! No, he never," I said, flapping my hands around to emphasize... something. I was shocked by his admission. "Wait, wait. *Wait*. You, Tiller Raine, big beautiful NFL superstar, have never had penetrative sex?"

He set his jaw and folded his arms in front of his bare chest. "My dick penetrated your mouth as recently as this morning," he said stubbornly.

I rolled my eyes. "You know what I mean, and stop acting like I'm making a judgment here. I live in a glass house, in case you didn't notice."

"Yeah, what's up with that? How is it possible you've never fucked someone before like that?"

"I told you, I'm not a big hookup person. I want a relationship. And with Nelson, I just... didn't trust him enough. Part of me worried he'd go tell everyone that he 'tapped that' or something." I shrugged. "He was the kind of guy who bragged about everything. I didn't want my ass to be one of the things he bragged about having."

Something dark passed through his expression, but I had no way of knowing what had sparked it.

"Anyway," I continued, "I guess I wasn't ready. What about you?"

He pulled me over to the bed and nudged me into it before climbing in beside me and pulling the thick duvet over us. I sighed and settled against his warm body, not realizing until then how chilly it had been in the room without my clothes on.

"I had a boyfriend in high school, but we were so hopped up all the time, just the idea of anal sex usually made us blow." His chuckle was deep and relaxed. "We lived for blow jobs, hand jobs, and frotting, to the point there wasn't really ever a need for more. Maybe we were too intimidated to try it, I don't know. But I didn't miss it. Then in college, I got backroom blow jobs at parties and stuff all the time. I even got them from some women when I was horny enough, which was usually after a game." Tiller stopped and tilted his head. "Wait. What about all those fucking guys who're always getting all up in your business at Sidecars? I fucking hate that."

It was true. For some reason, our favorite sports bar was like a magnet for weirdos. I'd never understood how the place attracted so many gay and bi guys, but maybe it had something to do with it being Tiller Raine's local hangout. If they couldn't have him, I was the next best thing. "I'm your sloppy seconds," I said without thinking.

His eyes turned stormy. "The hell you say."

"I meant, I *get* your sloppy seconds." I crawled on top of him and straddled his hips. His now-flaccid dick was warm under my ass. I rocked a little bit to get it going again. "I think you're the draw to Sidecars, and then they see me in all of my skinny, geeky splendor and decide this," I said, gesturing to my pale naked chest, "beats that," I said, gesturing to his firm, rounded pecs, "every day of the week. Who the hell needs NFL muscles when they can get sauté muscles instead?"

I flexed my biceps until we both burst into laughter.

Tiller grabbed me around the waist and flipped us over until I was solidly, deliciously under him. His dick was plenty hard by now, and he pressed it into my inner thigh with a groan.

"I've always preferred sauté muscles," he teased in a low, seductive voice. "And watching other men hit on you at Sidecars makes me want to punch something. Jack Wooden was the worst. He showed up there every fucking night during baseball season because he knew we came there to watch the Rockies games and he wanted to get in your pants."

I thought about the good-looking high school teacher we'd met through one of Tiller's teammates. "Aww, he's lonely."

"He's horny. Not the same thing."

I ran my hands up into Tiller's thick hair. "He was sweet. Except he always sat too close to me."

Tiller's eyes bugged. "Babe, he sat close to you so he could cop a feel of your butt. Every time you stood up to go to the men's room, he stared at your ass like a damned proctologist."

"That explains what happened," I muttered under my breath.

"Ya think?" Tiller was on a roll. "He tried asking you out every which way. You finally agreed to a date—at Sidecars on Rockies night, which was hilarious—and when he took that to mean he might actually get you to suck his dick in the back hallway, what the fuck happened?"

I felt my face heat even more than it already was with his big dick pressing its thick length against my leg. "I needed a wingman?"

He grinned like the Cheshire cat. "You needed a bodyguard. A big, strong man to come save you from that pushy punk."

I ran my fingers down his neck to his chest and rubbed them against his nipples. "I actually think he was more excited to get into a bar fight with the great Tiller Raine than he would have been to get his dick sucked by some no-name."

Tiller leaned down until our noses were practically touching. "You are nowhere close to being a no-name. And if you'd sucked anyone's dick in the back hallway of my favorite bar, I would have had to find a new favorite bar."

Suddenly, I remembered the night he started seating me on the inside of a booth at Sidecars. We'd always sat at a high-top table before that, but he'd complained one night he didn't like having his back to the room. When he'd moved us to a booth, he'd nudged me in first, every time. Now I saw it through a different lens.

My chest filled with warmth. "You sneaky little shit."

His brows lifted. "Who, me? How so?" He narrowed his eyes. "Wait, did Sam tell you about Lonny? That traitor."

Lonny was another Sidecars regular who was always trying to get in my pants. "What about Lonny?"

"What were you talking about when you called me sneaky?"

"Nothing. What about Lonny? Whatever it was, Sam didn't tell me."

"Good. He wasn't supposed to." He leaned down and sucked on

my collarbone a little. It made me gasp, but I was determined to hear the story. I yanked him back up by his hair.

"Not so fast, Casanova. Tell me."

He sighed and propped his head in his hand. "I overheard him asking Sam for your number one night, after you'd already shot him down a million times, so I gave him Bret McGraw's personal cell number."

I thought of the big-ass left tackle who was probably the only player on the entire Rigger roster who didn't hesitate to spout anti-gay bullshit under the guise of his devout faith. This, while the man slept around on his wife at every single away game and had arranged for at least one Rigger cheerleader to get the Plan B pill. And it hadn't been because of the generosity of the man's spirit.

I couldn't hold back a giggle. "Poor Lonny. I hope Bret wasn't too hateful to him."

Tiller scoffed. "Lonny lost any chance with me when he cupped your junk right after you'd politely told him no to a drink."

I wrapped my legs around him. I wanted to hump his dick, rub my body all over his until we both came, screaming. But I wanted information even more. "You saw that?"

Instead of answering, Tiller took my face in his hands and kissed me deeply. The taste of him, the feel of his warm exhalations and his strong fingers on my face were enough to make me lose my train of thought.

When he pulled back, his eyes were laser-intense on mine. "I watch you all the fucking time," he admitted. "I didn't even realize I did it at first. Sam asked me what was going on between us, and I looked at him like he was crazy."

His words surprised me. "When was this?"

"Two years ago. When he found out I was taking you home for Fourth of July."

My heart fluttered around like a sheaf of paper caught up in a wind turbine. "Your cousin's wedding?"

He nodded. "I wanted you with me. I wanted... I wanted you with me."

It had sounded like he was going to say something different there but changed his mind. And that was fine, because the words he'd said were enough for me to finally stop riding this line between talk and action. I wanted him. And I wasn't willing to wait any longer.

I knew this wasn't real or permanent. I knew it was a stolen moment where we were only slaking a temporary thirst before returning to our real lives and the rules we needed to abide by. But I still wanted it. Desperately.

"Kiss me again," I whispered. And he did. Only, he didn't start with my lips. He started with the top of my foot and spent the next hour dropping openmouthed kisses along every single inch of my body until I was gasping and begging. A pool of precum puddled on my stomach, but every time I reached for my dick to give it some much-needed attention, he batted my hand away.

When I was finally on the verge of coming untouched, I whimpered one final "Please, Tiller. Please make me come. Please."

And he took me into his mouth and down his throat until the sparkles at the edges of my vision became my entire world.

The following morning I woke up confident enough to try my spinach-and-herb soufflé idea. I'd picked up the ingredients at the local market our second day in town, but I'd been putting off making it for fear of fucking up. Somehow I'd gotten it into my head if I could successfully make this soufflé, I would be good enough to follow up with Gary and Erica Civetti. If the soufflé flopped, I wouldn't call. I knew it was silly, but that's where my brain was.

Waking up in the arms of a man like Tiller Raine was enough to make me feel invincible, though, so we were doing this.

I started the process with a strong cup of coffee and some final research about the use of potatoes to help keep the soufflé from flopping.

"It's fine," I murmured to my notes. "It's going to be fine. If it doesn't work, I'll just have a mediocre list of recipes in a mediocre cookbook and no future as a professional chef in my own restaurant. No problem."

Tiller had gotten up early to do physical therapy with the hand specialist. When someone named Winter Waites had been the only available specialist in the area, I'd assumed a busty blond woman was going to show up at the door with an annoying giggle and a side job on Pornhub.

But no. It hadn't been a busty blond. It had been a jacked one. The muscular guy had a scruffy blond beard and a nice enough haircut to make me give him the side-eye.

A hundred bucks said he was gay.

And he was currently in the basement gym alone with the hottest man on earth, the man I'd had in my mouth only two hours ago. The man who'd whispered words into my ear while I was sucking him off —words about wanting to slide his dick deep inside me and stay there forever.

I shuddered and wiggled my hips because I wasn't thinking about that right now. I was working.

My back teeth ground together as I yanked the spinach package open. Green leaves spewed everywhere from the bag like it was rice-throwing time at a vegan wedding.

"Dammit," I growled, trying my hardest not to remember the biceps on the physical therapist. "Why couldn't it have been an old guy with yellow teeth and a giant, hairy mole on his... anywhere."

I gathered up the spinach leaves and chucked them in a colander to rinse. This recipe needed my attention because if I couldn't get it right today, it would need to be scrapped from the project.

Once everything was prepped, I started the roux. The faint sounds of acoustic guitar came from my Bluetooth speaker, and I noticed it had started to snow. The fire was low in the fireplace, but it still cracked and popped periodically. I could get used to this. The clean, crisp mountain air was a refreshing change from Houston's heat and smog, and the small-town feel of Aster Valley had been a charming surprise. Rather, me finding it appealing had been the surprise.

I'd always pictured myself a city guy, but maybe things had changed in my life. While getting dressed up and going out to a nice restaurant was still a treat from time to time, I actually much preferred staying in and hanging out with good friends. These days, I tended to avoid crowds and any restaurant with a long wait.

Was I getting old or just settling into myself? Did it matter?

I folded in the last of the egg whites and poured the mixture into the soufflé dish before smoothing over the top and placing it in the oven. Now it was time to work on the pork tenderloin I was making to go with it.

This kitchen was a dream. I'd already moved some things around to make it work better for me, but overall, it didn't need much to be perfect for me. The commercial aspects of it made me ache to cook for a crowd, and I found myself wishing our friends could come over for dinner if only so I could make a feast.

I daydreamed about running it as a bed-and-breakfast and cooking for my very own guests. Of course, in my dream Tiller ran it with me as if we were stereotypical gay dudes from a charming small town in New England. In the fictional scenario, the large red barn out back doubled as a special-event venue with views of the slopes and the trees, maybe even a field of wildflowers in summer.

It didn't matter, a dream was a dream and what happened in Vegas stayed in Vegas. While I cooked, I mentally created menus for different seasons. There'd be a harvest-themed menu in autumn, a cozy comfort menu for winter, maybe a lighter, plant-based selection for spring, and then a fresh fruit and vegetable offering in summer. Maybe cutie-pie Truman at the spice shop would sell me some of the bounty from his gardens, or maybe he could at least show me how to grow some veggies myself.

I was deep into a mental image of Tiller shirtless and sweaty in my fictional veggie garden when the object of my lust appeared.

"Something smells good," Tiller said, setting his water bottle on the counter as he walked up to me. "Is that your soufflé?"

He wrapped one arm around my waist before leaning in and

kissing me full on the lips. I stared at him in shock and then turned to face the hot therapist who'd followed him in.

"Oh," Tiller said. "This is Winter. Did you meet him the other day? Winter, this is Michael Vining."

I was still speechless from the semi-public kiss, so I simply stared at the man.

Winter grinned. "Yeah, we met. Tiller's right. Smells amazing in here. He told me you're a chef who specializes in feeding pro athletes. That's killer. I'd love to pick your brain sometime. I work with some of the Broncos and Rockies players in the off-season whenever they get out this way, and I've got a few pro skiers in Steamboat who could really use some dietary fine-tuning."

I must have had a weird expression on my face because Tiller's hand tightened on my hip, and he met my eyes. "Babe, Winter and his husband live right around the corner in that cabin with the red roof. Remember we saw it yesterday on the way back from breakfast?"

Babe? I liked it, but was he really not concerned about claiming me in front of a complete stranger? Wait. *Husband.* Hot therapist was taken.

I shook off my stupidity and was blessed with brain waves. "Yes! Good. Oh, hey. Would you two want to come over for dinner tonight? I'm making enough to feed an army, and we could really use some taste testers for one of my recipes."

Winter's eyes widened in delight. "Oh, hell yeah. Let me text Gent to make sure, but I think we're good. That would be amazing. What time do you want us here, and what can we bring?"

After arranging the details, we sent Winter to his final appointment of the day. When we returned to the kitchen, I asked Tiller about it. "You're not worried he's going to tell someone we're... whatever we are?"

Tiller grinned at me. "What are we, Mikey?"

I flapped my hand in the air between us as if that answered it. He raised an eyebrow.

"Gah! Don't make me use words. The 'babe' thing. The kiss. You know what I mean."

He leaned in and kissed me again, wrapping his arms around me and leaning me backward a little bit so I was off-balance. I clung to him and went with it, enjoying the way he took charge of my mouth. By the time we came up for air, I didn't care who the hell knew.

"Winter's husband is a celebrity, so he gets it," Tiller said. "Besides, once I found out he was gay, I got an itch to make sure he knew you weren't available. I didn't realize he was with someone until later."

I could get very used to being unavailable as long as it meant Tiller Raine kept kissing me.

13

TILLER

Spending the evening with Winter and Gent was way more fun than I'd expected. When Mikey had first floated the offer of dinner to Winter, I'd bitten back a wince. I wanted Mikey all to myself right now. I knew this time in Colorado was limited, and I wanted to spend as much of it as possible alone with my favorite person. There was an unspoken understanding we wouldn't be able to continue this... whatever it was we were doing... when we returned home.

But Winter and Gentry were great company, and seeing Mikey's pride as he served up each dish and answered Winter's questions about his cooking was worth it. He was in his element. Mikey loved feeding people and having willing tasters to experiment recipes on.

Mikey sat down after serving dessert. "Is it true everyone in Aster Valley is gay?" he asked with a teasing smile. "We've been here like forty-eight hours and we've only met gay dudes. Not that I'm complaining."

Gent chuckled. He was the lead singer of one of Mikey's favorite bands, and when Mikey had opened the door earlier to see the singer/songwriter standing there, he gasped loudly enough to wake hibernating bears nearby. It had only taken a couple of glasses of wine to calm Mikey down enough to remember Gentry Kane was a regular guy despite being the lead singer of GUS. "Then you've had an unusual experience. When I moved here, it felt like Pim and Bill were the only gay guys around. They'd dealt with some homophobia early on, but it started getting better several years ago. I think Truman's the only one who's had any bad experiences lately, but I think that has more to do with his history here than his sexuality. Our friends Mindy and Mia are always mistaken for sisters, but that's because they really do look alike. For the most part, it's becoming an artistic little town that seems to be attracting more and more LGBT folks."

Mikey frowned. "What do you mean about Truman? Does he get bullied?"

Winter leaned in to reach for the wine bottle. As he poured his husband a refill, he began to tell us the story of Truman's role in the ski slope shutdown.

"This was right before the Salt Lake Olympics. Langdon Goode was training here before heading off to Salt Lake. Truman's dad managed the resort at the time. Anyway, Truman was a kid—maybe four or five?—and had always wanted to try his grandfather's old metal sled. So one night he snuck it out and took it for a spin on the slopes. The moon was pretty full, I guess, because he said he saw a mountain lion at the edge of the slope. Scared him shitless. He took off running for home, not even thinking about the sled he left behind."

Gent took over the story. "Poor kid. It snowed all night. Goode was excited for the first run on fresh powder the next morning. He had special early access to the lift. Took the run down and just so happened to ski right into the hidden metal sled."

Winter shook his head. "Fucked up his knee. ACL, MCL, the works. Not only was he done for the season, he was never able to get back to the same level again. Ruined his career."

I winced. I'd heard a hundred stories of pro athletes experiencing a career-ending injury, but it never got easier to hear. Especially when the kid was on the verge of finally realizing his dream in the Olympics.

Mikey sighed. "Poor Truman. He was just a kid."

Winter nodded. "Apparently, the whole town blamed him, and his parents were the worst of the whole lot. As soon as they were put out of business, they upped stakes and moved away. Durango, I think? Truman had a shit time of it after that from what I've been able to glean from other people in town."

Mikey leaned forward. "Why'd he come back here? I'd think he'd want a fresh start somewhere else."

Gent was the one who answered. "His aunt owned a large property with a greenhouse at the edge of town. She grew vegetables and sold them at the local farmer's market in the summer. She died a few years ago and left him her place."

"But he's so young," I said. If he'd been around five before the 2002 Olympics, that would put him in his early twenties.

Gent nodded. "He was eighteen when he inherited the property. Moved back when he was nineteen. We think it was to get away from his toxic family. He hasn't been to college or anything. He's completely self-taught."

I was impressed. And I could see the same thoughts running through Mikey's head. We'd liked the guy, and hearing his story made me want to protect him from anyone who would blame a kid for an honest mistake. I couldn't imagine carrying the burden of the accident around like that.

"And he's still getting hassled for it here in town?" I asked.

Gent held up his hands in a shrug. "He says no, but Pim and Bill have witnessed some bullshit from a group of assholes called the Stanner brothers. Their dad, Gene Stanner, was the head mechanic for the lifts. When the lifts stopped, Gene's employment stopped. Instead of finding another job nearby in Steamboat or at any of the other three hundred ski lifts in Colorado, I guess he just stayed here and whipped up a boatload of hate instead. It doesn't help that the sheriff is Erland Stanner, Gene's brother."

"Fuck," Mikey said. "Poor Truman."

Gentry sighed. "Yeah, the rest of us try and look out for the kid as much as possible. Pim and Bill treat him like one of their own."

Mikey quickly turned the conversation around to what eligible bachelors might be in town for us to set Truman up with so he could have a built-in bodyguard. Gent laughed and shook his head. "Truman already has a boyfriend."

We both stared at him in surprise. "He does?" Mikey asked. "Who?"

Winter responded. "Mr. Balderson, the librarian. Bit of a May-December situation, but who am I to judge?"

Mikey asked a million nosy questions and ended up in a full-on Aster Valley gossip session before long. He got the scoop on everyone in town which was pointless since we were only here for a few more weeks. But I could understand his interest. The people of Aster Valley were diverse and unique. Winter described artists and homesteaders, outdoor enthusiasts and small-business owners. It sounded like a close-knit place with tons of personality, and I could immediately picture Mikey thriving in a place like this. It was much more suited to his eclectic, creative self than hanging out with a bunch of football players in a big city.

Which, of course, made me unsteady. What if the Civettis really did have an opportunity for Mikey?

Gent leaned over and spoke softly just to me. "How long have you two been together?"

He caught me by surprise. "Oh. We're not really... I mean..."

Understanding crossed his face. "You really like him, though."

"So much," I said without thinking. "More than I even realized."

He moved his chair closer to mine and hid his words behind a sip of his wine. "Is it the job? Because I totally get it. We had a similar situation because of my job. The media had a field day when they discovered I was in a serious relationship."

Mikey stood to clear the table while he was still chatting happily with Winter. We tried to get up and help him, but he waved Gent and me off. "Stay where you are. Winter said he'd help. I want to write down a recipe for him anyway."

Once they'd moved from the dining room to the kitchen, Gent turned back to me. "I thought you were out, though?"

I sighed and leaned back in my seat. "I am. That's not the problem. Mikey is my coach's youngest son."

Gent winced. "Oh. Shit."

"Yeah. But there's more. Mikey had a relationship with the last football player he worked for, and I think he's embarrassed by hooking up with me because he's afraid people will think less of him for sleeping with his boss. Twice."

"What are you going to do when you get home?"

I closed my eyes and rubbed my hands over my face. It was nice to finally be rid of the sling. "Beg him?" I suggested with a laugh. "I can't even think about the possibility of this being temporary. But I can't ask him to hide either."

Gent seemed to think it through for a minute before meeting my eyes with a twinkling glance. "Then we need a plan."

As we brainstormed and laughed together, not really coming up with any kind of actual plan other than Gent's advice to fuck the media and do what made me happy, I realized how refreshing it was to be around guys I could be completely open with. Even though they'd been strangers only that morning, Gent and Winter were easy to be around. My closest teammates all seemed pretty cool with my sexuality, but it was different being with guys who really got it. I didn't have to put any of my thoughts or actions through a filter, and I hadn't realized how exhausting that was.

Once they'd said their goodbyes and Winter had said he'd be back for another therapy session the following afternoon, Gent and Winter hopped into their pickup truck and headed down the drive into the starry night.

"God, that was fun," Mikey said, turning back into the warm house. "I like them a lot."

I agreed. "And your soufflé was puffy enough to impress the pants off them."

Mikey's reaction was oddly pensive, but I knew deep down he was proud of himself for how it had turned out.

I reached out for Mikey's waist and turned him back toward me. "C'mere."

His lips tasted like sweet chocolate from the cup of cocoa he'd had after dinner. I kissed him as long as I could until he started getting antsy.

"Take me to bed," he said, ripping his lips off mine. "Now. Please."

I chuckled and tightened my arms around him. "That was really nice." Before he had a chance to think I meant the kissing, I continued. "Dinner with another couple, I mean. It felt..." I shrugged and felt my face heat. "It felt really normal and... I don't know. Grown-up? Is that cheesy?"

Mikey stood on tiptoes to get closer to meeting my eyes. "Yes, but I agree. It kinda felt like a double date. I thought it would be weird, but it wasn't. Makes me wish we lived here. Everyone's so nice and welcoming."

I couldn't tell if he was being serious or not, but I liked the idea we were of the same mind about it. Life here in Aster Valley was very different than our life back home, and I was grateful we had several weeks left to enjoy it.

Suddenly, I remembered how close Christmas was and how much Mikey adored the holiday. Despite being in the middle of the season, Christmas was a big deal at our house back home. Mikey usually decorated like a pro, setting up several trees around the house and twirling garland and lights everywhere. If we happened to be home for Christmas Eve, he made a huge feast and invited everyone over.

"Let's go get a tree tomorrow before the game," I said excitedly. "We'll pick up lights and decorations in town and put it in the kitchen near the fireplace so we can see it every night."

His eyes lit up until he remembered something. "I told your parents we'd go there for Christmas Eve and Christmas morning. Your sister and the kids are coming over for brunch. There's no reason to decorate this place if we're not going to be here."

I pushed his hair back from his forehead and dropped a kiss on the smooth skin there. "Don't care. We'll still do a tree here, okay? We can enjoy it until Christmas Eve."

The idea of missing the game tomorrow made me itchy, but I tried not to think about it. Winter had told me my arm and shoulder were doing better than expected, and I was in good shape to bump up a level on the conditioning. My hand was another story, but we were working on it. All I could do in the meantime was keep up my food intake and exercise, study the game film the coaches sent me, and be ready to return as soon as I got the green light.

"I'd like that," Mikey said. "And Tiller?"

I looked down at his sweet brown eyes framed by his adorable, nerdy glasses. "Hm?"

"I've been thinking about it a lot today. Actually, I haven't been able to stop thinking about it, and maybe that says something slutty about me, I don't know—although, that's not very sex-positive of me, so I take it back—but anyway." He gasped in a breath. "Where was I?"

"Pretty much, I'm still back on the word slutty," I admitted. He was clearly flustered. "Talk to me, Mike."

We were still standing in the large entry hall, so I pulled him by the hand toward my bedroom. When we entered the large space, I sat him on the edge of the bed and squatted in front of him, holding his hands and meeting his eyes. "What's going through your head?"

"I want to have sex," he blurted.

I blinked at him. "Ah, maybe I'm an ass for making assumptions, but I sort of figured we'd get naked at some point tonight and..."

Mikey shook his head. "No, that's not what I mean. Fucking. Anal. Like... *sex*."

He seemed so flustered. I hated seeing him dance around his words with me. "You want me to fuck you, or were you thinking—"

His head snapped up. "Yes! That one. The first one. I want you to fuck me. And you don't have to worry. It's not that I don't know if I'll like it. I, um, I use a dildo and stuff at home. I just... I just haven't been with someone I really wanted to do it with. But..."

He didn't have to say it. Things between us were good. Really good. And I'd never felt more comfortable with someone in bed before the way I did with him.

"You sure?" I asked, smoothing my thumbs over the back of his hands. "Because you know I'll be super fucking happy with anything we do. I don't need—"

"Stop talking. I'm sure. You're killing me." Mikey rolled his eyes and threw himself back on the bed. "This is excruciating."

I stood up and crawled onto the bed over him, peering down at his closed eyes. Dark eyelashes brushed the tender skin beneath his eyes. I pulled off his glasses and dropped a kiss right there. And then another on the other side. When I was done kissing his entire face, I carefully placed his glasses on the nightstand and began undressing him.

"Is this why you didn't eat dinner?" I asked.

Mikey's face flushed deep red, and it sent streaks down his throat. "Maybe. I was hoping you hadn't noticed. Can we not talk about it, please?"

I ran a finger along the side of his neck and felt my heart kick up when he shivered beneath me. "Talking is important. I hope you know I'm not easily bothered by stuff." I didn't want to embarrass him, but I also wanted him to know I was on board with fooling around with him no matter what.

His neck tasted warm and sweet. I moved my mouth down to his chest so I could tease a nipple lightly with my teeth. Mikey's legs came up to wrap around my back, and his dick arched up into my sternum. I leaned down and ran my tongue around the head, capturing the salty taste of him. Naked Mikey was a feast for the senses. I loved the way he felt and smelled and tasted. The sounds of pleasure he made hit me square in the groin, and watching his skin tighten into goose bumps ramped me up even more.

While I sucked on his dick, I reached for the bottle of lube on the nightstand and used it to quickly slick up my fingers.

As soon as I slid the first finger inside him, I knew we weren't going to make it. He was so hot and tight, and the whimpers coming out of him were so fucking sexy, I had to reach down and clasp my own cock to keep from coming all over his leg.

"Christ," I said, pulling off just enough to take a deep breath. "You're so fucking sexy."

"Flip around," he said urgently. "Wanna suck you, too."

Our height difference didn't make it the smoothest, but we more than made up for the awkward position with straight-up enthusiasm. I'd never felt so free and open with a sexual partner before—that was a given considering I'd only had quick hookups in the past—and this was wild and thrilling.

I doubled down on my attempts to drive him out of his mind. My finger searched for his spot while my throat worked him over.

"Fuck!" As he came, he replaced his mouth on my dick with a tight, talented fist. The squeeze, coupled with the taste of him in my mouth, brought my climax screaming over me.

So much for our big sex plans. The orgasm wiped me out. I lay there panting like I'd just run for an eighty-yard pass and hauled ass to the end zone for a touchdown in double coverage.

"Sorry," I said, even though I wasn't.

He let out a breathless chuckle. "Pretty sure my brain is in a thousand pieces right now. No sorry needed."

I moved around to face him on the bed and brushed my palm down his face. "We had plans for more."

Mikey's face relaxed into a tender smile as he turned to press a kiss in my palm. "I know where you live. I'll take a rain check."

My heart did a little spinny number at the idea I'd get more chances to have sex with Mikey V. The very thought of pressing my dick inside of him made me almost get hard again, but I didn't quite have it in me. I was tired from the long day and ready to curl up around Mikey's hot little body and lose myself to sleep.

"Thank you for today," I said as I moved us under the covers of the large bed and arranged him the way I wanted him. His limbs were like jelly, and he stayed exactly where I put him.

Just as I was drifting into sleep, he murmured something against my chest.

"What was that, baby?" I asked in a soft voice.

"I'm really hungry."

I laughed so loudly, I woke us both up again. We finally got out of bed and made our way into the kitchen for a midnight snack where we spent another hour talking about what a nice time we'd had with

Gent and Winter. This "time out of time" in Aster Valley was so different from our lives in Houston.

It was bittersweet, because I could see Mikey thriving away from his family and among kind people who had nothing to do with football and who showed interest in who he was and what he enjoyed doing. Aster Valley was good for Mikey, but it wasn't until the following day it finally sunk in. Mikey moving to Aster Valley wasn't just an idle thought, but a distinct possibility.

14

MIKEY

I knew it wasn't going to last. This floaty feeling of hope, the naive expectation we could make things work between us. The stupid, desperate desire to have Tiller Raine as my actual boyfriend.

I was on my knees in the snow, getting ready to pull Tiller's hard cock out of his jeans and warm it up with my mouth when his phone rang.

"Ignore it," he hissed. His fingers tightened in my hair. We'd been halfway through a nice early morning stroll in the snowy woods behind the house when the shrill sound pierced the silence and made me almost tumble onto my ass.

I tried ignoring it, but as my tongue curled around the head of his dick, it went off again. He fumbled it out of his pocket, cursing. It continued to ring. I finally huffed out a cloudy breath and stood, brushing my knees off and reaching out to close his pants.

"Not so fast," he cautioned. "It's Markus. I'll get rid of him."

I tried not to roll my eyes. Leave it to his agent to cockblock me.

"Markus, now's not a good time." His voice was rough and sexy. I closed my eyes and spun away from him to get my libido in check. The resentful part of me was feeling bitter about the reminder of our real lives back home. It was bound to happen at some point, but up till now, I'd made myself scarce when he received a call from work. I didn't want to hear about the Riggers. I didn't want to know about the film they'd sent him to study.

Maybe it was selfish, but for once in my fucking life, I wanted someone all to myself without sharing him with fucking football.

"It's going well, actually. The physical therapist was here and—"

He stopped talking, presumably when Markus interrupted him.

"Yes, but—"

After another minute, I heard Tiller sigh. "Mm-hm. Okay..."

If his agent was trying to convince him to come back to Houston, come back to work... I was going to lose my shit.

Two can play at this game.

I stepped close to him and dropped to my knees again. Tiller's eyes widened comically, and his head began shaking emphatically.

But he didn't step away.

I pulled him back out and went to town on his dick. His hand clutched at my hair as if he was going to use it to pull me off, but he didn't. He gasped and groaned, quickly explaining to Markus he'd tripped over something. I heard the sound of Markus's raised voice warning him against more injuries.

I wanted to laugh. I wanted to fist pump. But more than anything, I wanted to stay out there under the bright clear winter sun and bring Tiller Raine to his knees.

He made a choking sound before trying to answer one of Markus's questions. "I need to come. I mean *go*. I need to go. Oh *fuck*. No, my... foot. It's fine. Oh god. No... it's... lemme call you back."

As soon as he ended the call, he dropped his phone in the snow, thrust into my throat, and roared. Birds shot from the trees, and I almost sputtered in laughter. Despite the call from Markus, I felt free. Just the snow, the sun, the birds, Tiller and me.

It was a life I could get very used to. Even if I had to wait years for the dream to turn into a reality.

"Christ, Mikey," he croaked after his body ceased its involuntary movements. "I almost said your name by accident while I was on the phone with him."

"Sorry."

I wasn't sorry.

"C'mere." He pulled me up and kissed me, nuzzling his cold nose against my warm neck. "God, you're good at that."

I indulged in the feel of his arms around me, trying my hardest to forget about the phone call, but I knew it wouldn't last.

"I have to call him back," he said after a few minutes of post-oral snuggling. "He said Gonzales wants me on the line during the game doing some analysis."

He searched my eyes for something. Disappointment? Anger? Judgment?

"I understand," I told him, trying to smile. "It's your job. Of course I understand."

His hands came up to cup my cheeks. They were warm and tender, causing me to close my eyes and sink into his touch. "Let me call him back, and then we'll go get the tree. We can decorate it during commercial breaks."

Even though I knew that was a pipe dream, I agreed. It would give me something to do during the game instead of stew in my bitterness and daydream about a life I probably would never have. Reality had sunk in overnight, and I'd realized one casual conversation with strangers wasn't likely to turn into a real opportunity here in Aster Valley.

We headed back to the house and cleaned up before bundling up in tons more layers and heading to the diner to ask for a recommendation for a Christmas tree farm nearby. When we walked into the diner, the place was packed. It shouldn't have surprised me since it was a Sunday, smack-dab in the center of prime brunch hours. Thankfully, the football game wasn't scheduled until midafternoon, so we had enough time to do our shopping before needing to return to the house and get Tiller settled with his headset.

"Ooh!" Pim said, spotting us as soon as we came in. He excused himself from the family he was seating and came bustling over to us. "You won't believe what I overheard this morning. A hoity-toity couple from Big City, USA, was in talking all excitedly about a chef from Texas they wanted to convince to help them open a B&B right here in our very own Aster Valley! Can you believe it?"

I blinked at him, unable to process whether he was teasing me or being serious. Pim shook my shoulder and grinned wide. "They were talking about you, hon. Isn't that exciting? I told Bill it would be ah-mazing to have you two move here and take up residence out at the old Rockley place. Do you knit? Does one of you knit? Well, it doesn't matter. I can teach you. We'll have a knitting night at your place in front of the fireplace. Get a few big sofas, some snacks... I can picture it now. We'll have to order in wine by the case, but maybe the big box store out by..."

I let his voice fade out while I let the thought sink in. Maybe... maybe this was a real opportunity. Could it be?

If they were truly interested in moving forward with their idea, was that something I wanted to seriously consider?

I glanced at Tiller, who looked as shell-shocked as I felt. He was being oddly quiet. My heart squeezed at the sight of him, hinting at the answer. I wasn't sure I was ready to consider moving away from him.

"Pop, take a breath and let them sit down first," Solo said with a chuckle.

I swallowed and shook my head. "Oh, no. We actually came to ask about finding a Christmas tree."

Solo pointed us in the right direction and even pulled a flyer out of somewhere with the tree farm information on it. After gently extricating ourselves from Pim's excited chatter, we followed the directions out of town and eventually pulled down a narrow lane decorated with red-beribboned wreaths. Snow weighted down piney branches interspersed between naked aspen trees. I let go of thoughts of the bed-and-breakfast idea and let myself live in this moment with Tiller.

When we got to the end of the lane, there was a big open parking area filled with minivans and SUVs. Kids ran around excitedly in thick parkas and colorful hats while a bonfire crackled from a stone ring nearby. It was everything I'd always wanted to have in a Christmas tree excursion but never had.

"This is amazing," I said in an awed voice. "They're toasting marshmallows. Look!"

Tiller's voice rumbled with laughter. "This is what it's like visiting a real Christmas tree farm and not one of those home store lots in Houston."

I hustled out of the vehicle and reached for Tiller's hand to yank him toward the trees I could see beyond the parking area. His laugh followed me down the long rows until I finally stopped and stared at the view I spotted beyond the last tree in the row.

A horse-drawn sleigh moved across a snowy field in the distance with the jagged peaks of the Rockies in the distance.

"Tiller," I breathed, pointing with one of the bright red mittens I'd purchased at the gift shop next door to Truman's spice store. We'd already been back to see Truman twice since our first full day in Aster Valley, and he'd introduced us to the woman who owned the shop. "Look."

He slid his arm low across my back as we stood at the edge of the tree farm looking at the sight. "Truman said there was someone here who did sleigh rides. Did you want to book one?"

"Oh, no. God no," I said quickly. "I hate horses. But it's pretty from afar, isn't it?"

He laughed again, a sound that was beginning to feel like oxygen to me. Necessary... and thankfully plentiful.

"Very pretty." He turned and kissed me slowly on the cheek. "But not as pretty as you. And not as pretty as this giant tree is going to be in our house."

I turned to look at the one he pointed to. He was right. It was gorgeous. I didn't correct him when he called it our house because I wanted to pretend it was.

It could all be pretend until the real world threatened to interfere again.

Which, of course, it did only a few hours later. This time it was my dad.

Coach had discovered the truth about our time in Colorado.

15

TILLER

Watching Mikey at the tree farm had been a joy, but even being able to go out into the snow and select a tree for the first time in years was special. I hadn't realized how much I missed it.

We got the tree back to the house, surprising Mikey with the unique trick of blowing all the snow off the branches simply by driving with the tree tied to the roof. On the way back, we stopped at a store to grab lights and decorations, but we ended up having to hustle back so I could get the tree inside the house before calling into the coaching staff and turning on the pregame coverage.

Despite having to work, I enjoyed every minute of the domestic scene that followed. Mikey spent the first hour of the game prepping and cooking something in the kitchen while the tree dried off in front of the picture window between the sitting area and the kitchen.

At one point he brought me a crudité plate with little pieces of salami, cheese, and olives on it, and I snacked in between conversations with Gonzales. So far, Brent Little and Derek Mopellei were working well together, and thankfully the run game was also bearing fruit. We were up by three points going into the second quarter when Mikey asked if I could talk on the phone and string lights at the same time.

For the next hour, I used the Jaguars' possessions to focus on helping Mikey with the tree and then stopped to watch the game as soon as the Jags scored and the Riggers got the ball back. While I enjoyed Gonzales asking for my advice and treating me like a key consultant on the Riggers' passing game, I was selfishly annoyed it was causing me to miss out on giving Mikey and the holiday decorating my full attention.

Unfortunately, a late hit penalty halted our momentum right after the two-minute warning in the fourth quarter. The setback made the final half hour of the game excruciating. Gonzales didn't listen to my suggestion to trust Brent in the slot, and he advised Coach to call a running play instead. It wasn't enough. Time ran out without a touchdown, and we lost 20-27.

By this point, Mikey had disappeared from the kitchen area completely, and I could see the familiar veins popping up on Coach's head on the high-def television. He was pissed. And Mikey had bolted.

I wondered how many times Mikey'd had to bear the brunt of a Rigger loss in his lifetime. How many times had he been left with a Sunday night depression at the very least and a raging father at his worst?

After hanging up with Gonzales, I blew out a breath and ran my hands through my already messy hair. I'd spent the last half hour pacing and barking into the phone. My adrenaline was pumping, and my stomach hurt. I hated this part. My father had always warned me that high highs meant low lows.

Ups and downs are what make the roller coaster, son. But it's a hell of a ride, ain't it?

I rubbed my hands over my face and wondered, not for the first time, how men like Coach Vining could survive this kind of stress long-term. It wasn't healthy.

After calming down and drinking the rest of the water from my water bottle, I shuffled back toward Mikey's room. He wasn't there. I looked around the house until finally spotting him out back under the fading light of the sun setting behind the mountains.

He was building a snowman.

I gathered up some items, threw on my boots, hat, and parka, and hustled out to join him. "Hey. What're you doing out here?"

His face lit up so bright, I sucked in a breath. Mikey was gorgeous. The cold had pinked his cheeks, and playing in the snow had obviously brightened his mood.

"What does it look like I'm doing?" he asked with a laugh. "I've never gotten to do this before."

I pulled a scarf and hat out of my coat pocket. "Here. He looks cold."

Mikey laughed and wrapped the scarf around Frosty's neck before plonking the hat on his head. "What else? He needs eyes."

I pulled out the baggie of whole black olives. "Done."

He accidentally mashed a few in an attempt to fix the olives to Frosty's face, but we finally figured it out. Next, I handed him a carrot for the nose and a red Twizzler for the mouth.

Mikey's eyes narrowed as he flapped the Twizzler at me. "Where'd you get this?"

I grinned at him. "Since when are you allowed multiple hidden candy stashes?"

His hands fisted on his hips. "Since I'm not paid a zillion dollars to be in tip-top shape. In fact, professional chefs are expected to be... rounded."

I snorted. "You're the furthest thing from rounded I've ever seen. Besides, Twizzlers are only forty calories per stick. Do you know how easily I can burn off forty calories?"

"By giving one small, rounded chef a very enthusiastic blow job?" he asked innocently.

I ignored his suggestion, but my dick definitely did not. "And do you know why I know how many calories are in those things?"

"Because you're a sneaky sneak?"

"Because my... Mikey keeps a giant bag of these fuckers hidden inside an empty laundry detergent box in my laundry room."

His eyebrows shot up. "Since when do you go in the laundry room?"

Did I dare admit the truth? "Since I had a legit wet dream about you maybe a year ago and was too embarrassed to let you see my sheets."

His eyes twinkled, and his lips curved up. "No! About me? Really? Tiller Raine, you dirty dog. Raine was spankin' the main vein."

"You're a shit poet."

Mikey threw his arms out and spun in a circle in the snow. "Raine came in pain as he claimed my name!"

"This... was a mistake." I tried to bite back the giant grin threatening to overtake my face.

"Tiller fondled his pillar of a willer. Wait. That was terrible."

"*That* one was terrible?"

His eyes flashed in the low light. "Raine, no need to explain."

"Make it stop," I groaned.

"It's plain you strained to obtain me in vain. Instead... your fame was a stain on your counterpane. For shame."

I stalked toward him and placed my hand over his heart. Just as his face began to soften with affection, I shoved him on his back in the fluffy snow.

"Ack!" He flailed for a second before realizing he'd fallen in the perfect position for a snow angel. He began moving his arms and legs through the fresh powder. "Thanks, Raine!"

I climbed on top of him and shut him up with a kiss before he could keep rhyming. By the time I was finished kissing him, he couldn't have rhymed if someone had been there with a rhyming thesaurus and a million dollars. He was glassy-eyed and dazed. I wanted to devour him.

I stood up and grabbed his hand, pulling him up with me. "C'mon. Let's get you warmed up inside." In my mind I was already conjuring up images of stripping him down and shoving him into a hot shower, bending him over and sliding my way deep into his body to warm him from the inside out.

As I imagined how the scene would play out, we walked back to the warmly lit lodge hand in hand. Mikey asked me in a soft voice how the game ended up, and my dream snapped like a fragile soap bubble.

"Oh. We lost," I admitted, noticing the tension in his body pick up. "Ran out of time."

"Shit, Tiller. I'm sorry. Does it mess up your playoff chances?" Mikey reached for the door and pulled it open, letting out the warmth and the fresh piney scent of the new Christmas tree. Oddly, it smelled like home. Like the kind of place I wished was our home. I wanted more days like this with Michael Vining. Days of snowy adventures and holiday decorating. Listening to him putter around in the kitchen while football was on the TV. Watching him laugh and try something new for the pure joy of it.

I wanted more time with him, full stop.

"Tiller?"

I looked up from kicking off my boots onto the nearby mat. "Yeah, uh... It depends on how everyone else does tonight and how the Titans do tomorrow night against the Chiefs, but we still have a shot at the division title. If the Titans win and we don't want to rely on a wild card spot, we need to beat the Steelers which won't be easy."

My phone was ringing from farther inside where I'd left it on the kitchen counter. Mikey glanced in that direction and then sent me an understanding smile. "I'll hop in the shower while you take your call."

I leaned in and kissed his red nose, wanting so badly to tell him how much he meant to me, how incredibly special this time out of time was, and how I wanted desperately for it to become real when we got back to Houston.

But I didn't. Instead, I made my way to the kitchen and swiped my phone before looking to see who it was.

"Where in the Sam Hill are you?" Coach shouted through the phone. "I been trying to get ahold of you for thirty fuckin' minutes."

I was shocked by the vitriol in his voice, but then I reminded myself how much pressure he was under to make the playoffs. The loss would be sitting on him hard.

"After I got off the phone with Gonzales, I went outside to cool off.

Why? Did something happen?" God, please don't let someone in Mikey's family be hurt or sick. "Is everyone okay?"

"I even tried getting ahold of Mikey to see if he knew if you were even still in Denver."

Warning flags began waving across my mental landscape. Of course Mikey wouldn't have told him we were off together, just the two of us. Coach thought I was at home with my parents. "Oh ah... What did you need, Coach?"

"I need *you*. Get back here. This injured reserve bullshit isn't working for me. We'll have to figure something out."

At first, I thought he was joking. "I thought Brent and Derek did a great job tonight. It looks like—"

"I don't give a shit what you think. Just get back here in time for Sunday's game against Pittsburgh. Tell your parents I'm sorry you can't stay."

He had to be joking. I still didn't have full feeling in my hand. Winter had said I was improving, but I still had at least three weeks before I'd be healthy enough to even think about playing. He'd even mentioned possible nerve damage if I returned to the field too soon.

"Coach—"

When he cut me off, his voice was low and hoarse. No doubt he'd been screaming the second half of the game. "Just get back here."

"Tiller!" Mikey cried, running into the room in nothing but a towel. In his hand was a familiar piece of brushed nickel from the bathroom sink. Thank god I wasn't on a video call. "The faucet came off in my hand, and I can't get the shutoff valve to turn!"

The silence from the other end of the line was chilling. "Is that my son?" he finally asked in a low murder voice.

"Yes, sir."

My words caused Mikey to freeze in place. His eyebrows winged up so high, it would have been laughable if I didn't feel like my stomach was going to turn inside out.

Coach's voice was tightly controlled. Barely. "Put him on the phone."

I took a deep breath and held the phone out to Mikey. *Your dad*, I mouthed unnecessarily.

He approached the phone like it was made out of stingers. After handing it to him, I leaned over and pressed a long kiss to the top of his head before taking the faucet handle from him and making my way to the bathroom.

Coach's call was like a cooler full of ice water dumped on our time together, but not the celebratory kind that brought with it happiness and good tidings of great things to come. No, this was the regular kind of brutal wake-up call that reminded me why exactly we couldn't be together.

I had a job to do. While this time in Aster Valley had been amazing, I couldn't forget that my life was centered around football right now. I was under contract to the Riggers, and it was my job. Even if I wasn't ready to get back in the game yet, Coach could demand my presence on the bench whenever he wanted and I had to go.

After turning the shutoff valve and screwing the faucet handle back on, I tested the sink and made a mental note to tell the real estate agent about it. Thinking about this place being under new ownership soon made me feel a little off. I had a fantasy of bringing Mikey back here one day to stay longer. He'd love it here in the summer when the wildflowers were in bloom and the wind meandered through the aspen trees. Maybe we needed to find another place in Aster Valley to rent during the off-season.

"I hate him."

I spun around to see Mikey's face flush with anger. His eyes shone with something closer to sadness and disappointment. I pulled him into a hug. "I'm sorry."

"He doesn't care about me at all, and I just... I don't know why I keep trying." His voice was muffled against my shirt, and his hands clutched at my sides.

I ran my hands in strong circles along his back. "What did he say?"

"He just... he thinks I'm..." He shook his head and stopped talking. I pulled back and tilted his chin up with my fingers.

"Tell me."

"He thinks I'm following you around like a puppy. He said it's pathetic." His voice cracked. "He... he thinks I'm trying to find fame by association... like some kind of user? I think? He says it's time for me to move on and find a new job."

I felt my entire body begin to buzz with anger. "That's absurd," I bit out. "You're the furthest thing from a user I've ever met. Hell, it took a year before you'd even let me pay for your coffee when we stopped by Starbucks."

Mikey tried pulling away from me, but I held on tight. "Let me go," he said. His chin was wobbly, and his eyes were blinking rapidly.

"No," I said softly. "Never."

He closed his eyes and leaned his face back into my chest. After a few deep breaths, he murmured, "I'm sorry."

"For what? For your dad being an asshole? Me too. For people making jackass assumptions when they don't know their ass from their elbow? Me too. For family butting their damned noses in where they don't belong? Me fuckin' too."

I tried to stay gentle with him, but inside I seethed. How dare Coach Vining make Mikey feel small when he'd already spent his entire life trying to fill impossibly large shoes?

Mikey sniffed and looked back up at me. "Do you want to get drunk in the hot tub?"

I barked out a laugh and then snuck in a quick kiss because his lips looked too tasty to resist. "Absolutely. Let's go."

It took him exactly two and a half glasses of crisp white wine and three repeats of Billie Eilish's "Therefore I Am" played at top volume on the Bluetooth speaker to loosen up.

"I think maybe he's right," he said, holding up his hand with a splash. "Wait. Hear me out. I've been your personal chef for too long when it's not exactly what I wanted to do with my degree."

My heart dropped. "Go on."

"I've always wanted to cook for groups of people. Like... maybe have my own cafe or restaurant."

I knew this about him already from listening to him talk to Sam.

They'd taken some business classes together at the community college to help Sam's work as a contractor and Mikey's hope of owning his own restaurant one day. But, was it selfish of me to wish that was still further off on the horizon?

"You deserve to follow your dreams, Mikey," I said instead of begging him to stay with me like an asshole.

He firmed his jaw and nodded, as if to himself. "Yeah. Yeah, I do."

I took another big slug of water. After allowing myself to slow-sip one glass of wine with him, I'd quietly switched back to ice water. "What are your dreams? Where do you want to be? What do you want your life to look like?"

Mikey glanced at me out of the corner of his eye before turning to look out at the distant slopes, barely illuminated under the bright moonlight. After a moment, he closed his eyes and leaned his head back.

"I want my life to look like this," he said slowly, as if testing every word before sending out into the world. "A cozy lodge I can turn into a gourmet restaurant. A town with enough tourist traffic to support fine dining but not attract much competition at first. Friendly people who notice when you do or don't show up. A gay population who makes me feel like I'm not weird or different. No offense, but a place that doesn't live, eat, and breathe football..."

"None taken," I murmured. "I get it. I'd love to have my very own snowboard mountain and time to get a puppy. And all the Nutella crepes and coffee I can stomach." I winked at him.

"I've been saving up for my own restaurant for seven years now, and I think I'm finally ready. No, scratch that. I know I am. I was ready three years ago."

I didn't want to hear the answer, but I asked the question anyway. "Then why did you stay?"

Mikey shrugged. "Same reason you kept me on long after you needed a chef."

"For your egg surprise?"

He punched me lightly, so I grabbed his fist and yanked him in close for a kiss. After a while of wrestling and exchanging lazy kisses, I got up the nerve to ask him.

"Does that mean you want to move to Aster Valley?"

I wanted him to say no, because I wanted him with me. But I also wanted him to be happy.

"No. Maybe. Yes. I don't know. I have a lot to think about. But at least we have the rest of the month here."

I agreed, swearing silently to myself as I remembered Coach's demand that I return home. I covered up my discomfort by making a stupid joke about how I hoped Stacy the real estate agent wouldn't simply drop by unannounced again.

But when the doorbell rang the next morning again, this time it wasn't Stacy. It was ten times worse.

16

Moose Raine was a giant of a man. He'd been a linebacker for Nebraska in college but hadn't been picked up by anyone in the league after graduation. Instead, he'd gotten a job in mid-level management at a bottling company and had low-key resented it for twenty years. When Tiller had finally hit it big in the NFL, he'd offered his dad the chance to retire early and coach youth football full-time as part of a charity foundation Tiller had set up.

I'd always thought Moose's efforts to push Tiller were the common desire for a parent to live vicariously through the child's success. In his case, it had paid off. Now, Moose got to live his dream, too, and tons of kids got the chance to pursue football instead of getting into trouble after school. Win-win.

I knew Moose loved Tiller. He was proud of everything his son had worked so hard for. But I often wondered if Moose cared a little too much about Tiller's work and not enough about the man himself. What would their relationship be like when Tiller was done playing football? To Moose, football was everything.

I wasn't sure Tiller felt the same way deep down. But maybe that was wishful thinking. During my phone call with Coach yesterday, my father had made it very clear that someone like Tiller Raine didn't have the time to spend coddling a needy hanger-on. He was clearly disgusted with my trailing after Tiller as if I was one of his groupies.

Needless to say, I'd ended the call feeling about a centimeter tall. My father always had a knack for making me feel small. It was one of the reasons Sam couldn't stand the man. It was also one of the reasons I realized it truly was time for me to pick up stakes and make a life somewhere outside of Texas.

And if I chose Aster Valley, I knew I'd have friends right off the bat. It was just a matter of asking some of the Aster Vallians what they thought of the idea of my restaurant. Hopefully the real estate agent could help me do the right kind of research.

"We came as soon as Coach called," Moose said, nudging Jill into the foyer before holding the door open for Tiller's sister, Stephanie, her husband, Luke, and their two daughters, all of whom seemed to be carrying tinfoil-covered dishes.

I stood there agape as Tiller's entire family trooped into the lodge. "Uh, hi?" Tiller was still asleep in my bed, and I'd only been up long enough to make some gingerbread cookies so we could decorate them for gifts for Winter and Gent and maybe Truman and our new friends at the diner.

Jill stopped and gave me a hug. "Merry Christmas, sweetheart. Sorry to spring this on you at the last minute, but we didn't want to miss seeing you now that Tiller's heading back to Houston sooner than we expected."

I didn't freak out at the news of Tiller's return to Houston because I honestly assumed she was mistaken.

"Mom? Dad?" Tiller said, walking around the corner pulling a long-sleeved T-shirt on over his low-riding pajama pants. I said a little silent prayer of thanks for the quick display of his killer abs and sexy-as-hell happy trail. "What are you doing here?"

He glanced at me like I'd somehow have the answer. I shrugged and shot him a "your guess is as good as mine" glance.

"So, we'll do Christmas real quick before you have to catch your flight," Jill said merrily, leaning in to press a kiss to Tiller's cheek. "Hi, love. How are you feeling?"

He frowned and looked at me again. This time I recognized nerves in that expression on his face. There was something he wasn't telling me. "I'm feeling fine," he grumbled.

"What flight?" I asked.

We all made our way into the kitchen sitting area since Tiller and I had made it our de facto hangout spot. I immediately went into my usual host mode, helping everyone find a place for their dishes and then offering drinks around. It looked like they'd brought a ready-made spread from a honey ham–type place which made me shudder. If only they'd given me some notice, I could have whipped up something homemade.

Jill followed Tiller to the stone hearth as he began building a fire. "Do you really think you're ready to go back?"

"What flight?" I asked again, feeling a little light-headed.

Tiller's nostrils flared. "Nothing. No flight."

Jill frowned and glanced over at Moose. "But Coach Vining called your father last night. He said they needed you back for next Sunday's game."

I felt the blood rush from my face, not because my father was an asshole who seemed content to put Tiller's health at risk, but because Tiller clearly knew and chose not to tell me. "Excuse me."

I turned to make my way back to my bedroom as calmly as I possibly could. Tiller's voice sounded oddly loud in my ears. "Mikey, wait."

I waved a dismissive hand over my head without saying a word and kept walking. It was fine. He didn't owe me anything. It wasn't like we were... anything to each other. Well, except I did still work for him, and technically, I was the one who was supposed to make the travel arrangements. Even though I knew I was overreacting, the fact he'd hidden this from me stung like a bitch.

I spun on my heel and jabbed a finger in his chest when he came closer. "Fuck. You."

"Baby, wait."

"Do *not* 'baby' me. Don't. What? Did you think I couldn't handle a change of plans? That I was going to curl up into some kind of fragile ball of crybaby if you—" I suddenly realized his entire family was standing at the entrance to the back hallway gaping at us. "Never mind," I choked out before turning into my bedroom and throwing the door closed.

Everything in my body wanted to curl up into a fragile ball of crybaby.

Tiller caught the door before it slammed and followed me in, closing it carefully once we were both inside.

"Michael." His voice was soft, but it held five years of emotions. I met his eyes, and my heart thudded to a stop. I didn't want him to call me that. I never wanted him to call me that. "Please stop."

I crossed my arms in front of mud thundering heart. "It's fine."

He stepped closer and reached for my upper arms. "It's definitely not fine. I didn't tell you he wanted me back because I was in denial about it, okay?"

I saw the mixed-up feelings behind his eyes, and suddenly I wanted to let him off the hook. I didn't want him to be emotional over me when he had a job to do.

"Tiller, it's okay," I said more sincerely. "It just surprised me, that's all. I should have known he'd call you back. There was no way you could actually spend a month away during the damned season. I was a fool to think you could."

His arms slid under mine and wrapped around my back, pulling me in for a tight hug that lifted me to my toes. "I'm sorry," he said into my neck. The rumble of his familiar voice against my chest loosened some of the tension between us. I didn't want to fight. I wasn't mad at him. I was mad at the circumstances. And furious with my father for treating people like his own personal chess pieces.

"Me too."

His lips moved along my neck up to my ear and down along my jaw to my lips, leaving tiny kisses in their wake. "One more night, though. Think we can make it count?"

I would not cry. I would not feel sorry for my pathetic, lovesick ass who'd dreamed of more than only one more night with this kind and sexy man.

"Damned right," I said despite the tightness in my chest and the churn in my gut. I wasn't giving up my chance at having sex with Tiller Raine, and now our only remaining chance was tonight.

With his family here.

"Are they staying?" I asked.

Tiller sighed and shrugged. "Who the hell knows? Let's find out what they have in mind."

He kissed me firmly on the lips before turning around, but I grabbed his hand. "Wait," I hissed. "What... what are we going to tell them? About us?"

His grin was easy, and it made my stomach tumble the way it did to the millions of people who saw the same smile on billboards and in magazine ads.

"No need to tell them anything. They already know you're my... Mikey."

What did that even mean? "Huh?"

Tiller's eyes sparkled like he was sitting on a delicious secret. "Babe. They've teased me for having a crush on you for at least two years. Ever since I brought you home for my cousin's wedding."

That didn't make any sense. "But that wasn't a date... Was it?" Holy fuck. Had I been missing out on dating this man for two whole years?

"No, but apparently, I shot you puppy eyes all night and snapped when anyone got too close to you."

My heart stretched its wings and did a little joyous loop-de-loop. If only it was sustainable. But the fact he hadn't acted on it in two years was proof it wasn't. There were reasons we couldn't do this long-term.

I blinked up at him, deciding to take it one day at a time and push off the fear and stress for a future version of Mikey who would—please god—be better equipped to handle it.

"Thank you for coming after me," I said, leaning up to kiss him again. "Let's go have a very Rainey Christmas."

When we returned to the kitchen, Luke and Jill were in the kitchen sorting out the food while Stephanie sat on the floor in the sitting area setting up a Connect Four game for the kids. Moose had the remote control and was flipping between sports channels.

As soon as Jill saw me, she bounced on her feet and clapped her hands. Her eyes jetted back and forth between Tiller's and mine. "Oh, please, please," she said under her breath. "Please make an announcement."

Tiller's large hand slid against mine, our fingers twisting together naturally. "No announcement, Mom. We're just... enjoying spending time together."

She clasped her hands together over her heart and gave us a look of true affection. It was the kind of maternal moment I rarely had with my own mother, not because she didn't love me but because she simply didn't stop and pay attention to those kinds of things. She was flighty at the best of times. But it felt nice to be loved by Jill, and even Moose tended to stop and ask about me whenever we were together. He'd never once treated me like Tiller's employee. He'd always welcomed me to their family as a real friend.

Moose called over from the sofa. "Stop giving the boys a hard time. Mikey, please tell me that's your gingerbread I smell. Ever since you sent some in the mail last year, I haven't been able to get them out of my mind."

I couldn't hold back the grin. "I'll make sure you get the first ones. Maybe the kids want to help me decorate them later."

The kids shouted their agreement without leaving the game. Moose turned to Tiller. "So Coach told me the team docs want to reassess you. Get you back out there sooner. Isn't that great?"

"They want you to *play*?" I blurted. I'd assumed they just wanted him back on the bench or in the booth consulting. It had never occurred to me they wanted to put him back out there before he was ready.

Tiller held up a hand. "Coach was just upset after the loss. I don't think he really means to play me. The local rehab guy told me I still had at least three weeks before even considering getting back on the field."

Moose balked. "Bah, that man doesn't know pro football. He's just some local yokel. You gotta trust the league docs to know what's right. And they say it's time to get back to work, so that's what you're gonna do."

Tiller snuck a glance at me, making my stomach drop. It hadn't hit me until then how often he looked to me for an opinion. It made me feel smart and competent, not to mention special. I didn't want to let him down.

Unspoken words flashed quickly between us. Tiller's shoulder sure as hell wasn't ready to be tested against the brutal challenge of a pro football game before it was fully healed.

But I wasn't about to interfere with the man's career. I gritted my teeth and tried smiling at him in a way that agreed with trusting the pros. He winced but continued looking at me for a beat. Suddenly, his face softened and he reached out a hand to my hip. His touch made me suck in a breath.

His thumb slid under the edge of my shirt and brushed the skin of my hip just over my waistband. "It's okay," he said low enough only I could hear it. "I'll call Krystal and ask her what the team PTs are saying. Sound good?"

I could barely breathe, but I managed a tiny nod. He smiled. "Good." His hand squeezed on my hip before he took his phone out of the room.

I busied myself helping reheat the food and asking Jill and Steph for help preparing the table for a big midday meal. After the board game, Luke had taken the kids outside to see the views of the barren slopes through the naked trees at the edge of the property. It was a beautiful, sunny day. Hard to believe it was cold outside when the sky was bright and blue like that. I decided to enjoy this day as much as I could since it was our last one here.

When everything was underway, I snuck out to shower and dress in my room. When I came out of the bathroom with a towel around my waist and water still dripping off my hair, Tiller was sitting on the edge of my bed. I could tell immediately from his body language that the news wasn't good.

He held out his arms for me, and I walked right into them,

squeezing him in a hug as tightly as I could. His big, warm hands moved up and down my back before settling on my butt possessively. I finally said to hell with it and knelt up to straddle him. My towel popped open and fell off, leaving me completely naked on his fully dressed self.

"You're so fucking sexy," Tiller said in a rough voice. "Please don't tell me this is over. Please."

His voice broke a little on the last please, and it crushed my heart and gut at the same time. "I don't... I don't know what to say." I was mixed up and twisted. My history of hopping into bed with football players was embarrassing as hell, and the fact I'd slept with my previous boss was mortifying. I felt like a user. A fraud. Something horrible.

Tiller's hands came around and cupped my face. His expression was fierce, and his lips were tight. "Let me say it another way. This. Is. Not. Over. Do you understand? I refuse to let... *circumstances* be the deciding factor in whatever is happening between the two of us."

I could tell he'd wanted to say *your father* in place of *circumstances*. He was smart not to. The specter of my father in this situation was the main factor in my mixed feelings. And I hated that. I was a grown man, for fuck's sake. Why did I still give him this much power?

Because of what he can do to Tiller's career.

"What did they say when you called?" I asked, stepping around his question like it was a live ordnance.

His nostrils flared, and his hands moved down my shoulders and arms to wrap around my waist again. "I guess the team PTs have a different definition of range of motion than Winter does."

"Maybe we should call Winter and ask him for advice?"

Tiller leaned in and kissed me firmly on the lips before pulling back and shaking his head. "I think that's a good idea. But, if there's any chance I'm going to get put in, I need to be studying film with the coaches. Honestly, I was always surprised he let me come here in the first place."

I looked down and noticed his T-shirt was on inside out. I

smoothed the back of the hidden graphic. "Well... he, um, kind of thought you were visiting your family."

He chuckled and leaned in to kiss the side of my neck. My dick began to fill as if this wasn't a ridiculous time to get turned on. We were talking about my father, and his own father was in the other room for god's sake.

"I see that now," he said. "I told him I'd be back in time for a meeting tomorrow afternoon. So let's enjoy the day with my family and then head home in the morning, okay?"

"Should we ask if your parents are spending the night?" I asked as he leaned back in to nip at my neck. If I had to sleep apart because his family was here, I was going to feel very, very sorry for myself.

"Yes, but since we don't have access to many rooms, you and I will have to share a bed. Shame."

He looked so damned proud of himself, I couldn't help but laugh. "We'll muddle through."

The holiday meal we sat down to an hour later was much more fun than I'd expected. I should have known, since I'd always had fun with Tiller's family in the past. Stephanie was a public defender, who always had hilarious stories from work. She had us all rolling with laughter when she told us about an unnamed client who'd led the police on a low-speed chase through Cherry Creek State Park, obeying all of the traffic signs and even stopping to let a deer cross the path at one point before finally giving up with an exasperated "Fine, y'all win" as she got out of her minivan and threw herself face-first into the nearby snowbank.

Steph's husband, Luke, watched her with affectionate pride. I'd always appreciated how well suited they were for each other, but now I couldn't help but notice the little signs of love and attention. Luke made sure Steph's drink was refilled. Steph reached over to dust a crumb off Luke's shirt, her caress lingering on his chest for a few moments afterward. They finished each other's sentences and laughed at each other's jokes.

It reminded me not everyone was lucky enough to have that kind of connection. Two of my four brothers were in serious relationships. Eddie was married to Ashlynn, who none of us liked. She was sarcastic and mean to my mom and oddly flirty with my dad. Wally had been dating Oaklyn for at least five years. They'd met at a Clemson football game when he'd come back as an alum and she'd still been there as a cheerleader. She seemed to take great pride in dating one of the team's biggest stars even though Wally hadn't seen the inside of a uniform in years.

And then there was my mom and dad. Thirty years of her putting up with his controlling, opinionated, football-saturated bullshit. I didn't know how she did it. He was often kind and tender toward her, but there were also times he was an absolute jackass.

I wouldn't say I'd had great examples in my life of true love like the kind I saw between Luke and Steph and the kind that had seemed evident between Winter and Gent last night. It was the kind of love that made it seem like each of them felt honored to have been chosen by the other. Maybe it was something newer couples had, but I was fairly sure Tiller's sister had been with Luke for going on ten years.

After the meal, we took a walk through the snow to the edge of the slopes where the old ski mountain was laid out in all of its snowy glory. The sun shone on the bare aspen trees, and the cables from the original ski lift sparkled in the afternoon light.

"It makes me itch to strap on a board," Tiller said with a smile, turning to his sister. "Maybe thrown down with Steph if she still has some skills."

Stephanie's cheeks were pink from the cold, and her eyes were bright. "Name the time and place, *brah*," she said with a laugh. "I'd like to see your epic wipeouts after all this time."

They started telling stories of their adventures on the slopes. When Tiller had been in high school, Stephanie had been at Colorado College. She and her friends would plan ski outings to nearby Breckenridge and invite Tiller and his friends.

"I can't picture Julian skiing," I said, thinking of the buttoned-up business executive I'd met several times. He was one of Tiller's close friends from childhood, and he'd stayed with us several times when his job brought him to town.

Steph turned to me. "Oh no. Julian loves to ski, and he's really good at it. But the one you really need to see is their friend Parker. That man is hot shit on skis. He's also not bad-looking in tight ski pants..."

Luke leaned over and swatted Steph's ass. "I'm not bad-looking in tight ski pants either, wench."

Steph chuckled. "True. We should plan a weekend soon to take the girls. I'd be happy to stare at your ass as I follow you down the mountain. We should take the girls before it gets crowded over the holidays."

I could see Tiller's disappointment at not being included. It was the same every season—the most we got was a quick visit and meal with our families between games. I didn't much mind because I wasn't as close to my family, but I knew it bothered Tiller. He'd never complain about it because Moose had told him again and again that football was only temporary. There'd be time later on for the other things in life.

"That league paycheck will make for plenty of good Christmases and ski trips after you're retired, son," he'd said only an hour or so ago when Tiller was grumbling about missing Santa gifts on Christmas morning with the girls.

I'd gritted my teeth and kept my mouth shut. After Tiller retired, Santa would no longer be visiting the girls. Unless Tiller had his own kids or Steph and Luke had more, that would be that.

I realized Jill was trying to get my attention. "Have you ever been skiing, Mikey?"

"If you mean water skiing, then yes, ma'am," I said politely, shooting her a wink.

Steph's face lit up. "Oh man, we need to get you some lessons. It's too bad Tiller can't teach you. He's so patient. I wish he could teach the girls."

I sensed Tiller's funk deepen, so I leaned down to scoop up some snow before carefully packing it into a ball while he wasn't looking.

While moving closer to Tiller, I said, "I think I might rather be the guy back at the lodge with hot cocoa than the guy flying down the slopes on waxed sticks. No offense."

Bam. I nailed Tiller directly between the shoulder blades with my snow missile and then took off running toward the girls. Tiller squawked in shock and immediately promised retribution. His nieces proved to be crappy human shields and even crappier snowball throwers, so we went down in a cold and wet blaze of glory once the snow started flying.

Even as I dragged my freezing, teeth-chattering ass back to the lodge an hour later, I knew the pain had been worth it.

Tiller had gotten a fun day in the snow with his family, even though it hadn't included skiing or snowboarding. It wasn't exactly what he'd been missing, but it was enough.

We all took a break to shower and dress in comfortable clothes before meeting back up to watch the Monday night game between the Titans and the Chiefs. A lot was riding on the result of this game since the Titans were in direct competition with the Riggers for a spot in the playoffs.

I busied myself washing dishes and starting a butternut squash soup we could have for dinner in case anyone got hungry after the big midday meal.

When Moose started yelling at the television, I snuck away to my room and stripped the sheets off the bed before packing my things. I started a load of laundry and moved my stuff into Tiller's room, all the while hearing cheers and groans from the other room as the game progressed.

I didn't want to watch it. If Tiller wasn't playing, I didn't much care, and honestly... I was angry at the game. Angry at my dad and the kind of people who prized the game enough to push players like Tiller into playing before they were properly healed.

I knew the drill. This game was about money, and Tiller Raine put fans in the stands and money in Rigger pockets. No one wanted to come see Brent Little fumble the ball when they thought Tiller would catch every damned pass thrown to him. It wasn't true, of course, but fans tended to think in extremes.

Sure enough, when I came back to the kitchen, the Titans were ahead and Moose was grumbling about how much trouble the Riggers would be in on Sunday without Tiller there to save the day.

No pressure.

I glanced at Tiller, who was clearly agitated as well. His hair looked like he'd been on a ride in a convertible for about a thousand miles of rough road, and even now, his fingers threaded through the thick locks as he paced back and forth.

I swallowed a sigh. If there was one thing I was used to, it was close football games and the stress of losing late in the season when every game seemed to count even more. Despite my history of hooking up with football players, I'd never wanted to end up with one. This tension was a lot to deal with, and I'd already put in a life-time's worth of hours watching boys throw balls around in the grass.

But this was Tiller's livelihood and his passion. He cared about the game, about helping his team. He wanted to improve and be the best at it he possibly could.

I grabbed some baby carrots and homemade dip out of the fridge and called Tiller over to the kitchen island to have some. He dropped a haphazard kiss to the top of my head with a mumbled thanks, grabbed the bowl, and returned to his pacing area.

This time, the loud crunch of carrots punctured the sound of the crowd in Kansas City. I knew from experience it helped Tiller to have something to do when he was anxious about a game he was watching. He took out his frustration on the carrots while I went back to tending the soup.

Despite the shouted coaching help from Moose and the softly muttered curses from Tiller, the Chiefs lost to the Titans in the final two minutes of the game.

If the Riggers lost the following week at home against the Steelers, they could be in danger of missing the playoffs. There was no doubt in my mind this loss would make my father even more deter-mined to get Tiller back on the field as soon as possible.

Thankfully, our impromptu pity party was interrupted by Winter Waites a little while later. Even though I knew he'd only been doing his job when he'd sent a status report back to the team medical professionals the day before, I still partially blamed him for the sudden end to my little fantasy vacation with Tiller.

As Winter and Tiller walked past me to the basement door for their workout session, I heard Winter ask, "Why is Mike looking at me like he wants to toss my body parts into a meat grinder?"

Tiller sighed and turned back to give me a sympathetic glance before opening the basement door for Winter. "We're going back to Houston earlier than we expected."

Winter stopped in his tracks. "Why? Is this because of the loss yesterday?"

"No. Apparently my hand therapist thinks I'm ready to be back on the field." Tiller said it in gentle, teasing way, but Winter balked.

"What the hell? Who? Not me. Jesus, Tiller. Are you kidding? They're not going to put you back in yet, are they?"

The physical therapist's shocked response made my stomach hurt. It was as I suspected. My father wasn't about to risk qualification for the playoffs. Even if it meant putting Tiller's health in jeopardy.

17

TILLER

I shouldn't have been surprised by Mikey's terrible mood leaving Colorado, but somehow I still was. He was pissy and short with me as if I'd been the one to call myself back to work. Apologies piled up on the end of my tongue, but I bit them back. There was nothing for me to apologize for. I was following orders—his father's orders, no less.

I still hated to see him unhappy.

Leaving him at the airport was hard as hell. The team had sent a car for me, so Mikey would have to drive the SUV back to the house with our luggage on his own.

"Will you be home for dinner?" Mikey asked hesitantly. We stood outside the door of baggage claim trying desperately to figure out how to say goodbye to each other under these new circumstances— whatever those happened to be. I wasn't quite sure yet what we were since it was both temporary and something I never wanted to end.

"Markus is in town," I said. "He wants to catch up over dinner."

Mikey's face was neutral while his eyes were anything but. They sparked with a mixture of uncertainty and annoyance. He hated my agent, and the feeling was most likely mutual. Markus worried Mikey was some kind of mole sent by Coach V. to keep an eye on me in case I ever got the urge to leave the Riggers. Which was laughable. Not only did I not want to leave, Mikey was the last person who'd give his father insider information about me.

He cleared his throat. "Yeah, fine. Maybe I'll have Sam over if he's not stuck on a jobsite."

"Mikey," I said softly, leaning down to whisper in his ear. His body leaned toward me with or without his permission. "I'll be home for dessert. Will you wait up for me, please?"

He shivered and pulled back, sniffing as if none of this mattered. "It depends on how late you get in. I'm kind of tired."

I grabbed the front of his shirt and pulled him close again, not giving a shit who saw. This time, my lips brushed his ear, and he made a noise in his throat that went straight to my cock. "If you go to sleep before I get home, it had better be in my bed. You got me?"

His eyes fluttered closed for the briefest moment before he opened them again and stared at my chest. "Mm-hm."

I let go of his shirt and smoothed the wrinkled fabric down, pressing my hand firmly over his heart for a long beat. "Look at me."

He tilted his head back until he met my eyes.

"I would kiss the fuck out of you right now if I could," I told him in a low voice. "You know that, right?"

He nodded and sighed. "Yeah. Okay. Good luck today. Text me and tell me what they say. If Dad tries to play you this weekend, I might have to..." His voice trailed off as he hopefully remembered it wasn't his place to get between me and my coach even if the coach in question was his dad. "Cry," he finished.

Not being able to kiss and hug him killed me. "Call Sam, okay? Have some fun. Maybe contact your publishing lady to ask about the cookbook photo shoot."

He waved me off. "Go. I'll be fine."

As I watched Mikey walk away, trailing both of our suitcases behind him, I realized a chunk of my heart was going with him. I ducked into the town car and thanked the driver for waiting for me before I settled back into the plush leather seat for the drive to the practice facility. I needed to get my head back in the game. Markus would be willing to go to bat for me if I truly felt like I wasn't ready to return to regular play, but if the team PTs thought I was ready, maybe they knew better than I did.

I wouldn't know until I got out there and tried.

Of course the first person I saw when I arrived was Coach V.

"Thank fuck. Get your ass in there, we're about to start." He slapped me on the back and nodded toward the film room. When I entered the room, half the team was already milling around. There were shouts and catcalls as everyone's eyes landed on me, and the warm welcome was nice. My friend Peevy jogged over and threw his arms around me with a mock wail. "Where have you been all my life? I missed youuuu!"

Antone walked by and pinched my ass. "Good to see you back, lazy-ass."

"Fuck me," someone said from up in the tiered seats. "It's the prima donna herself, come to save the day."

Someone else added, "You know things are shit when Coach calls babygirl back from vacay."

I shot a bird in their general direction and smacked Antone on the ass before following him up to the third row to take our seats. Peevy took the seat on the other side of me and leaned in to ask if I'd hooked up with any hotties from high school on my visit home.

"I didn't really go home. Mikey and I rented a cabin in the mountains," I said without thinking. The guys on either side of me went strangely quiet. "What?" I asked.

"You banging your assistant, Raine?" Peevy asked.

Antone's forehead creased in concern. "Better yet, you banging Coach's baby boy?"

I swallowed, frantically searching for an answer that wasn't a lie. "Why are you asking me that after all this time? Mikey always travels with me."

Antone sat forward. "Raine..."

Before Antone could warn me off something we all knew was stupid and inappropriate, Coach V. came in and told us all to shut up and listen.

It was hard to concentrate with the sting of Antone's unspoken rebuke in my ears. Every time I focused on Coach, I couldn't help but see him as Mikey's dad instead of my boss. He did the same odd little head tilt Mikey did when waiting for someone to answer a question, and he used the expression "You snooze, you lose" just like Mikey did every time I complained about not getting one of his peanut butter brownies before everyone else ate them all.

For an hour and twenty minutes, all I saw was proof I was banging the boss's boy. It was like sitting in a courtroom while the prosecutor trotted out every single piece of irrefutable evidence against the defendant. And I was the defendant.

I squirmed in my seat and jostled my leg until Peevy clamped his giant hand down on my knee and squeezed to get me to stop. When the meeting finally finished, I blew out a sigh of relief until Coach called out, "Raine, Mopellei, meet me in my office."

The cool, modern hallway leading from the film room to Coach's office filled as players made their way to different post-meeting appointments. Some went to the locker room to change out for practice, some headed to the trainers or the weight room, and a few walked in the same direction I was going in order to meet up with the assistant coaches. Derek Mopellei caught up with me and asked how I was feeling. I could see the hope in the quarterback's eyes.

"Shoulder feels stronger," I said. "But my hand still feels numb and tingly sometimes, and my grip isn't where it should be."

He nodded. "Okay. We'll go out there and run through some passes. Figure out what we can do, alright?"

I hated to disappoint him, but I wasn't quite as optimistic as he was. Instead of trying to temper his expectation, I simply agreed and followed him into Coach's office.

When I stepped into the room, I immediately looked in the direction I always did. There, on the bookcase to the right, were framed photos of the Vining family. There was a shot from Eddie in his orange-and-white Vols uniform, a photo of Jake in his Bengals uniform grinning wildly at a playoff win a few years ago, one of Wally in cap and gown at his Clemson graduation with his arm around his coach's shoulders, and one of Richie in his A&M wrestling singlet holding a medal of some kind.

The only photo of Mikey was a family group photo taken at Eddie and Ashlynn's wedding several years ago. In fact, with the exception of the Bengals playoff shot, all the photos on display had been around longer than I'd played for the Riggers. I wondered why he didn't have a picture of Mikey's graduation from Texas A&M. I knew Mikey had walked in his graduation because he had photos from it in a collage on his bedroom wall.

When Coach came in and closed the door behind him, I had to bite my tongue against the desire to ask him why he didn't seem as proud of his youngest son as he was of the other four. Was it because Mikey wasn't into sports? Was it because Coach had simply overlooked his youngest or lost interest when Mikey came along? Or was there something else there, the seemingly shorter attention span for a son who didn't seem to have much in common with his dad?

The thought made me feel unexpected rage.

He started off talking to Mopellei. "Derek, I want you to get in some practice with Brent regardless of what happens with Raine. You have more than one wide receiver, and I'd like you to get to a point where you don't play fucking favorites when you're under pressure in the pocket. When you've got that shit squared away, you can watch Raine's practice and give me your thoughts on where we are."

Mopellei shifted in his seat. "Yes, sir."

Coach V. flapped his hand. "Get out of here. Brent is already warming up. If he asks you about Raine, tell him to mind his own damned business."

Mopellei shot me a wink on his way out. I could tell he thought everything was going to be A-okay now that I was back. I didn't want to disappoint him. Derek and I had been a smooth, successful team for several years now. It wasn't easy creating that kind of comfort level with someone new.

Coach faced me. "I want you to see Krystal and Ben when we're done here. They're going to do an assessment, then get you warmed up for some light practice." Coach took a seat behind his desk and tossed his phone down on the cluttered surface. "How are you feeling?"

I opened my mouth to respond, but he kept talking. "Because I gotta tell you, we need you out there against Pittsburgh. You know as well as I do, we can't win with the running game, and Brent isn't quite there yet, especially in the slot. It's getting in Maple Leaf's head. I need someone who can do both. If we can't pull out a win this week, there'll be a lot of disappointed fans—not to mention management— looking for someone to blame."

Had his low-key threat been a little more obviously directed at me, I might have said something defensive, something like a team loss can't come down to missing a single player. But I simply nodded instead. "Yes, sir. I'll do my best."

Honestly, I didn't know how I was feeling. I wouldn't truly know how it felt until I tried catching some passes. I was willing to suit up and give it a try to find out.

"Good," he said, nodding firmly. "How's Moose? How's Jill?"

Coach had always been extremely welcoming to my family. Ever since he met them at the draft, he'd made them feel like part of the team. The only thing that kept my father from fangirling all over Coach Vining was the fear of losing access to his bragging rights.

"They're good. We had a big meal together yesterday to celebrate Christmas. My sister and her family came, too."

He sat back in his chair. "Good, that's good. Thank god it falls on a Tuesday this year. My wife has rented a big house on the water in Galveston for the week, and I'm hoping to sneak out there for at least the night. She has some crazy notion of a beachside Christmas. I don't know. I just do what she says."

"That sounds nice. Mikey didn't mention it."

His forehead creased. "Not sure he knows about it, now that you mention it. He told us he was visiting a friend in Colorado." He lifted an accusatory eyebrow at me that I chose to ignore.

Even if Mikey was supposed to spend the holidays in Colorado, I still knew he'd feel left out when he found out they'd made plans without him. It annoyed me. Now that I saw more clearly how Mikey was treated like the black sheep in his family, it pissed me the hell off.

"Don't you think he'd like to have the choice? Maybe if he knew you were all going to be together, he would have wanted to join you."

I knew right away, I'd crossed a line.

"Maybe you need to stop worrying about family issues involving your employee," he said carefully, emphasizing the last word as a stark reminder of the warnings he hadn't needed to give me early on.

Because every jackass these days knew not to fuck their employee.

I mumbled an apology and stood up, trying not to remind him he'd been asking about his own employee's family not three minutes earlier. "Yes, sir. I'd better get to work."

His icy glare met mine. "Damned right."

When I hauled my exhausted and disappointed ass out to the parking lot at the end of the day, I remembered I didn't have a car. Thankfully, my agent was leaning against a rental parked right up front. He lifted his head up from scrolling through his phone when I called his name.

"There he is," Markus said with a big smile. "Good to see you, man. Please tell me you're in the mood for steak because I'm starving."

Nothing sounded better to me than a tender filet and a loaded baked potato, but I knew it wouldn't make me feel good for long. "Let's head to Taste of Texas. They have steak and a huge salad bar."

We hopped in the car, and I pulled my phone out to text Mikey.

Me: *Headed to ToT. Want anything? It'll be a while, but I can bring takeout.*

I didn't get a response right away, so I slipped my phone back in my pocket.

"How're things going?" I asked as he made his way out of the parking lot.

"Excellent. I signed the point guard at UNC, and everyone wants him. Oh, and thanks for sending me the info about that kid in Indiana. I sent someone to watch one of his games, and he's got an incredible arm. I'm headed out there Friday to check him out."

"Good. I couldn't believe it when I saw him throwing practice passes at that Colts game. He's a water boy or something, I guess. Goes to a no-name school, right?"

He laughed. "You could say that. He's a Hoosier."

It felt good to laugh. Markus went immediately into a discussion about Indiana's poor football history and what they needed to do to fix things. That led to a discussion about the Riggers and what *we* needed to do to fix things. As I followed him into the restaurant, I knew the questions were coming. Thankfully, we were stopped by fans several times on the way to our table. When we finally sat down, he pinned me with a look.

"They need you back out there against Pittsburgh. Tell me how it went. What did the docs say?"

I tried not to let my earlier panic return. "I have radial nerve damage. Everything else is pretty good, but my grip is for shit. I think that's why the Colorado therapist and the team PTs disagreed. They learned my shoulder was doing well but didn't trust his assessment of my grip."

"What does that mean for Sunday?"

I shrugged. "I managed to catch some stuff in practice, but I certainly wasn't back to normal. I guess it'll depend on Coach's assessment of my current-level injured versus Brent's current-level healthy. He's going to let Mopellei chime in, too, which probably means they'll put me in."

"What's your gut telling you about playing this weekend?"

I appreciated Markus not jumping on the bandwagon to get me back on the field, but at the same time, his interest was mostly selfish. I would make him more money the longer I stayed healthy. Going back too soon and fucking up my arm might be great for the Riggers' season, but it wouldn't be great for my long-term playability. I wondered which of those two things Coach would choose if he had to make a tough call.

"My gut is telling me I don't want a career-ending injury, and right now this feels like it's on the cusp of becoming one. Hell, I feel like I've been hit by a truck, and this is after a light practice and all the TLC afterward with icing and whatnot." I held out my hand and made a fist before opening it back up and trying to hold it steady. It wobbled a little after the PT session and practice. There was no telling what a full-length pro game would do to it, especially against Pittsburgh's defense. And what if Mopellei threw me the ball on a critical play and I botched it?

I met Markus's eyes. "The hand specialist in Colorado said if I got hit again before it fully heals, it can cause permanent nerve damage. The team docs couldn't disagree."

He studied me for a minute before pulling out his phone to type in a note. "Okay, here's what we're going to do. I'm going to get you in to see a private specialist who's not affiliated with the team. We'll get another opinion and then reassess. Sound good?"

I breathed out a sigh of relief. "Yes. Thank you. That's a great idea."

Before he finished typing, he muttered under his breath. "Let's hope we can find someone who doesn't have loose lips."

By the time we finished dinner and Markus dropped me off at home, I was ready to collapse. We'd gotten up early in the morning to make the drive to Denver, and it felt like it had been the longest day in history.

The kitchen light was already out, leaving only the night-light by the stove. I grabbed a protein bar and bottle of water before trudging upstairs to my room. When I saw a sleepy, sexy Mikey snuggled deep in my bed with his dark-framed glasses perched on his nose and an iPad propped on his chest, I felt an overwhelming sense of relief.

"Hey," I said in a rough voice.

Mikey put the iPad on the bedside table and sat up, revealing a worn Riggers tee that gaped over his bare collarbone. Suddenly, it seemed like my whole entire body clenched with need, only this wasn't some kind of physical or sexual need. I needed him here, like this, for me to come home to.

Forever.

Fuck.

"You okay?" he asked, frowning a little and tilting his head.

I shook my head, dropped my stuff in a nearby chair, and kicked off my shoes before stripping down to my boxer briefs and striding over to him. He opened the covers to invite me in. I saw his bare legs below his rucked-up boxer briefs. He was so beautiful, so hot and tempting and *there*.

"I need you," I said, reaching out to pull his shirt off. When it pulled off his head, it left his hair every which way and knocked his glasses askew. "Sorry, baby," I murmured. "I just—"

He knelt up to kiss me, stopping my words and giving me permission to touch him again. I wrapped my arms around him and laid him back down on the soft sheets before propping myself on top of him carefully and continuing to kiss him.

Within moments, we were humping against each other, pressing hot cotton between us while we devoured each other's mouths. I wanted more. I wanted to taste him and suck him, make him come and then do it all over again.

I moved down the bed and pulled the elastic band of his underwear away from his hard cock. After stripping them off him, I nuzzled my nose in the crease of his leg. Fuck, he smelled good. Traces of my own soap lingered on his skin, and I felt satisfied, like it was a sign of possession or some caveman shit like that.

I hadn't expected to jump on him like this when I got home. In fact, I was shocked I had the energy for it. But connecting with him, pressing my skin as close to his skin as possible and breathing in his very exhales... it was like sliding into my own bed after weeks away. He was comfort, he was home. He was mine.

"Come up here," Mikey said between gasping breaths. "Fuck. Fuck me. Fuck."

I couldn't figure out if it was an exclamation or a request, but I moved back up his body and kissed his soft lips again. A little bit of late-day beard stubble scratched at my chin, but I didn't care. I could be scratched raw from his stubble all over my body and still feel giddy with the taste and smell and feel of him.

"Want you inside me," he begged again. "Please."

I pulled back in a daze, long enough to look down at him to see if he truly meant it. I hadn't intended to fuck him for the first time without at least making some kind of plan, but at this point, I was ready to throw plans completely out the window so I could feel the hot, tight squeeze of his body.

"You sure?" It was all I could give him. A lame-ass escape hatch he'd better duck out of quickly if he didn't want me inside him.

He nodded emphatically. "More than." He nodded toward the bedside table where I noticed a bottle of lube and three foil condom packets lying in wait. The man had plans.

"I guess you're sure," I said with a grin, lurching to the side to grab the supplies. I was relieved to see proof this wasn't a spontaneous decision. I didn't want him to have any regrets.

When I got back to him, I nipped at a spot on his neck before moving down to tweak his nipple with my teeth. The feel of Mikey's sexy legs wrapping around me and his hard dick arching up into me made my brain fog. I squeezed a dollop of lube onto my fingers and reached for his hole, brushing his balls with my thumb as I began to smooth my slick fingers on his skin.

The sounds he made—whimpers, sighs, and moans—made me feel powerful, and I wanted to pull more out of them of him. I felt euphoric. We were okay. Being back home in Houston didn't mess everything up. Mikey was still in my bed, and all was well.

"More," he urged, grabbing my wrist with a strong grip and pushing it into him. The move made me so hot, my dick jerked against his leg.

"Fuck, baby. God." I squeezed my eyes closed for a second. "You're gonna make me come."

His channel was hot and tight. Every time my fingers brushed over his spot, his groan of pleasure was so dirty, I was surprised I hadn't already shoved myself inside him in desperation.

When he was finally ready and we'd both ramped up to a hair trigger, I leaned up to his face again and kissed him tenderly. "Thank you," I whispered against his lips. "Thank you for being here with me right now."

Mikey's eyes widened in surprise, but then they softened. "Nowhere else I'd rather be."

I leaned back and pushed his knees up before moving my dick to his hole and pressing into him. We went slowly, which took super-human levels of self-control because he felt so fucking good.

"Christ," I hissed when his body tightened impossibly around me. "Fuck, oh god. *Mike*."

His eyes shone as he blinked up at me, and I actually thought I'd reached the penultimate moment in my life. Here it was. I had everything I could ever want. No one else on earth was as lucky as I was.

And it was true. I only needed to hold on to it.

18

MIKEY

After having sex with Tiller on Monday night, I walked around like I'd won a damned beauty pageant. Even Sam noticed when he came over on Wednesday night for dinner. Wednesday nights were usually mediterranean salad night which he loved for some reason.

"Why do you look like you just scored a multimillion-dollar recording contract from a homemade YouTube video?" He threw his leather jacket over a nearby chair and reached for one of the apple slices I had cut up for Tiller. Tiller hadn't come in from practice yet, but he was expected any minute.

"What? I'm not. No reason," I stammered, turning to make a cup of coffee. If I busied myself with the coffee maker, maybe he wouldn't see the blush steal across my face.

When he spoke, his voice was slow and precise. "I'm thinking... you had a man's penis in your little virginal asshole."

I blew out a breath like the air had been punched out of me. "You don't know what you're talking about." And that wasn't a lie. He didn't know jack shit about what Tiller and I had been up to. Over and over again.

I turned around to scowl at him. "How do you know I hadn't had anal before?"

He lifted an eyebrow. "I didn't. But the particular use of past perfect tense in your question reveals I was correct. Who has the lucky penis?"

This wasn't happening. Tiller was going to walk in and catch Sam interrogating me about anal sex. My face was on fire. I changed my mind about the coffee and went to the refrigerator to stick my face inside.

"Please tell me it wasn't Colin Saris," he said. "Because I never told you this, but he cornered one of the team interns in the bathroom at the Halloween party and asked him for a blow job. The guy's a pompous ass."

I opened my mouth to respond, but he was still talking.

"The ball boy was cute, though," Sam muttered. "Real enthusiastic."

I turned and stared at him. "Are you fucking kidding me right now?"

His grin was rare, but when he flashed it, it made even my heart flitter wildly. I always assumed it was because he was a pretty stoic person most of the time, but maybe he just had an award-winning smile. "Yes, I'm kidding. Come on, Mikey. You know I would never take advantage of a situation like that."

I rolled my eyes and inserted myself back into the fridge. It was true, though. Sam was the most protective person I knew. Our friendship had started when he'd decided to become my own personal bodyguard at school when there wasn't another Vining around to do it.

"Do you think this is a good idea, Mikey?" His voice was serious this time, as if he knew exactly what was going on. I realized right away, he obviously did.

"No," I said peevishly, slamming the fridge closed after yanking out the banana pudding I'd only made an hour ago. "Of course it's not a good idea."

I grabbed a spoon from the drawer and dug it into the bowl, pulling out the cool yellow pudding and shoving it in my mouth.

Sam stared at me. "Is that my dessert?"

I shook my head. "No," I said around another big bite.

He stood up and reached for the glass bowl. "It is! That's the dessert you made for me tonight. Asshole. Give it here."

I yanked it out of his reach and cradled it. "I need it. Man can't live on salad alone."

Sam's eyes were still wide in surprise. "You're eating your feelings. You never eat your feelings. Something about the destructive psychological effects of conflating neural pathways blah blah blah, I don't remember the psycho-nutritionist bullshit, but the bottom line is you don't eat your feelings. Ever."

I picked out a particularly squishy vanilla wafer and spooned it in my mouth. "It's just really good pudding," I mumbled pitifully.

"Which is why, if you don't mind, I'd like to have some later. After I eat the required polite serving of mediterranean salad. The only fucking reason I eat that damned salad is because you make dessert on salad night."

I gaped at him before I started laughing. "I thought you liked my homemade salad dressing."

"I do. But not enough to cancel a date for. Now that pudding...? That's enough to cancel a date for."

I sighed and handed over the bowl. Instead of digging into it, Sam carefully snapped on the lid and returned it to the fridge for later.

"Tell me why the hell you finally slept with him after five fucking years?" he asked, returning to his seat at the island.

I glanced at the back hallway to make I didn't hear anything from the direction of the garage door. "Because he's so damned beautiful and sweet and kind and fit and sexy and gorgeous and so fucking sweet. And kind." I stopped to inhale. "And... and I want him so badly. I can't stop. I can't stop wanting him. Help."

Sam sighed. "Mike. I told you from the very beginning to go for it. He adores you. When you're in the room, he can't look anywhere else. It's been that way for years."

He'd said that before, but I'd always thought it was complete bullshit. And even if it wasn't, I'd sworn off messing around with my dad's players. Well, except for Colin because I didn't much care if he ended up traded to Seattle and I'd been horny at the time.

"He's my boss," I said for the millionth time in five years.

Sam reached for another apple slice. "Do you want me to list the famous boss/assistant couples throughout history? Because I can't. I don't know any off the top of my head. But I'm sure there are many. And if you're not okay with it, quit. You can make a living on your catering easy peasy."

I heard the distant rumble of the garage door opening. Suddenly I found myself scrambling around, running in a circle because I couldn't remember what I was doing. "Act casual," I hissed, reaching for anything I could find to look purposeful.

Sam stared at me. "What are you doing?"

When Tiller walked in, I froze. He looked up from the mail he was carrying and smiled at Sam before turning to me and tilting his head in confusion. "Why are you holding salad tomatoes up to your ears?"

"Oh, ah... They'd make really good earrings, don't you think?" I wiggled them around a little like they were the dangly kind.

Sam snorted and shoved the apple slice in his mouth, no doubt to keep from calling me out for shits and giggles.

"Never mind," I muttered, tossing the tomatoes back onto the cutting board. "How was work?"

My heart still thundered unevenly in my chest. He was *right there* and so fucking pretty. Familiar in a way that made my heart squeeze.

Tiller grinned which made me want to climb him like a tree. Preferably naked.

"Fine. Mopellei's wife is pregnant."

I thought of the Canadian quarterback who I still held a stupid grudge against for getting Tiller hurt—yes, I knew it wasn't his fault —and his friendly wife.

"That's exciting," I admitted. "Zauna always gets heart-eyes when she's around the other players' kids. She'll be a great mom."

I was excruciatingly aware of the physical distance between Tiller and me. My fingers itched to touch him, and I had to hold my body still to keep from swaying toward him.

Meanwhile, Tiller had no such awareness. He tossed the mail down on the counter, strode over to me, grabbed the back of my head in one giant paw, and kissed the ever-loving fuck out of me.

Right in front of Sam.

It took about one nanosecond for me to forget about Sam, salad tomatoes, where I was, my own name, and anything else not related to Tiller Raine's tongue in my mouth. When he pulled away, I was pretty sure I was a puddle of goo on the floor.

"Alrighty then," Sam said in a voice laced with dry humor. "That happened."

"Um..." I tried getting the goo back together and reassembling some form of human brain with it. "Um."

Tiller smiled affectionately and leaned back in to kiss me next to my ear. He whispered, "I've been waiting all day to put my hands on you. I couldn't wait a second longer."

I blinked up at him like he was Elvis Presley found alive and well and sitting on forty some-odd years of new music. At least that's what I assumed I looked like. Surprised stupid and pretty fucking happy.

"Do you want me to pretend to go in the other room?" Sam asked. "Because I can do that."

Tiller laughed and let me go. "No. Sorry. It's fine. How'd it go on the Kelsey job? Did you find a new carpenter?"

As they started talking about Sam's current construction project, I wandered around in a lovestruck daze, cutting veggies and preparing the big salad. I daydreamed about what it would be like to live this life for real. To have my good friend and my... Tiller here with me all the time. I mean... I already had them, but it was different if Tiller and I were a thing.

Which we weren't.

But this was a daydream, and good shit was allowed to happen in Vegas. I went along on my merry way, tossing in red onion slices, fresh mozzarella, and marinated olives until the huge bowl was full. I moved on to making the dressing in the blender as their conversation moved to football.

"They going to put you in?" Sam asked.

I felt Tiller's eyes on me. "Yeah."

"You okay with it?"

"Depending on what the specialist says, I guess so. Coach was pretty insistent that the team needs me."

And Tiller would never dream of letting the team down.

My back teeth ground together, but I kept my mouth shut. Not only was it not my place to interfere with his career, but he also hadn't asked me. I'd known this was coming, and I was doing my best to be okay with it.

I was for damned sure not okay with it.

Sam glanced up at me. "We going to the game?"

I swallowed thickly and looked back down at the blender controls as if they contained the secret to world peace, eternal life, and flawless laser hair removal. "Ah, no. Actually, I booked a flight back to Aster Valley."

The silence in the room was so thick, I thought it might strangle me. And, quite frankly, I deserved it.

Because I hadn't actually booked shit. I'd made it up on the spur of the moment when I thought about sitting in that stadium box watching Tiller get smashed to bits by another linebacker. I may not have been the world's biggest football fan, but I knew the Steelers' secondary well enough to know they ate cement blocks for breakfast just like the guys on their defensive line. And one more hit like the one he got against the Raiders and he could kiss his hotshot career goodbye forever.

Because of my dad and his incessant need to win.

"Really?" Tiller asked. I couldn't quite figure out his mood from his tone, and I sure as hell wasn't going to look at him. I'd probably break. I'd blubber out an apology and promise to come to every football game played on earth for as long as I lived.

"Mm-hm." I busied myself adding more fresh parsley through the little hole in the top of the blender lid.

"Are you going to talk to the Civettis about the lodge?"

It hadn't even occurred to me, but now that he mentioned it... that would be a good excuse for my trip. I shrugged. It wasn't a lie if I actually did it.

"Wow. That's... No one would do it better than you would, Mikey."

I couldn't read his eyes. "I mean, it's all up in the air..." As in, I'd just invented it. "Who knows if or when it would even happen?"

He cleared his throat and nodded. "They'd be fools to turn you down. Have they made an offer on the property yet?"

Every question made my guilt flag flap more briskly in the lying-liar wind.

"I'm, ah, not sure?" I glanced over to see Sam's knowing gaze piercing me. I shot him a look that warned retribution if he narc'd on me. "Anyway," I said, looking everywhere but at him, "let's eat."

After dinner, Sam and Tiller went into the movie room to watch *SportsCenter* before our scheduled movie night. I snuck off to my room to do some quick emailing to see if I could arrange a time to talk to the Civettis.

I had mixed feelings about it. When the Civettis had originally floated the idea, I'd assumed it was too good to be true. Then, when Pim had confirmed the Civettis' conversation in the diner, I'd realized maybe there was something to it. But the truth was... I hadn't wanted to truly consider a life away from Tiller. I still didn't.

My hands shook as I typed my request for a meeting. Even if the Civettis didn't have any serious interest in me, it was a good excuse to go to Aster Valley and avoid the game. I wasn't Tiller's boyfriend. Not really. And if I went to that game, in front of my family no less, I'd be an obvious nervous wreck. There'd be no way my mom and brothers wouldn't notice. My mom probably wouldn't care. She adored Tiller. But my brothers? They'd notice and care very much. More than that, they'd tell Dad.

And Tiller would be shipped out, especially if his hand didn't fully recover and his stats started to suffer from his injury. Being traded while down with an injury would be a huge step down in his career. Speculation would run rampant about the exact nature of his hand and the possibility he'd never be the Super Bowl–winning, Heisman-winning man he'd been before the bad hit.

I couldn't let that happen.

My stomach wobbled with nerves. I wondered what would happen if I made a plea to my dad, if I told him this time was different. Unlike with Nelson, I had real feelings for Tiller. Surely my father would understand that? But what if my floating the idea was enough to make him take action against Tiller? Even if he didn't trade him, he could treat him like shit on the field.

My father was a professional. Wasn't he? Maybe not. I remembered every clip from a game where my dad had lost his cool and gone apeshit on the sidelines. Hell, there was probably a video montage on YouTube of all those stellar moments spliced together.

My father was *not* a professional. He was an emotional child fairly often, especially if the stakes were high. And right now, the stakes were high. The Riggers were on the cusp of losing their playoff spot and not even getting the chance to defend their Super Bowl title. I knew the pressure was intense on the team and its coaches.

But I was his son. That had to count for something, right?

In the end, it didn't even matter. Because he found out in the stupidest, most unexpected way.

19

TILLER

I wore the wrong damned shirt. The stupidest thing I could have done and I didn't even know it was a thing.

"What the fuck do you have on?" Coach V. barked at me when I walked into the locker room on Thursday. I looked down at the old Rigger shirt I wore.

"A T-shirt?"

He walked up and got in my face. The scary vein popped in his neck, reminding me of the game against Arizona last year when I'd truly thought he was going to have to be taken out on a stretcher. "And do you know whose T-shirt that is?"

I thought back to this morning when I'd tried swallowing his son's load while doing sixty-nine on the kitchen floor. Some had dribbled onto my shirt. I was already late because of the sixty-nine, so I'd grabbed a clean tee from Mikey's room instead of heading back to mine.

"Is it Mikey's?" I asked carefully. "Maybe he got his mixed up with mine in the laundry."

"It's mine, actually." His voice was scary low. "We will continue this conversation in my office."

I followed him dutifully, wishing I could quickly text Mikey to ask him what was up with the shirt. He and I both had a million Rigger T-shirts. How could Coach possibly know this one wasn't mine?

When he closed the door behind me and grunted at me to take a seat, I started to sweat. His eyes were like lasers of death, looking deep into my soul and finding a wasteland of immorality.

"Before you ask, that shirt is from Coach Warren's retirement party. That's how I know it's not yours. It was before your time. Explain to me why my son is doing your laundry."

Was that all? I could handle that. "Because he likes to. Because he fired my housekeeper and the three other people I tried hiring to replace her."

I wanted to ask him how it was any of his damned business, but I wasn't that stupid. Until he asked the next question.

"Are you sleeping with my son?"

I almost swallowed my tongue. "Wh-what?" I spluttered. I tried letting my shock that he had the balls to ask that question masquerade as surprise at the very suggestion I would do something so inappropriate and unprofessional as to sleep with Michael Vining.

"Answer the question," he growled.

I wanted to ask for a time-out, a recess, a stay of execution, anything that might buy me a little time to contact Mikey in a complete panic. Regardless of how inappropriate the question was, I could not lie to my coach's face.

The laser eyes started cutting into my soul. "If you lie to me, Raine, I will know it and we will be done here. Do you understand?"

"I understand," I managed. "But I also feel like you're crossing a line."

I didn't die. Instead, I simply sat there while the eyes carved more of my soul away. "And do you not feel that sleeping with your coach's son is crossing a line? Do you not feel that sleeping with an employee is crossing a line? In fact, some consider that crossing a *legal* line."

"I care about your son," I said with as much conviction as I could muster. It was the truth. I cared about Mikey way more than I ever expected to when I first saw his little supposedly quiet self in Bruce's office five years ago. "Very much," I added softly.

His nostrils flared as he finally moved his laser stare onto something else across the room. It could have been the family photo from Eddie's wedding, but I wasn't sure.

"You're dismissed."

I opened my mouth to ask if he meant I was dismissed from the team or simply his office, but he beat me to it.

"Get your gear on and give me a reason not to send your ass to Buffalo right this fucking minute."

I lit out of there like my feet were on fire. After changing out and meeting with the PTs for a special warm-up and stretching, I met up with Mopellei and Brent out on the practice turf. Of course, it was the worst practice day yet. I felt like I dropped damned near every pass and even tripped over my own feet at least twice.

I wasn't sure how much it mattered, though, since Coach never showed up to watch.

When I got home, I was tired, sore, and grumpy, not to mention scared as hell of admitting my mistake to Mikey. But he wasn't home. I knew he was probably out delivering the meal he'd agreed to make for his parents' next-door neighbor, but I'd hoped he'd be home by now.

I wanted to hold him and ask his advice about his dad. Maybe try to find out if he was ready to put a label on our new relationship and approach his family as... *family* instead of their son and his boss.

I'd never felt like Mikey's boss. To be honest, if anything, I'd felt like his employee. Mikey had always been the boss in our house. I did what he said because I knew he always had my best interest at heart. He always had, even when it was simply a working relationship.

After pulling out some leftover salad and spying a dinner plate he'd left for me in the fridge, I shoveled food down until I'd cleaned the bowl and plate of every morsel. The house was too quiet without Mikey there. I changed into pajama pants and wandered into the movie room to watch *SportsCenter*. When I'd caught up on all the news and was in the process of trying to decide whether I wanted to watch an action movie or put on one of Mikey's cooking shows, the man himself appeared and walked right over to climb on top of me.

"Hey," he mumbled into my chest.

He smelled faintly of the garlic bread he always made to go along with chicken parm. He'd most likely cleaned the kitchen after stashing the meals in his car so I wouldn't smell the delicious food he'd made and get envious. I'd enjoyed the salmon, sweet potato, and asparagus he'd left me, but I would have much rather dug into the hearty Italian food. One day I'd get to enjoy his food without having to worry so much about my performance, but that day was not today, especially in the run-up to the playoffs.

I wrapped my arms around him and held on tightly. "Hey. Thanks for leaving me dinner. I was starved when I came in."

He lifted his head up and frowned at me. "Of course I left dinner for you. It's my job."

My stomach dropped like a rock at the reminder of our tenuous working relationship. I didn't want him to cook for me because he was getting paid, and I often forgot he was getting paid since he was the one who did the paying. Mikey handled all of my bills, including his own payroll. It meant it had been easy for me to stop thinking of him as my employee. The reminder didn't sit easy on my gut.

I scraped my top lip with my bottom teeth. "Well, thanks. It was really good. How was your mom? Did you see her when you dropped off at the Niberts'?"

He shook his head and smiled. "No. Mrs. Nibert insisted on besting me in, like, ten games of backgammon while catching me up on all the drama from Bible study which included, but was not limited to, several people coveting their neighbors' wives. At one point I thought I heard Mr. Nibert walk by muttering something about Proverbs 21:9, so I might have to dust off my Christianity and look that one up. Suffice to say, by the time I got out of there, I didn't have the mental fortitude to visit my parents, despite their repeated attempts to get me to stop by."

I leaned in and kissed his lips, taking my time to refamiliarize myself with the taste and feel of him. The conversation ahead of us wasn't going to be nearly as easy and enjoyable as this.

When the kiss turned heated and Mikey's hips started pressing into my lower belly, I pulled away. "I need to talk to you," I said, before I could convince myself sex would be way, way better than discussing his dad.

His forehead creased in concern. "That sounds ominous."

I shifted us up so we could talk face-to-face instead of in a tempting snuggle. I decided to throw out the bad news quickly before I had a chance to talk myself out of it. "Your dad knows about us."

Mikey blinked at me. "That's not possible."

I saw his face drain of color as my words sank in. "I'm sorry," I offered. "It's my fault. When I grabbed a Riggers shirt out of your room this morning, I didn't realize it was anything other than one of the many team shirts we have."

"Warren's retirement," he muttered, putting the pieces together. "He was Dad's mentor. *Fuck.* But, wait... that doesn't mean anything. Why would that mean anything? I do your laundry."

I ran a finger along a rip in his jeans without looking up at him. "I tried that. It didn't work. He asked me point-blank if I was sleeping with you."

He slapped my hand away from his jeans and pulled his legs closer into his body. "And you denied it. Right?" His voice sounded frantic, almost manic. "Tell me you denied it. Please."

His reaction surprised me. "Of course I didn't deny it. I'm not going to lie to my boss's face. But I didn't confirm it either. I told him he was crossing a line."

Mikey's laugh was humorless. "I'm not sure he gives a shit about crossing lines."

"No," I agreed. "He definitely didn't appreciate that." His brown eyes flashed with worry. I wished like hell I could reassure him, but I couldn't.

"What happened next?"

I swallowed around the lump of nerves in my throat. "I told him I had feelings for you."

The silence that followed wasn't reassuring. My heart began to thud dully in my chest. *Say something*, I urged silently.

"What was his response?" he finally asked. I could see mixed feelings warring in his eyes. On the one hand, he wanted to assert his independence from his parents, say his dad's opinion didn't matter. On the other, he always wanted their approval after decades of being treated like the one who never did anything worth noting.

"He wasn't happy," I said, clearly hedging.

Mikey picked at his fingernails. "And did he... say anything about trading you, or...?"

I laughed. "Other than threatening to send me to the losing-est team in the league?"

His eyes flashed to me with worry, so I tried reassuring him. "Babe. He's not really going to send me to Buffalo. It was just his way of telling me he wasn't happy."

He moved away from me to the other end of the sofa and hugged his knees. "You don't know my dad. He'll do just about anything to keep me from being happy."

I wanted to touch him, to hold him and reassure him everything would be okay. But I couldn't deny he knew Coach V. better than I ever would. "Why?" I asked. "Because you're gay?" I was still unsure about where Coach stood on it. He'd been very accepting of me these past five years, but I couldn't deny some of the times he'd seemed to gently discourage me from being public about my sexuality. It was almost done with kindness, like not wanting me to be bullied by naysayers or hounded by the media. Like he was looking out for me.

But maybe I'd been wrong about that all along.

"He doesn't come right out and say it," Mikey explained, waving his hands around as he got more heated about the subject. "He says all the right things and is supportive on paper. But whenever Mom talks about me finding someone or mentions wanting to plan another wedding for one of her kids—since I'm the one most likely to involve her in the planning—my dad says things like, 'There's no need for a big wedding. Mikey doesn't need all that.' Or he'll say, 'Can you imagine the media firestorm? Coach's gay son gets married in lavish wedding? I'm not sure that's a good idea. It'll only bring Mikey under attack by those hooligan reporters.'"

That was similar to my own experience with him. "So it's the publicity factor he's most worried about."

He sighed. "Which is why he can't stomach the idea of me dating a player. What will the media say?"

"He's not wrong, you know. Not only would the media be all over a gay player with an actual, real-life boyfriend, but they'd also lose their shit over a Riggers player dating the coach's son."

I watched him for his reaction, and it was pretty much what I expected. "We shouldn't be doing this," he said with a pitiful note of pleading in his voice, as if he couldn't bear to stop and was hoping I'd have the strength to stop it for him.

He was going to be wildly disappointed. I didn't have the strength to stop it, and moreover, I didn't have the desire to.

"I strongly disagree," I said as calmly as possible. "We're two consenting adults."

He lifted an eyebrow at me. "We're boss and employee."

"You're fired," I said between tight teeth.

Mikey barked out a surprised laugh. "You can't fire me. I quit. And anyway, I'm going to be a famous cookbook author now, so I don't need no stinkin' personal assistant job."

This wasn't a total surprise. I'd been dreading and hoping for it since he'd talked about his dreams back in Aster Valley.

It was odd that he hadn't mentioned the job opportunity in Aster Valley, but maybe he didn't want to jinx it. Hearing him talk about flying out there to talk to the Civettis had both crushed me and made me proud. I wanted him to be happy, and I knew turning that lodge into a B&B was his dream come true.

But I didn't want to lose him. If he was going to pursue his dream that far away, I wanted us to figure out a way to do it together, to make the distance work until I could retire and join him full-time.

I couldn't wait any longer to touch him again. I crawled across the leather sofa and forced myself between his bent legs until I was propped on top of him. "Please don't leave me," I said softly.

He studied me as if processing my request and carefully parsing his words. "I don't want to leave you."

I chose to ignore the clanging warning bells going off somewhere deep inside my brain as he inserted the word *want* in there. As if he'd do it anyway. Instead, I leaned in and kissed him, telling him with my slow perusal of his lips that he was more important to me than any nosy reporter could ever be.

Mikey's hand came up to cup the side of my neck. "You could always come with me."

These words hadn't been tested. They were raw and real, but they were also impossible. "I can't." They were the hardest words I've ever said.

"I'm sorry," I added in a near whisper.

He shot me a smile as fake as a dollar-store Santa. "Nope. Of course you can't. I'm sorry for asking. I didn't really mean it. You have football. I know how important it is to you. Giving it up for... this... would be ridiculous."

Every cell in my body begged me to disagree with him, to tell him I didn't want football if I couldn't have him, too. But it wasn't that easy. Football was everything. It had been everything for as long as I could remember. Football was how my father and I communicated, how I proved my worth to the world, how I made my friends and family proud. It was how I convinced myself that I was a hard worker, that I had dedication, drive, and commitment.

"Not ridiculous," I finally said. "Just not... realistic. Not right now. But maybe we can figure out a way to make it work."

"Maybe we can," he said, leaning in to kiss me again.

By the time we finished our long stay at first base, I was itching to steal second.

"Take off your clothes," I urged, moving onto my knees on the carpet in front of the sofa. "Want to suck you off."

Mikey scrambled out of his shirt and jeans, revealing a tight little pair of navy-and-orange striped briefs. I chuckled. "I didn't know you had Rigger undies. You're full of surprises."

"Santa brought them in my stocking last year. I'm not sure Santa knows any other colors besides navy and orange, to be honest." He shucked the briefs down and dangled them by a finger before flinging them across the room with abandon. I was fully on board with his "fuck it" attitude, and my dick was beginning to think there was entirely too much chitchatting going on.

I sucked on the tip of his dick and watched for his reaction. His eyes rolled back in his head as he groaned and reached his fingers into my hair. "Holy fuck, you're good at that," he said on an inhale.

I pressed my palm against his bare stomach and pressed him back into the sofa while I moved my mouth up and down on his hard shaft. He was a mix of clean and musky, and I wanted to lick and suck him all over.

I pushed his knees up until his feet rested against the edge of the sofa cushion. My tongue continued teasing his dick while I reached blindly under the sofa for the bottle of lube we'd left there the night before after Sam had left. He'd come over to watch a *Fast and Furious* movie which meant I'd sat there watching hard, sexy bodies on screen for two hours while Mikey squirmed against my side. As soon as Sam had left, I'd pretty much gone feral all over Mikey's person before fucking him loudly into the floor on his hands and knees.

I glanced down at his hole to see if it was still abused from the night before. As soon as I caught a glimpse of it behind his sac, I felt my dick scream against my blue jeans. *Fucking pants.*

The button was impossible to pop open while I was also trying to find the lube, so I gave up on my search, ripped opened my jeans, and then pushed Mikey's knees to his chest to get a better look at his hole. It squeezed tight when I yanked him forward until his ass was also at the edge of the cushion. Mikey made a nervous, squeaky sound before covering his eyes with his hands. Streaks of flushed pink peeked out from behind his arms, all down his neck and onto his chest.

I told him how sexy he was, how much he drove me out of my mind with need, and then I leaned in and ran my tongue along his rim. The noise he made was carnal and raw, desperate. But he didn't beg. I could tell he wasn't completely comfortable with this yet, so I took my time, interspersing licks and teasing nips between words of wonder and appreciation.

When I opened him up farther with my tongue, he finally broke. "Please. Oh fucking god, that feels good. Don't stop." His words became slurred the more I sucked him with my mouth and jacked him with my hand. When I finally found the lube and pressed slick fingers inside him, he mumbled something about wanting to rim me, too, show me how good it felt.

Before he could finish his thought, I must have hit just the right spot because he cried out and came all over my hand and his front. Fuck, he was stunning. I could watch him take his pleasure all day, every day and still be happy.

I scrambled to stand and whipped out my dick, using my cum-slick hand to jack myself over him. It took a pitiful number of strokes before I was busting a nut all over his stomach and chest while he lay there panting.

The sight of him naked and flushed, covered in our combined fluids, made my orgasm last even longer.

My feelings for him were stronger than ever, and I felt incredible relief knowing he wouldn't leave me because of his father's media concerns. I'd come out a long time ago for a reason, and I wasn't going back in the closet now for anyone.

"Let me grab a towel," I said roughly before leaning down to run a finger through the mess. "Before this makes me hard again and I flip you over and take your ass."

His eyes heated, and his dick tried to rally against his thigh. "Jesus," he muttered. "You're going to kill me."

I stood up with a chuckle and made my way to the nearest bathroom where I wet the hand towel and brought it back. Once I had us both cleaned up, I lay down on the sofa and pulled him on top of me for a cuddle. I wanted to hold him for a little while.

SportsCenter continued playing softly in the background as I tried to muster up the energy to reach for the remote to change it. The orgasm, mixed with the relief that Mikey hadn't stormed out or broken up with me, made me relaxed to the point of dozing.

Just as I drifted off, I heard his soft voice muffled against my chest. "I have feelings for you, too."

I fell asleep with a giant smile on my face and Mikey V. exactly where I wanted him. In my arms.

Everything was going to be okay.

20

MIKEY

I didn't sleep well, despite pressing myself closer to Tiller than the small Super Bowl tattoo he had on his calf. Usually, sleeping against him was as good as being knocked out with hard drugs, but I couldn't stop the anger welling inside me. I was almost thirty years old, well beyond the age when my parents should have a say in who I dated or slept with.

At first, I'd wondered if I was making too much of it. I certainly didn't want to get into World War Three with my father over a temporary hookup with Tiller. But after the way the gentle giant had claimed me in front of Sam the other night and talked about enjoying the double date as a couple with Winter and Gent, I thought maybe it was okay for me to assume this was more than a temporary fling.

He'd told my father he had feelings.

So I waited until he'd downed his breakfast and headed out to a doctor's appointment before I started trying to come up with a plan. Meanwhile, Gary Civetti called to arrange a meeting in Aster Valley on Monday. They were still in the area and were excited to hear from me. I went ahead with my plans to fly out in the morning so I wouldn't be tempted to go to the game on Sunday. Even if my parents knew about Tiller and me, I still wasn't ready to see him put himself in the line of fire against the Steelers.

Once I made my travel arrangements, I grabbed my keys and set off for my parents' house. I wanted to get it out in the open, tell Mom and Dad that things were real this time. Tiller wasn't a fling like Nelson had been. He was the real deal. This wasn't a crush or a lark. This was someone I had true feelings for. I didn't just like Tiller Raine. I loved him.

I jerked to a stop in the back hallway just as I was reaching for the door to the garage.

My stomach tumbled in crazy loops as the knowledge of my certainty hit me all at once. It was true. I loved Tiller. Desperately.

The breaths came quick and sharp. *Oh fucking hell, I'm in love with Tiller Raine.*

I reached out and grabbed the wall next to me as my head spun. Why was this such a surprise? I'd had a crush on him for a long time. Even though I'd been in denial most of the five years I'd worked for him, there was no denying how close we'd become in that time.

What if he didn't feel the same way? I knew he cared about me. He was a kind man, and we were close friends if nothing else. But what if... what if he didn't care about me *like that*?

I entered this little janky mental cycle in which I had to remind myself he'd told my father he had feelings for me, and then my brain countered the reminder with all the reasons that probably hadn't meant what I'd thought it had meant.

"Fucking hell," I muttered to the garage door. "What am I saying? He looks at me like I'm a piping hot supreme pizza and he's spent days eating nothing but raw beetroot."

I finally got ahold of myself and made my way out to the SUV. Sliding into Tiller's "backup" car was always a treat. It was smooth, buttery leather with a hundred percent less shitmobile ambiance than my ancient Volkswagen Golf. I loved the SUV so much, Tiller had suggested I change the tag to a personalized one that said MIKEYV. I may have even considered it for a brief moment while petting the steering wheel one day, but in the end I'd reminded myself I was perfectly happy with my shitmobile. Most days, anyway.

Not today. Today I needed all the Big Dick Energy I could gather. I had plans to march into my father's house and declare my relationship none of his beeswax. For that, I needed to get into the mindset of a pro football player with a giant ego.

I also needed an iced coffee from Starbucks and possibly one of their cookies.

Once I was well armed, I made my way into my parents' house and called out. "Mom! Dad! I'm here."

Crickets.

I finally found my mom out back talking to Mrs. Nibert over the fence. I tried turning back around before either of them saw me, but it was too late.

"Mikey!" Mom called out with a smile. "Come see Mrs. Nibert's odd gourd."

I waved and smiled. "Oh, no, thank you! I saw it last night."

Mom frowned at me in disapproval. "What in the world has gotten into you, Michael Vining?"

Oh lord. This wasn't how Big Dick Energy was supposed to work. I sighed and wandered out into the yard. "Yes, Mother."

Twenty minutes later, after I'd seen more late-season gourds than anyone had a right to make someone look at, my mom finally followed me inside and told me Dad had headed into work already.

Hellfire and damnation. I could have avoided all of this nonsense if I'd headed to the practice facility first.

I decided to float a test balloon. "Mom?"

"Mm-hm?" she asked while dropping a complimentary gourd in the trash can and washing her hands at the kitchen sink.

"I'm kind of... seeing someone."

"Oh honey, that's wonderful," she said, looking up as she dried her hands on a dish towel. She looked truly happy to hear it. I wasn't surprised she hadn't known. My parents didn't have the kind of relationship where they talked about mushy-gushy things like dating and relationships. Theirs was more of a "What time are we meeting the Niberts for dinner at the club?" kind of marriage.

"Yeah," I continued. "But I kind of need some advice."

Her face dropped. "Sweetheart, I'm not sure I know how to advise you about dating a man." Then she seemed to realize what she'd said. "Well, I guess I do, but it's been a while since I've dated one myself."

"Not that kind of advice," I said. "I'm dating a player."

"Meaning he dates lots of people?"

Bless her heart. You could trace my mother's entire family tree going back hundreds of years and you'd never find an Albert Einstein perched on a single branch.

"No, Mom. Meaning, he plays football for the Riggers."

"Oh. *Ohhhh.* Hm." She pinched her face together while she thought it through. "Are you worried you don't have much in common?"

I blinked at her. "Well, I wasn't. Until you said that. Jesus, Mom."

"Honey, why don't you tell me what the problem is, exactly?"

"Dad's going to freak out. And I don't want him to retaliate on Tiller because he's dating me."

Mom clapped her hands together and smiled. "It's Tiller? Oh, I love him. He's so handsome and kind. What a nice boy. Plus, it doesn't hurt he's one of the most successful NFL players in your generation. How exciting! Tell me everything."

I loved my mom. She had her fair share of pros and cons, but in general, her heart was usually in the right place. "I really like him, Mom. He's so sweet and thoughtful. He treats me like the most important person in his life and we're not even really dating. At least... we haven't said we are."

"Will dating Tiller interfere with your job?"

She meant my job working for him. I still hadn't told my parents about the cookbook deal or my dream of opening my own restaurant, but they had to know I had a ton of savings built up by now. Enough to give me options. "No, because I quit."

Her eyes widened in surprise. "Why? Mikey, that job is perfect for you. You love working for Tiller."

"I love taking care of Tiller. It's not really the same thing. Yes, I did love working for him, but I don't want to work for him if we're dating."

"What are you going to do for work?"

I took a seat on one of the stools at the island. "I have plenty of savings. I'm fine."

Mom straightened a pewter basket that had fake fruit in it. "Where are you going to live? Do you want to come back here while you look for a place?"

It had never occurred to me that I'd need to move out of Tiller's place, but if I no longer worked for him, what did that mean exactly? I couldn't exactly go from a live-in personal chef to a live-in boyfriend without an actual conversation.

Could I?

"I'm not sure, but it doesn't matter right now anyway," I said dismissively. "I'm headed back to Colorado. I actually... have a lead on a possible job there. I don't know. We'll see." It was at least a quick way of getting her off my back about work.

Her face lit up. "Oh honey, that's fantastic. Although... I'm not sure I'd be okay with you living so far away. I'd miss you terribly."

While it was nice of her to say it, I wasn't sure I believed it. She rarely called me or invited me anywhere. She definitely enjoyed it when I came over for a visit, but it was never reciprocated despite my inviting her over for meals many times to taste-test new recipes or even have an old favorite I knew she liked.

I guess part of me was wondering if the worst came to pass—if Dad sent Tiller off to another team in another city—could I, would I, go with him? The answer was yes, if he'd have me. At this point I knew well enough to know I didn't want to be apart from Tiller at all. In fact, I couldn't even imagine it.

Life without Tiller? No, thanks.

"Bring him to Galveston," Mom said. "We have plenty of room."

I tilted my head at her. "What do you mean, Galveston?"

"You know, the big rental house we arranged for Christmas." She flapped her hand as if she'd already told me this, but I would have remembered. She definitely had not told me this.

"No, I don't know."

She fussed with a houseplant on the counter in front of her. "Well, your father and I have rented a house on the water for the week of Christmas. All your brothers are coming so we can have a big family do. Won't that be nice?"

I refused to have hurt feelings over being left out. "Were you going to tell me about this big family gathering? Ever?"

Maybe I wasn't as mature as I'd hoped.

"If I recall, you were supposed to be in Colorado for the holiday. It must have slipped my mind. But the two of you can come now, and you can introduce Tiller to your family."

"They all know him already, and I'm not sure Coach would be as welcoming as you are."

"Nonsense, dear. You don't give your father enough credit. He wants what's best for you."

I didn't bother to argue with her because part of me wanted her to be right. She wasn't.

After I left my parents' house, I headed straight to the Rigger practice facility to try and catch my dad during the hours he was in his office. Once midday came and went, he was usually on the field or working with special teams.

I ignored the little floaty hearts swimming around in my heart when I saw Tiller's old pickup truck with its illustrated bumper sticker that featured an oddly sexual-looking pile of fresh veggies on it that read, "I feel good from my head tomatoes." I'd gotten it in a welcome letter when I'd registered for a nutrition seminar, and Sam had dared me to put it on the truck one night after we'd had a little too much red wine.

The fact Tiller had laughed and kept it on his grandpa's beloved truck was a testament to his love of people over things. I loved that about him. He was one of the highest-paid players in the league, and you'd barely know it from his worn jeans, team tees, and half-broke Chevy.

Seeing the familiar pickup truck boosted my confidence. Tiller and I had been in each other's lives for five years now. This wasn't a flash-in-the-pan situation with a stranger. His position on the team was solid. My career as a professional chef had several different lucrative possibilities, meaning I didn't need to work for him anymore to make a living. We would be fine. There was no reason not to support us in a relationship.

I smiled at the security staff as I entered the building and stopped several times to exchange pleasantries with players and members of the staff as I made my way down to Dad's office. His assistant, Noreen, was almost as bad as Mrs. Nibert when it came to bending an ear, so I tried nipping a chat in the bud by walking right past her with a wave as if I was in a great hurry.

"He's in a mood, hon," she warned as I sailed past.

And he was.

"Goddammit, where is the injury reserve update I asked for?" he shouted through the open door. Noreen continued typing calmly on her computer as if she couldn't hear him. She'd been working for him long enough to have learned how to set boundaries by now, and one of them was not responding when he bellowed from the other room.

"You busy?" I asked, poking my head in.

"Mikey? What are you doing here? Is everything okay?"

To his credit, he stopped blustering and immediately stood with a look of concern on his face. I waved him back down. "Everything is fine. I just came from the house. Mom and Mrs. Nibert were comparing gourds, and I heard way more than I wanted to about Mr. Nibert's sciatica."

He nodded absently and sat back down. "What's on your mind?"

After a moment in which I tried to gather my thoughts, he seemed to catch on to the upcoming topic of conversation. The crease of concern on his forehead turned to a slash of annoyance.

"Close the door."

I did as he said and moved to take a seat in front of his desk. It reminded me of the time I'd come here to ask if I could take a part-time job in high school at a local bakery. It would have meant waking up at four in the morning and getting most of my schoolwork done in the afternoons so I could get to bed at a decent hour.

He'd said no with the excuse that I didn't need a part-time job as long as he made ten million dollars a year. I'd sat here and argued that all four of my brothers had been allowed to have jobs in high school, but none of my arguments had worked.

"I'm in love with Tiller Raine," I said, clasping my hands together in my lap so I didn't use them to throw myself out the window in an effort to escape my big scary confession.

He barked out a laugh. "No you're not. Don't be so dramatic."

I swallowed the sting. "I am. And I'm here to ask you, man to man, to respect that this has nothing to do with his professional life."

My father leaned forward on his elbows and steepled his hands together. "It has everything to do with his professional life, and for you to imply otherwise only goes to show how naive you are. This cannot happen. It *will not* happen. Do you understand what I'm saying?"

I felt my intestines wobble. My dad had always had the ability to intimidate the shit out of me. "Why not? Explain it to me. What does it matter to you who he dates outside of work?"

Because I sure as hell knew my dad didn't care about *me* nearly as much as he cared about Tiller Raine and his effect on the team.

"You may think I'm some controlling asshole, Mikey, but this is me looking out for you and him. Tiller is on target to be one of the greats. Do you get that? He has already had a once-in-a-lifetime career, and if it continues, he'll be a Hall of Famer the likes of which the league hasn't seen before. Do you have any idea how little time he has to concern himself with a relationship and all the media bullshit it would bring? How can you be so fucking naive?"

"Coach, you can't expect him to spend the next several years without a love life. You'd never ask that of any of your other players!"

"Can't you find anyone else to date besides people you work for? Christ, Mikey." He ran a hand down his face.

"I don't work for him anymore, so there's no issue there either."

"Find someone else. Someone who has the time and energy to give to you. Not someone who lives, eats, and breathes football."

"I don't want someone else. I want him."

I started to feel the familiar helpless feeling I used to get when trying to reason with my father when he'd already made up his mind. It brought panicky feelings that usually made me more emotional which was the last thing that I needed when dealing with him.

"Too fucking bad. I told you when I sent you over there that there was to be no inappropriate conduct. Why do you see the need to sleep with every goddamned player on my roster? Can you tell me that, huh?"

His voice was rising, and I felt myself shrink back into my seat. "Please keep your voice down so we can talk about this reasonably," I said as calmly as I could. "I have not slept with every player on your roster."

He gave me a look that called bullshit. It made me wonder how much he knew because if he was aware of the Colin hookup some-how, then I could understand him thinking three players was an unusually high number, especially for someone like me who purported not to give a shit about football players.

I tried not to feel like a ho-bag. In what universe was three hookups in six *years* some kind of promiscuous pattern? And since when was a man's sexual pursuits anyone else's business to judge? Especially his father?

The fact I was even in here making my case made me ill.

I stood. "Never mind. I thought if I told you how much he meant to me, it might make a difference. I can see this is a simple case of double standards. What's fine for the straight player isn't okay for the gay one. Nothing I say is going to change your mind." I bit back the part about haters being haters and bigots being assholes.

"I resent your accusation. I have supported you since the day you came out. Hell, I recruited the first out player to make a name for himself in football for Christ's sake! This isn't about his being gay. This is about him dating my son. If you care about him, if you love him like you say you do, you won't pursue this."

I glared at him. "If you care about *me*, if you love *me* like you say you do, you won't ask me to give him up."

"This isn't about you. This is about your life and his football career. What, are you going to put your own damned dreams on hold for him? How many more years, huh? And what about him? Do you honestly think you're more important to him than football? Jesus, Mikey. The man is a Heisman winner. He was the Super Bowl MVP last year. He is going places in this league most players don't even dream about, and you think a dalliance with you is worth throwing all of that away for? Besides, there's no happy future for you with someone like him. Even if you were a woman, I'd tell you to walk away. This man lives, eats, and breathes football. The next ten years of his life will be spent doing something you don't even *like*. He needs to stay focused on his career, and you deserve better."

"Bullshit. You've never told a single player of yours to walk away from someone they loved. In fact, you claim married players are ten times more reliable and stable."

"Now you're talking marriage?" he shouted. "Are you fucking kidding me?"

My face ignited, and I tried not to cry. He made me feel like I was stupid for even thinking a man like Tiller might want to marry me one day. And maybe I was. Maybe I was assuming way too much about what was happening between us.

I felt like a fool.

"You say you care about him and his career," I continued, "but you're planning on playing him Sunday even though the medical professionals said another hard hit before he's fully healed could result in a permanent injury. Explain that to me."

"I don't have to explain shit to you, Michael. But I'll tell you what. You walk away from Tiller Raine and I'll sit him this weekend. I'll give him another week to rest before putting him in. How'bout that?"

My jaw dropped. Was he seriously bribing me with Tiller's health?

"Not only that," he continued, "but I'll green-light this little cookbook project of yours that you didn't see fit to inform me about before using the Riggers' name to get yourself a publishing deal."

I stared at him in shock. "I don't need your permission to publish a book."

"No, you certainly don't. But you need my permission to get endorsements from the Riggers and Raine. The legal department was contacted by the publishing house just last week. It seems they needed approval before being able to present you as the personal chef to Rigger superstar Tiller Raine. And without being able to mention your Rigger clients, good luck selling books."

A hot tear escaped and slithered down my cheek before falling into my collar. I clenched my hands and teeth together so hard, I felt numb.

My father sighed. "Listen, Mikey. I don't want to fight with you. Believe it or not, I want the best for you, and I'm proud of you. It sounds like you took the bull by the horns with this book deal. But I can't have you say you're a professional chef to our star wide receiver when you're really nothing more than his boyfriend. Do you really want your relationship to keep you from this dream of yours? Think it through. Do you want to put your own damned dreams on hold while you're in the shadow of his?"

I didn't say anything. I could barely breathe, much less continue to argue. He always made me second-guess myself. It made me feel powerless and small.

"Just slow it down, okay? Get out of town for a little while and get some perspective. Maybe head out to the Galveston house your mom arranged. Let Tiller get back to work and focus on staying healthy and getting us to the Super Bowl. Maybe after the season we can reassess."

There was a knock at the door. I jerked in my seat before frantically swiping at my cheeks with the backs of my hands. Of all people, it was Tiller who popped his head in after my father's shouted "Enter."

"I wanted to talk to you about my arm," he said, obviously not noticing me yet. I didn't turn around. He would notice right away I'd been crying, and I couldn't bring myself to tell him any of what my father had said.

Dad said, "Give me a minute, Raine. Wait outside."

"Mikey?"

I squeezed my eyes closed and tried not to shed more stupid fucking tears. "Yeah. Hey," I said, still not turning around.

"What are you doing here?" He walked over and put his big hand on my shoulder.

I shook my head. "Uh," I croaked before clearing my throat.

Dad cut in smoothly. "He came by to tell me about a friend of ours who's having a health scare. Mikey's very close to the family. Give us a minute to finish up, Raine."

Tiller squatted in front of me and reached for my chin to force me to face him. Before he got that far, my dad barked at him. "Raine! Out!"

He left reluctantly, but I knew he'd be waiting for me just outside the door. I tried to pull myself together.

"Go to Galveston," Dad continued once he was gone. "Get your book done. I'll sit him this Sunday, but then he's going to have to focus on the playoffs. After the Super Bowl, we'll talk. You can't tell me he's not worth waiting two months for if you truly have real feelings for him, can you?"

He made it sound so easy, but I knew his words for the tempting lie they were. He wouldn't feel any differently in February than he did now.

He continued pounding more nails into the coffin. "His contract isn't worth shit right now as long as he's carrying that injury, and you know it. If I cut him loose now or trade him, he won't be in a position to get nearly as much money as before. We're talking millions of dollars, Mike. Is that what you want?"

He obviously didn't know Tiller very well if he thought Tiller cared about the money. Hell, the man already had more money than he could ever spend in a lifetime.

But Tiller cared about football. He cared about his stats and his reputation. The man beat himself up to be the best, and being traded away while down with an injury would gut him. He'd feel like he let the team down.

He'd feel like he let his family down.

I steeled myself and met my father's eyes, mentally begging Tiller's forgiveness for not protecting his career over my own heart. "I can't let you manipulate me like this, and I'm disgusted that you're even trying. It's clear where your priorities lie. Do what you have to do."

"Don't be rash. Take a day to think it through."

I'd done all the thinking I needed to do, and maybe it was overly sentimental and idealistic of me to think my feelings for Tiller were worth fighting for, but I at least knew I wanted to tackle this problem together. As a team.

I strode out of my father's office without looking back, and when I found Tiller pacing restlessly in the outer office, I walked right into his arms.

Everything would be okay. It had to be.

21

TILLER

When I was fourteen, I'd snowboarded right into a tree, breaking my leg so badly the bone had pierced through my skin.

Seeing Mikey Vining crying hurt ten times worse.

When the door to Coach's office opened and a bedraggled Mikey came out sniffing, I thought my heart would fly right out of my chest and land at his feet.

"Are you okay?" Before I could get the words out, he smacked into me, tightening his arms around me and holding on for dear life. "Baby? Is it bad? Is it Mr. Nibert?"

He shook his head against my chest, and I heart a soft sigh from Noreen's desk. When I glanced at her, she looked away quickly but not before I saw the affectionate look in her eyes. She'd always had a soft spot for Mikey.

I ran a hand through Mikey's hair before leaning down to press a kiss on his head. The familiar smell of his shampoo reminded me of home and sleeping in his bed. "Do you want to talk about it?"

He pulled back and wiped at his cheeks. The poor guy looked miserable. "No. Not really. Not right now. But will you be home for dinner?"

"Of course. I saw the ingredients for apricot chicken in the fridge.

I'm not missing that for love or money," I said with a grin, trying to cheer him up.

It didn't work. He looked even more miserable.

"What did the doctor say?" he asked.

My stomach dropped. I'd forgotten why I'd come to Coach's office in the first place. To plead my case.

"The specialist says I absolutely should not be playing yet. A dislocated shoulder should result in six weeks of rest regardless, but the bigger concern is this: if I get hit again before it's completely healed, the nerve damage could be permanent. That means permanent numbness and tingling in addition to loss of grip strength. The problem is, the team doctors are of the opinion none of this matters since it's my nondominant hand. Which makes no sense to me since I catch with both arms and hands. They're clearly more concerned about my ability to do my job than the risk of permanent injury. Not gonna lie. I'm scared of getting hit again, and I'm worried it's going to make me play too conservatively. If that's the case, they might as well have Brent out there anyway."

As I spoke, Mikey's face dropped in disappointment and worry. "Oh. Shit."

I ran a thumb at the dampness remaining under one of his eyes. "It's fine. I'm going to talk to Coach, try to plead my case. Are you really okay? Do you need me to bail on practice and come home with you?"

The question made his chin wobble a bit, but he gave me a smile. "No. I'll be fine. But... can you..." He swallowed and firmed his jaw. "Can you wait here for a minute? There's something I forgot to tell my dad."

I nodded and waited while he went back into the office for a minute. When he came out, he wouldn't meet my eye.

"Mikey," I said, lunging out to grab his arm before he raced past me. He winced and stopped in his tracks. Whatever it was going on with his family friend must have been bad. I hadn't seen him this upset in a while. "You sure there's nothing I can do?"

He shook his head and kept his eyes on the floor. "I'm sure," he whispered. "Go easy on your arm, okay?"

I nodded and leaned in to press a kiss to his lips. He melted against me a little bit and kissed me longer than I expected. When he finally pulled back, he looked dazed.

"I... I'll see you later," he said.

I grinned at him. "If Sam gets there before I do, tell him to keep his hands off my apricot chicken."

This time his smile was genuine and unforced. It made it easier to say goodbye to him and watch him walk away. My relief only lasted thirty seconds until I got into Coach's office and prepared to be disappointed.

But Coach surprised me. Before I even had a chance to tell him what the specialist said, he told me, "I'm going to play Brent, after all," he said with a big smile. "Give you another little while to get that arm back to full speed. No need risking permanent nerve damage. I still want you on the bench and focused, but I expect you to keep your flailing hands and strong opinions to yourself. Got me?"

I nodded. "Yes, sir. Thank you."

I wanted desperately to ask him what had changed his mind, but I wasn't inclined to look a gift horse in the mouth.

"Was there anything else?" he asked, reaching for the tablet he usually brought to meetings.

Only the teeny tiny issue of my sleeping with his son. But I wasn't stupid enough to upset the apple cart right now, especially if they were dealing with a family issue.

"No, sir."

"Then get out of here. I need to meet with the college scouting team, and I'm late."

I hustled out of there and down to the locker room where I got an odd smile from Colin Saris.

"That Mikey I saw in the parking lot?" he asked. My stomach curdled. I didn't like the look on his face, especially if the topic at hand was my... Mikey.

I nodded and reached into my locker for my turf cleats. "He was here to see Coach."

"Yo, listen... can I get his number from you? It's just that my, ah, ma wants to order some of his casserole shit for Christmas."

The man was lying through his teeth. "I thought you already had his number," I said, trying to keep my voice calm. These cleat laces were a bitch, so I yanked on them. Hard.

When he didn't respond, I glanced up and noticed him studying me. "Why you ask me that like that?"

"You know what?" I asked, feeling a head of steam building up. For as much as I'd never thought of myself as the jealous type, my gut was churning with green rage. "No. No you can't have his number. Not only that, but if someone else gives you his number, *lose it.* Got me?"

He studied me for a second before the edge of his lip curled up. "That how it is?"

I glared at him. "That's how it is."

"I see. What you're saying is to give it a little time. Alright. Can do, man. Can do." He laughed and turned away, shaking his head and moving on to talking smack about something else. I let out a breath and closed my eyes. *Asshole.*

I spent the rest of the day doing my job. Meeting with the PTs and trainers, practicing lightly, studying game film, and meeting with the assistant coaches. When the time came to drive home, I finally allowed myself to think about Mikey and how upset he'd been earlier. Part of me was disappointed he hadn't wanted me to comfort him, so I looked forward to spending the evening being there for him however he wanted.

Walking in to discover him singing to himself as he pruned his windowsill herb garden wasn't exactly what I'd expected. I'd thought he might be curled up under a blanket watching his favorite baking show or burning through old episodes of *Project Runway*. Instead, he seemed much calmer than he'd been before, although he looked worn-out.

When I set my keys down on the counter, he looked up and

noticed me. "Oh, I didn't hear the garage," he said absently before turning back to his plants. "Let me just finish trimming these really quickly and I'll get the chicken started."

I kicked off my shoes and laid my messenger bag on the counter next to my keys. Suddenly, I was hungry for something other than apricot chicken. "Is Sam here?"

"Hm? Oh. No. He had family stuff and said he might need to head out of town. But if he gets back before Sunday, he'll come to the game."

I stepped up behind him and wrapped my arms around his waist, leaning in to press a lingering kiss to his cheek. He always smelled a little like coffee at the end of the day, but today he also smelled like peppermint for some reason.

I couldn't wait to tell him the good news. "Tell him not to get too excited since I'll be riding the bench."

Mikey's body stiffened for a beat before relaxing back into me. He let out a deep exhale. "Thank fuck."

"Yeah, see? Your dad's a good guy. Said he'd rather give me the extra days than risk permanent damage." I licked and sucked a favorite spot on the side of his neck. "I appreciate him looking out for my career. Can you imagine if something happened and I had to retire at twenty-seven? I can't even think about it. Markus called to tell me rumor has it the recruitment team sent someone to check out that wide receiver at Oregon. I hope they're not considering trying to get him in case I can't come back at full power."

Markus had assured me the scouts were much more interested in filling in the holes in our secondary. In particular, there was a safety at the University of Wisconsin who was drawing everyone's eye this season. I hadn't even brought up the subject because I was all that worried. It was more nervous babbling because I was getting a weird feeling from Mikey.

Suddenly, Mikey turned in my arms and slammed himself into me in a tight hug, holding on as tightly as he would if we were falling into a sinkhole and had nothing but each other to grab onto.

"Baby?" I murmured into his hair. "Is this about the Niberts? Are you going to tell me what's wrong?"

"I'm just really glad you're not playing on Sunday," he croaked. "I was worried."

"Shh, it's okay. Now you don't have to run away to Aster Valley to avoid watching the game," I teased.

He still didn't look up at me. "I'm going to Aster Valley anyway. I have a meeting. I have a plane ticket."

I pulled back and reached for his chin, tipping it up until I could look into his brown eyes. "I know," I said gently. "I was teasing." I searched his face for information, but he mostly just looked tired. "Why don't you let me cook tonight? I'll turn on a show and wrap you up in your favorite blanket on your chair. Or you can go get in my bed and catch up on all the Words with Friends games you owe me."

He stood on his toes and kissed me softly. My dick perked back up as I roamed my hands all over his back and butt. When things started getting more heated, he pulled back with a laugh that made my heart feel lighter than it had all day. "Dinner first. Hands on butt after. And, no, you're not cooking. You're not the only one who likes apricot chicken."

I leaned down to kiss him again before letting him go. "How can I help?"

After he handed me some preapproved menial tasks—in this case getting out the silverware and pouring ice water—I decided to ask him one last time about whatever the bad news had been earlier. "So... the Niberts?"

He flapped his hand. "No. It didn't turn out to be a thing. I misunderstood and overreacted. I don't want to talk about it."

I changed the subject by asking him about the meeting he'd arranged with the Civettis.

"I don't want to talk about that either," he said with a nervous laugh.

"Why not?"

Mikey shrugged. "It's my dream come true, you know? But I don't know what their vision is, and I don't know if I want to work for someone else. I have a dream of how I'd do it if I was in charge. But what if their vision is different? What if they want to micromanage me? I wish I could afford to do it myself."

"Then do it yourself."

He looked at me like I had three heads. "I don't have that much money."

It was on the tip of my tongue to say I did, but I knew he wouldn't agree to letting me help him. If I gave him a choice.

I froze as an idea started to form in my mind. A way Mikey wouldn't have to give up his dream and I wouldn't have to give up mine. But there were too many unknowns—his family, my health, the situation with the Civettis—for me to talk to him about it. Yet.

"Then start small. Start with a small cabin and your catering business. Once people in Aster Valley discover your talent, you can grow until you open your own place."

"Can we talk about something else?" he asked.

I asked him about the call he'd had scheduled with his editor. Mikey's face lit up with excitement as he told me about his plans to meet some food stylists and photographers online the following week.

"The stylist can't Zoom until next Friday, but he's the one who did the styling for the Giles Gatterman cookbook."

"I don't know who that is," I admitted. "But from your smile, I can tell we're excited about it."

Mikey pointed to the kitchen shelf where his favorite cookbooks were stashed. "The orange one? The one that has your favorite beef-and-corn taco cups recipe in it?"

I walked over and wrapped my arms around him again. If he was here in the same room with me, I wanted to have my hands on him.

"Baby, I don't know where you get the recipes you make," I admitted. "Honestly, I assume most of them come from a combination of your imagination and sadistic experimentation, but the result is delish."

I pulled his earlobe into my mouth and sucked. He shivered before nudging me away. "Stop or we'll starve to death."

He was right. I left him alone long enough for us to get dinner on the table. While we ate, we talked a little more about his book plans. Mikey's responses were a little more short than usual, but I chalked it up to nerves. I knew how much was riding on this project for him. He'd spent so much time studying to be a nutritionist and practicing his culinary craft. Being able to put those things together by putting out this book was a dream come true for him, not to mention validation that he had something important to say.

"Will you get to travel around to bookstores and sign copies when it comes out?" I asked. "Is that something cookbook authors do?"

He nodded. "My publisher said they're planning a multicity release tour. They're even going to try and book me on some morning shows."

I pictured him dressed up and adorably flustered on the set of *The View*. "You're going to be amazing. I can't wait to get my own personalized copy and brag to everyone on the team that my boyfriend is a best-selling author."

His eyes widened in worry which surprised me. Maybe I thought he'd like the idea of being claimed as mine. "You can't tell anyone, um, yet. And we don't know it will be best-selling."

Oh. My stomach clenched a little. Maybe I was reading more into this than he was. Maybe I needed to slow down and find out what he was thinking.

I swallowed the bite of chicken in my mouth and tried to smile. "Pfft. Of course it will be. Publishers don't send authors on tour unless they think the book is going to do great. Are you supposed to keep it quiet? When can we tell people?"

He seemed uncomfortable and couldn't give me a straight answer. I knew the deal had already been published in some kind of book industry magazine because he'd squealed when he read it.

I put my fork down. "Mikey... I'm a little confused here. Are you upset at me referring to you as my boyfriend, or are you warning me about mentioning the book project?"

His hesitation made my stomach knot even worse. I pushed my plate away. "Talk to me."

"I don't know. I don't know what I'm feeling. I'm just... this is all happening fast, and with everything else going on—the book, your injury, the thing with the Civettis, my parents..." His eyes darted around, not really ever landing on my face. "And apparently my family planned a whole 'Christmas in Galveston' thing without telling me, so that made me feel like shit, too. Leave it to my family to plan a big family get-together and not include me. It was like my senior year in high school all over again when I came home late from a yearbook meeting to an empty house. I had to learn from the neighbors that everyone had gone to Disney World on the spur of the moment."

Now he was the one babbling. I hadn't mentioned the Galveston thing to him for fear of hurting his feelings, but this was the first I'd heard of the Florida story. "They left you and fucked off to Florida without you?" I'd heard some shitty stories about the Vinings overlooking Mikey or even borderline bullying him in some cases, but this was the worst.

He shrugged. "They thought I was with them. Supposedly, my brother Eddie told Mom I was in the back of the car lying down because I didn't feel well. When they got to the airport and realized he'd been lying, it was too late to go back for me. I guess? They offered to fly me out the next day, but I had a Calculus test."

Jesus. "Forget what I said about your dad being a good guy," I muttered. "I fucking hate your family."

At least it explained why he was in a strange mood. Family drama could do that to you. I knew especially from the many times my father had pressured me about football. Sometimes I questioned whether I did this job for him or myself. I loved football, but I didn't love prioritizing it above everything else in my life.

Mikey shoved his own plate away and stood up before coming over and squeezing himself into my lap. He straddled me with his back to the table and slid his hands up my chest before wrapping them around my neck. He looked so tired. I wanted to baby him and coddle him until he felt strong and happy again.

"I've had this fantasy low-key playing in my head today," he said, leaning in to press a kiss to the edge of my mouth. I tried turning my head to get another one full on the lips, but he dodged me with the barest hint of a teasing smile. "And I was wondering if maybe we could do less talking and more fantasy role-play."

I'd never done anything remotely resembling "fantasy role-play," but I had to admit the idea intrigued me.

"What exactly did you have in mind for this role-play?" I moved my arms around him and snuck my fingers down into the back of his pants.

"Well, I miss our house in Aster Valley, and I miss wandering through the snowy forest out back. So I was thinking back to that and started fantasizing about some poor, adorable fool—a Texan chef, probably—getting lost in the woods during a blizzard." He stopped and leaned in to nip a spot under my chin. "And a big, muscled guy— who looked shockingly like the Riggers wide receiver—came across the fool's little half-frozen self."

"Poor baby," I murmured, moving my finger along the crease between his cheeks.

"Right? And so I—I mean *the chef*—needed resuscitating, but not the kind with a Saint Bernard and wooden barrel of whiskey. This was the kind of reviving that required getting naked in a shared sleeping bag in a sex cave. By candlelight."

I huffed a laugh into his hair. "I like it so far. Continue."

Mikey's hands moved back to my chest and squeezed my pecs before moving down my stomach to my pants. "But no matter how much naked cuddling they did, and it was a *lot*, the chef still couldn't get warm."

"Oh no. What did the football-dude do? Was he able to come up with a better plan?"

Mikey nodded solemnly. "He did. He took one for the team and inserted heat directly into that poor little Texan using his giant *mpfh!*"

I slammed my mouth into his and stood up, ignoring our plates of half-eaten food abandoned on the table. Mikey's legs wrapped around my waist as I carried him to my room. We kept kissing like we were starving for it, like we hadn't had access to each other's mouths in days.

When I tossed him down on the bed, I stripped off my clothes as fast as I could while he did the same. I grabbed lube and a condom from the bedside table and climbed onto the bed on top of him.

Mikey was already breathless. "Did I mention the mountain man had to fuck the guy face-first into the floor of the cave? Because he did. Hard."

"Mm-hm," I grunted, pressing my throbbing cock against the inside of his thigh. "Poor dumb Texan needed to be taught a lesson about getting lost in the woods, didn't he?"

His eyes were bright with need as he nodded rapidly. "So, so much."

I leaned down and kissed him again before pulling back and shoving him over onto his front. He whimpered and pulled his knees up under him until his ass was on full display. I didn't wait. I leaned right in and licked a stripe up his crease. Rimming him was my new favorite thing. It made him beg and squirm until my dick was like granite.

This was so much better than talking about work or family or any of the million other things in our lives. It was pure connection. When Mikey and I were pressed close together like this with nothing between us, I felt the simple joy of being in the moment with him, of knowing we were each other's everything right then regardless of what came before or after.

"Please," he said on a gasp. "Don't fuck with me right now. I can't take it."

I didn't question him. Instead, I simply slicked up my fingers and prepped him quickly while leaning up to murmur words in his ear.

"Watching you beg with your ass in the air like this makes me want to come all over you. You're so fucking beautiful. I can't believe I get to be with you like this. That's it. Fuck, you feel good. Shit, oh god, Mike. Fuck. Let me in, baby."

I finally suited up and pressed my dick against his opening, running my hands up his back and into his hair before leaning down along his back and thrusting my hips forward some more.

Mikey sucked in a breath, and I stilled, waiting for him to adjust. When his hand came back and grabbed my leg, I knew he was ready.

I pounded that poor Texan chef into the floor of the cave like our very lives depended on it. Thankfully, we were alone in the house because Mikey couldn't stay quiet. He shouted and cried out until his voice sounded wrecked and my heart felt like it was going to pound out of my chest.

At one point I pulled out, flipped him onto his back, and shoved a pillow under his ass before finding my way back inside his hot body. He was sweaty and flushed, glassy-eyed and dazed. When I finally found just the right spot and hammered it over and over again while he jacked himself, his eyes widened and then squeezed closed.

His body contracted for a minute before his release hit. Watching him come was the best thing ever, and it always seemed to speed up my own orgasm. I came hard inside him until I felt as wrecked as Mikey sounded.

Sex with him was intense, whether it was hot and hard or slow and sweet. It wasn't transactional like the guys I'd been with in the past. It was a meaningful physical addition to the emotional connection we'd spent years building.

I finally felt like we were exactly the way we were meant to be: together in every way.

It was clear to me I was falling hard for him, and when I woke up to his sweet kisses a little while later in the silent early morning hours, I did my best to tell him so with the slow, tenderness of our lovemaking. I'd woken up spooned around his back, and, after sliding a condom on, I slid easily into his still-slick channel and rolled my hip gently in and out of him until I felt the hot drip of a tear hit my arm.

"Baby?" I murmured into the skin behind his ear.

He shook his head. "Keep going," he whispered roughly. "Feels so good."

I thought the tear was a happy one. It was only days later, after things had gotten weird between us again, that I began to wonder if the tear hadn't been a happy one after all.

22

MIKEY

Leaving the sleepy, warm embrace of the man I loved was pretty much the worst thing ever. But I'd made a deal with the devil, and it was time to pay the price.

I snuck out of Tiller's bed, away from his warm body, and made my way to my bedroom. I'd already spent most of the afternoon yesterday preparing meals to help tide him over while I was gone. He had much more knowledge and resources now than he'd had five years before, so I knew he'd be fine whether I'd cooked for him or not. But he was right when he said cooking for someone was how I showed them love. Even the fridge and freezer were full to the brim of his favorite meals.

After packing for longer than the original week I'd planned, I headed out to my car and tossed my luggage in the hatchback. The drive to the airport was uneventful, save for the mental cursing I did at my father.

Of course I'd agreed to his terms. When Tiller had come back from the specialist with fear in his eyes, it hadn't even been a question. I'd told myself it wasn't a big deal. I could change my mind at any time. It wasn't like I was giving Tiller up for good. As long as

Tiller didn't have to play this week, I could deal with the rest of it later.

In the meantime, I mourned the loss of my father, of the man I'd thought he was, had hoped he was. It was clear to me now he wasn't that man. Maybe he never had been. He cared more about his job than my heart, and that was an incredibly heartbreaking and bitter pill to swallow.

It was especially hard to take when I couldn't lean on Tiller for comfort and understanding.

So I was a sad sack as I checked my bag in the terminal and made my way through security, and I was extra pitiful at the gate when the agent called me up to give me an updated boarding pass reflecting the upgrade to first class Tiller had somehow managed from afar. I hated that I loved him. Worse than that, I hated that I was essentially lying to him. It wasn't fair, but neither was my father prioritizing his fucking playoff chances over Tiller's career.

When I boarded the plane, I stashed my carry-on bag under the seat in front of me, fastened my seat belt, and grabbed the blanket before curling up in a little ball and trying to close out the world around me. It didn't work.

"Hey, aren't you the guy who makes the couscous salad at Hilltop Cafe?"

I blinked up at the thirtysomething woman in yoga pants and a flowery tunic standing in the row in front of me facing backward. She had creamy brown skin and a shaved head that set off her big brown eyes and thick dark lashes. She was gorgeous, but after scrambling my memory, I couldn't place her.

"Uh, yes?"

She slapped a palm over her heart and smiled. "Thought so. I saw you deliver it one time. I am in love with that salad. I've been begging Sid to finagle the recipe out of you for months. I was devastated when I found out you weren't supplying it anymore."

I returned her smile and held out my hand. "Thank you for saying that. I'm Michael Vining."

She shook my hand over the top of her seat. "Konni Prater, nice to meet you. Hilltop Cafe is kind of my office," she said with a light chuckle. "I'm a writer, and for some reason I can focus more with the buzz of hungry customers around me. Sid and Marti are awesome to let me loiter in a back booth most days."

As other passengers continued to make their way down the aisle, Konni rifled through her bag before stowing it in the bin above her seat. When I saw her at an angle, I realized I did recognize her.

"Oh, I think I remember seeing you there. Do you wear glasses when you work?"

She grinned and nodded. "Yup. Kind of like yours. Love those, by the way. But not as much as your food."

As she winked and took her seat, I realized I felt a little better than I had before. There was more to my life than Tiller Raine, and I needed to remember that. Even Tiller wouldn't want me to spend my week in Aster Valley sniffling about him. I needed to embrace new opportunities and push all of this other shit to later, maybe after Christmas which was only a week and a half away now. I had my own talents and plans that had nothing to do with Tiller or football, and it was in my best interest to make sure whatever direction I took with my own future, I was actively choosing it instead of letting the tide of indecision take me.

When we landed in Denver, I said goodbye to Konni with a hope of running into each other sometime soon at the cafe. I headed to the car rental desk and got behind the wheel of a smaller SUV than before. I was on a Mikey budget this time, but I still had the Rockley Lodge to stay in since Tiller's reservation had been booked for the entire month.

As I made the drive through Denver and out the other side, I imagined what it would be like if we could return to Aster Valley and build a life there, just the two of us. Maybe if the B&B didn't work out, I could spin up my catering business again. Tiller could coach football or befriend Truman and help plant stuff. I wasn't sure what his role would be, exactly, but I definitely got the sense he'd be happy there. Not right now, while he was still playing professionally, but later. One day down the road.

The drive was gorgeous in the afternoon sun. Driving into Aster Valley was just as stunning the second time as it had been the first. It embraced me like an old friend, and I knew already I didn't want to leave. Friendly faces lined the streets outside the shops, and someone dressed like a reindeer waved from the street corner outside Truman's Honeyed Lemon.

After pulling down the now-familiar driveway to the lodge, I pulled out my phone and texted Sam. He'd already messaged to tell me he was back in Houston.

Me: *I'm going to stay in Aster Valley longer than a week.*

Sam: *Makes sense. You said you loved it there. You and Tiller can always go back after the Super Bowl.*

I bit my lip.

Me: *Do you think they'll make it?*

Sam: *Without Tiller?*

He followed it with a frowny emoji.

Me: *I was thinking about staying here through the end of the season. Let Tiller focus on football. The Aster Valley house is paid for through the new year. And then I can rent something smaller.*

The three typing dots appeared while I waited for the judgment.

Sam: *What does Tiller think about that?*

I couldn't exactly tell him about the deal I'd made with the devil to stay away. Before I could answer Sam, I got a text from my mom.

Mom: *Your father told me not to expect Tiller at Christmas. Did something happen?*

I'd never been able to understand how you could be married to someone and barely talk to them.

Sam: *Did you ask him or is this you running away from him?*

I decided to answer my mom first since it was way past time she got to be naively unaware of what lengths my father was going to for his precious team. My mom needed to know.

Me: *Yes, something happened. Dad blackmailed me. Said he would play Tiller on a bad arm and possibly even transfer him to a shit team if I didn't break up with him to spare everyone's reputation. Jesus, Mom! Don't you two ever talk? Do you have any idea the asshole you're married to? He also said he would yank the Riggers' endorsement of my cookbook deal.*

By the time I hit Send, I was pacing through the drifts of snow next to the wide wooden front door. I quickly pressed the button to call Sam so I wouldn't immediately see my mom's response. I needed to calm the hell down, and Sam was usually good for that. His deep voice was familiar and reassuring. "What's going on?"

"I just... I just think things have moved really quickly, you know? And Tiller has a lot on his plate. And I have a lot on my plate. And... and in Aster Valley everything is calm. I can focus on my cookbook project and just enjoy myself. It is *calm*."

When I heard myself repeat the word, it was like a lightbulb snapping on. Houston was noisy and busy, overwhelming and intimidating. Aster Valley was like a warm hug. Everywhere I went people were friendly and interested, the way Konni had been on the plane. That was an anomaly in Houston, but in Aster Valley, it was the norm.

I really did feel at home here.

Sam hesitated for a few minutes. "If staying in Aster Valley will make you happy, do it. Tiller isn't going to have much spare time in the next several weeks if the team makes it all the way through play-offs. You know that."

I did. It would be the four most important games of the season played over six weeks, and if I had to watch him put his body at risk in each game as the stakes raised exponentially higher, I wasn't sure I'd survive it.

Which, of course, made me second-guess whether the two of us even made a good match in the first place. It wasn't easy to watch him get tackled on a good day, but the older he got and the more injuries he received, the harder it would get to witness.

"I do," I said. "And I think he'll understand, especially if I tell him I need to focus on my own work for a little while."

"Of course he'll understand. But is that what you really want? To be alone in Colorado?"

His familiar steady calm grounded me. "I think so?"

"Are you sure you don't want to be here for the playoff games? You haven't missed one of his games in five years."

Guilt twisted my gut. It was true. Even when I hadn't been physically present, I'd still managed to catch his games. Maybe I folded laundry with the game on in the background, or maybe I tuned in on the radio when I delivered catering orders, but I always managed to catch the game when Tiller was playing.

"I won't miss it," I said lamely. "I just can't watch it live. Not knowing if he's going to be hurt."

"Fair enough." Sam hesitated. "Mike..."

I braced for words I knew I wouldn't like. "Yeah?"

"You should tell him."

"Tell him what?"

He sighed. "Tell him you're not running away."

But I was running away, and we both knew it.

Sam's voice softened. "Tell him you love him."

My chin wobbled. "I do love him." My voice was scratchy and pathetic. "But..."

"But what, babe?"

I blinked back tears before they could escape and freeze to my face. It was gorgeous and sunny, but cold as hell. "But I just don't know if I'm what's best for him. And I don't know if I can put off following my own dream so that he can keep his."

Sam's sudden and raucous laughter startled me. I firmed my chin and felt anger swell inside of me. This was no laughing matter.

"That's not how love works," he said. "If you love someone, you don't set them free like a damned butterfly. You chain them to your bed and use your mouth to convince them to stay."

The sniffly laugh that bubbled out of me felt irreverent and inappropriate. No matter how much I appreciated his plan. "I just want some time to think," I said at last. "I wasn't expecting this."

"Talk to him so you can tackle these things together. As a team."

"I know... I will... I just... I want to see what's what here first. Find out what my options are."

It was difficult to hear Sam with a truck honking nearby, but I thought he muttered something about spending five years in a bath and only now realizing I was wet. I wasn't sure what he meant exactly, but I knew I needed to go before I full-on cried and froze my eyeballs shut.

"Gotta go, Sam."

"Love you, Mikey. Be safe."

I nodded and gulped, grateful for my good friend. "Love you, too."

After shooting Tiller a quick text to tell him I'd arrived safely, I made my way into the house and crawled into Tiller's bed. It was blessedly still unmade and smelled of him. Thank god they hadn't sent in the housecleaners yet. I didn't care that I hadn't had lunch and it was only midafternoon. I was warm and a little numb, and all I wanted was to curl up into a ball and sleep with the faint scent of Tiller surrounding me.

The following day, I happened to visit Truman's spice shop while he was starting a class on using spices as antioxidants. After taking copious notes into my phone, I joined him and his friend Chaya for dinner at a brick-oven pizza place around the corner from his shop. Chaya was a surprisingly tall woman—originally from New Jersey—with a thick mane of dark, curly hair. If Truman was petite and unassuming, Chaya was his complete opposite. She and I talked each other's ears off, alternatively making Truman blush and laugh. It was a much-needed break to my internal tension, and I returned home to the lodge that night relieved to realize I hadn't once thought about the Riggers' game against the Steelers.

But I couldn't go to sleep without finding out who'd won and making sure Coach hadn't gone against our deal and put Tiller in. I quickly visited the ESPN site on my phone to discover they'd won and Tiller hadn't played. I closed my eyes and took a deep breath, thankful for both outcomes.

I'd successfully ignored the message notification on my text app all day, but now I clicked into it.

Tiller: *Good morning beautiful. Have a wonderful day. If you see anyone we know, tell them hi from me.*

Tiller: *Just arrived at the stadium. It's going to be a busy day, but I wanted to tell you I can't stop thinking about you.*

Tiller: *Oh, one more thing. I want you to know I support you in whatever you want to do. Follow your dreams. If that includes moving to Aster Valley, we'll find a way to work it out, okay?*

My heart thudded in my chest. Besides Sam, no one in my life had ever been so supportive of me. It made me feel... strong. It was exactly what I'd needed and wanted to hear.

A new text came in.

Stacy Clifton: *Can you meet me for breakfast tomorrow at the diner? Something's come up.*

My hands started to shake as I replied to the real estate agent. I knew she'd been helping the Civettis with some concerns about the property, and the reality of the real estate deal made me nervous.

What if the Civettis didn't want me after all? What if they did? Either way, it was time to move forward and see what the future held.

Me: *Sounds good.*

I responded to Tiller next.

Me: *Congrats on the win! Spent the day with Truman learning more about spices than you'd ever want to know. Sprinkle some nutmeg in your oatmeal. Helps with tissue damage.*

When I went to sleep, I felt calmer, more settled in my skin. I didn't know what the future held, but I knew it was going to be okay.

The next morning, when I sat down across from Stacy, my determination was tested.

"The Rockley property is no longer on the market," she said, right off the bat. "I'm so sorry. When I called the Civettis to tell them about it, they were in the middle of flying back to Chicago for a family emergency. They wanted me to make their apologies to you as well."

My heart fell. "I hope they're okay?"

"Oh, yes. I believe one of their grandchildren broke a bone, and the Civettis were flying back to help look after him. I'm sure they'll be in touch."

Pim came by with the coffeepot, all smiles. "Hey, Mikey. Great to see you. Where's your wingman?"

As he poured the coffee, I took a deep inhale and tried to recenter myself after Stacy's surprising news. Thinking about Tiller helped. "He's back on the roster for this week's game," I said. "So he's on his way to Buffalo."

Pim shivered. "Better him than me. At least in Aster Valley we get the sun with the cold. What would you two like to eat?"

After ordering, we took a few sips of our coffee in comfortable silence. I'd spent quite a bit of time thinking things through and was surprised to find myself almost relieved at the news the property had fallen through. Not because I didn't want the Rockley Lodge. I did. It was still my dream property. But the more I thought about it, the more I realized I wanted to run my own business rather than run the Civettis'. Tiller was right. I could start small with my own catering business. The upside to that plan would be flexibility. I could plan my business around Tiller's schedule so that we spent part of the year in Aster Valley and part of it in Houston. While I didn't really want to ask him for financial help, I'd be willing to ask him to cover the costs of the travel between the two places. I knew he wouldn't think anything of it. In fact, he'd insist on booking first-class tickets each way.

"You're smiling," Stacy said with her own smirk. "That's unexpected."

"I have an idea," I said. "And I'd love to get your help with it."

As I talked through my idea for trying to find a cozy cabin with the nicest kitchen possible in my price range, both of us got more and more excited. We talked for two hours, and by the time we paid our tab at the diner, we had a table full of scribbled pages from my notebook and tons of saved listings on her iPad to check out over the following days.

I spent the rest of the afternoon wandering through town and ducking into more shops to get a feel for the people of Aster Valley. Before I made an investment here, I wanted to be extra sure it was the right place. I already knew in my heart I wanted to buy a place here, but my heart couldn't be trusted. My heart was Vegas. Sometimes stupid shit happened in Vegas.

Everyone I met was amazing. I even ducked into the public library where an older man pointed me to the section on Aster Valley's history. I fell more in love with the town and became more sure of my plan. I couldn't wait to tell Tiller about it, but I wanted to wait until I had something concrete to share. Until then, I dodged his calls. Part of me knew I wouldn't be able to stop myself from telling him about my dad, and I worried Tiller would be mad at me for keeping it from him, not to mention making a deal with him in the first place.

But when Thursday came along, I finally had something exciting to tell him. I'd found a little fixer-upper cabin that might work, but I wanted to get his opinion about the plan before making an offer. Tiller had given me every reason to think we were together, and if I was going to make this big of a decision, I wasn't going to do it without him. Since he was probably already at the stadium in Buffalo, I shot him a quick text.

Me: *Good luck today. Call me after the game. I want to ask your advice about something.*

"Aww, his face just went all lovey-dovey," Pim said to Bill. I'd been on my way to take Truman some dinner at the shop, when Pim and Bill had spotted me on the sidewalk and offered to walk with me.

Bill reached out and ruffled my hair. He was a quieter, sweet sort of man who'd surprised me with physical affection as soon as he'd gotten to know me a bit better. He was a hugger with a great big belly and strong arms. He smelled like fried onions mixed with coffee, and it was like getting a hug from the diner itself.

Winter and Gentry had hosted me for dinner the night before and had invited several other LGBT families to join as well. I'd spent at least half an hour swapping recipe ideas with Bill while Gent had sat with Solo in the other room teaching him how to play the guitar and a woman named Mindy had talked Winter's ear off about the hand pain she was experiencing after taking a wood-carving class. The evening had been comfortable and friendly, exactly the kind of atmosphere I'd hoped to find there in Aster Valley.

I glanced at the phone in my hand and debated whether or not to text him I loved him. The tinkle of a bell rang in the cold mountain air as Truman stepped out of his shop and turned to lock the door behind him. It was quickly followed by the sound of my phone ringing. Since I was expecting a call back from Stacy with the answer to a zoning question for the cabin we'd looked at, I answered the phone without looking.

23

TILLER

"Sam, dammit, tell me what the fuck is wrong with him? He won't even answer my calls."

I'd completely lost my patience with Mikey. Something was wrong, and he wouldn't fucking talk to me. I'd almost decided to ditch practice on Wednesday and fly out to Colorado to shake him in person and ask him what the hell was going on. In the end, I forced myself to stay put since I was playing in the game Thursday and my team was counting on me.

But that didn't mean I couldn't shake down our friend for information. I left Sam a message Wednesday night but didn't get a call back until I was heading into the Bills' stadium late Thursday afternoon.

Sam had been busy with a family thing. I knew that, but I couldn't help but think he might know what was happening with Mikey.

"Tiller, take a breath." His voice sounded calm the way it always did. Sam was steady like a rock. "And then sit down. Because you're not going to like this."

My face started tingling with fear that he was going to impart some terrible news. Teammates jostled past me on their way to the locker room, but I ignored them. "Just spit it out."

Markus glared at me for taking a personal call this close to the game, but I waved him on ahead. He'd supposedly come to Buffalo to meet with another client of his, but I suspected he was really here in case he had to handle another injury involving his highest-paid asset.

He tapped his smartwatch and tilted his head toward the locker room. I waved him on again without looking up.

Sam sighed. "I'm not supposed to know this, and I sure as hell am not supposed to tell *you*, but you two fuckers need to get your head out of your asses before you get railroaded by external forces."

That didn't make any sense. My head wasn't in my ass. I was all-in with Mikey. Hell, I'd spent the better part of the week making plans to *show* him how all-in I was. "How so?"

"He accidentally sent me a text that was meant for someone else. But it looks like maybe his dad is threatening him to make him leave you."

"Leave m—" I stopped as I realized what he was saying. He didn't mean quitting his job as my chef and assistant. He meant walking away from the relationship. "How?"

"He told Mikey he would play you injured or possibly trade you. He said he would deny the Riggers' endorsement of Mikey's cookbook deal."

Sudden hot rage came over me. My personal life was none of my coach's business, but more than that, how could he be such an uncaring asshole to his own son? How could he deny Mikey a chance at happiness?

"Fuck." I felt like my back teeth were going to crack. I'd never felt so angry at my coach before, and that was saying a lot since he'd bawled me out plenty of times and run me until I puked.

As I made my way down the hallway, I tried to talk myself down from the cliff. Every part of me wanted to find Coach Vining and lay him out.

"Take a breath," Sam said.

My thoughts pinged around in my head like an exploding bag of Skittles. I didn't even know where to start. "Why does he even care?" I wondered out loud.

"Optics?" Sam suggested. "That's all I can figure. I'm not sure what angle bothers him, though. Is it the player with coach's son thing or the star player being publicly gay thing?"

"But I've been out the whole time," I argued.

"Not the same thing as being in an actual gay relationship. There will be photos of you together. It would mean putting your sexuality in people's faces. The media would have a field day."

I lowered my voice as I made my way to the locker room. "The media already has a fucking field day with my sexuality. How is this any different?"

My hands were shaking with the familiar rush of adrenaline, and I knew I needed to calm down if I had any chance of playing well in the game.

"I need to talk to him," I said.

"Do not confront Coach V. right now," Sam warned.

"No. I mean Mikey. I need to talk to him. Ask him if this is why he's been avoiding me."

"Feeling like you already know the answer to that. Calm down, play your game. Focus on your job right now."

He was right. I knew that, but I also knew I needed to hear Mikey's voice. I needed him to tell me he wasn't going to let his father get in the way of how we felt about each other.

"Okay," I said finally.

Sam let out a breath and sounded resigned. "You're going to go off half-cocked."

"Pretty much."

"Don't fuck up your career while you're angry. Promise me."

He was a good friend to both of us, and I valued his advice. "I promise. I just want to make sure Mikey's okay."

"Then call him. Tell him you love him and you'll call him back after the game to talk about it. Then go out there and kick ass, alright?"

I wasn't going to tell Mikey I loved him for the first time over the phone. After our strange final night together, his sneaking out the next morning to catch his flight, and his lack of availability to even talk on the phone this week, I had no idea how he was feeling about us. Not knowing had me completely fucked-up. And now this.

"Thanks, Sam. I really appreciate it."

"Good luck."

After the call, I headed toward my locker to stash my bag and peel off my jacket. Everyone I passed cheered or thumped me on the back to tell me how happy they were to have me back in the starting line. I smiled and nodded, murmuring my thanks until I got to the bench in front of my locker. I pulled out my phone and saw the text from Mikey to call him after the game.

Thank god. I didn't want to wait. I dialed Mikey's number as my heart thumped nervously, and Markus shot me another pissy look from across the locker room where he was talking to Antone.

"Michael Vining," Mikey said breathlessly when he picked up. I could hear wind and people talking, so I assumed he was outside or maybe in the car.

"Hey, baby," I said, closing my eyes to drink in the sound of his familiar voice. I missed him terribly.

"Tiller?" Mikey sounded surprised. "I thought you had a game. What time is it?"

"I'm in the locker room, but I wanted to catch you really quick before I dressed out. God, it's so good to hear your voice. How's your trip so far?" I wasn't sure why I was starting with a stupid question, but it just popped out. Maybe I needed another minute to get the balls to ask him about his dad.

Mikey hesitated. "Good. I'm on my way to give..." The rest of his words were muffled. I stuck a finger in my other ear to block out the noise from the guys around me.

"What? I didn't hear that last part."

"Sorry, was asking Truman to wait a minute. I'm just dropping—" The sudden sound of a car honk followed by screeching tires came through the line. It was followed by a gasp and Mikey's scream, the loud clatter of the phone hitting the pavement, and then muffled shouts and unidentifiable noises.

"Mikey!" I yelled into the phone. "Mikey, what happened?" The locker room around me went silent as I stood from my bench. It was a car crash, obvious from the horrible noises. "Mikey!"

"Tiller?" His voice sounded weak and faraway. I could barely hear him. "Call 911. Near... near... spice shop..."

Peevy's hand was on my shoulder, and his face was creased with worry. "What can I do?" he whispered.

My voice was thick with shock. "Find a number for 911 in Aster Valley, Colorado. I don't know how, but call them and..." My brain scrambled to think of what the name of Truman's shop was. "The Honeyed Lemon shop on the main street there."

Peevy immediately pulled out his phone, and I realized several other players were doing the same. I hoped they were trying to help rather than gossiping.

"Mikey?" I begged into the phone. "Are you hurt? Tell me you're okay."

All I could hear were the sounds of people shouting, muffled noises of people possibly trying to help, and other unidentifiable commotion. I kept my eyes closed as if that would help me hear better, but the only distinct voice I could hear was my own ragged one begging Mikey to answer me.

At one point, I thought I heard the sound of sirens. It was quickly followed by a more authoritative voice I hoped like hell was a cop or EMT. Part of me wanted to shout into the phone, demanding answers, but the rational part of me knew to stay quiet and let them do whatever needed doing.

Someone's strong hands guided me back down to the bench where I sat numbly and waited. People moved around me in the locker room, getting into uniform and talking quietly among themselves. Someone asked someone else if they should tell Coach, and Markus and Peevy both hissed a "no" before Markus suggested moving me to a separate room.

Derek Mopellei squatted in front of me and reached up to quickly thumb tears off my face I didn't even know had fallen. "He's going to be okay," he said in his calm manner. "Deep breath."

Finally, after an impossibly long time of listening to what was now clearly emergency response personnel, someone picked up the phone. "Hello?"

My entire body flooded with fear until I gagged with it. "Mikey, I croaked. "My... my Mikey. Is he okay? Is he...?"

"Sir, two hit-and-run casualties are being taken to Aster Valley Emergency. That's all I can tell you at this time."

"Is he—" The call cut off so quickly, I grunted in surprise. I tried calling it back, but there was no answer. "Fuck!" I shouted, wanting to hurl my phone across the room in helpless frustration.

Suddenly, I realized I was wasting time. I shot to my feet and grabbed my bag out of my locker cubby before bolting toward the door. A shout of "Where the hell are you going?" rang out as I sailed by. Markus tried to stop me, to tell me I needed to dress out in my uniform for the game, but I shoved him away. "Stop!" he tried again, so I spun around to face him.

"I'm going to Colorado. If you think this game is more important to me than that man, you're mistaken," I hissed at him. "And if Coach wants to fight me on this, I'm happy to trot out all of the medical specialists who advised me against playing. Now, go get Coach and tell him his son has been in an accident."

Antone's eyes were big. He stepped up next to Markus and shook his head. "No fucking way, man. We've been through this before. When we were in the playoffs against the Broncos—this was before you—his boy Eddie was in a motorcycle accident. Broke his tibia and needed surgery. We interrupted the game to tell Coach about it, and he still hasn't forgiven us. We lost by one point. He made it very clear that as long as Eddie was in good hands with the right medical care, there was no reason to interrupt the game. Fretting at his bedside could wait. Those were his exact words. Mikey understands that. He understands there's nothing Coach can do to help him in a hospital. He's no doctor."

Markus nodded. Even our kicker, old-timer Trace Elliott, nodded aggressively over Markus's shoulder. "He's right. Coach will fuck you up if you bring him this shit right now."

I stared at them, unable to grasp not wanting to know if my child was okay or not.

Markus continued. "What I'm saying is, Mikey will understand if you get to his hospital bed at midnight instead of eight. What's the difference?" He frowned and reached for his phone. "I'll find someone to go be with him."

I yanked his phone out of his hand and was about to throw it on the floor when I had an idea. "Not necessary. There's nothing you can say to stop me from going to see Mikey right now." I tried to say it in a calm voice, but I didn't feel one speck of calm on the inside. I felt terrified and angry. Terrified for Mikey and so damned angry that his parents wouldn't feel the same sense of urgency to get to him.

I hoped he never found out. My heart broke for him. He thought *my* dad placed too much emphasis on football, but it was nothing like this.

I made eye contact with Markus as I handed him back his phone. "You need to do whatever it takes to get me on a private jet from Buffalo to Aster Valley, Colorado, ASAP. If you do this for me, I will forgive you for telling me not to do this."

His jaw ticked for a beat before he nodded and took the phone.

I bolted out of the stadium while arranging for a ride on an app. As soon as that was done, I dialed Winter Waites.

"Hey, Tiller. I hope this means they're not playing you tonight." He sounded happy and relaxed which meant he didn't know what had happened.

"I need your help. Mike—" My voice cracked. I swallowed and banged the phone against my forehead before trying again. "Mikey was in some kind of accident in front of Truman's shop. He's being taken to the hospital. Can you... can—" I sucked in a breath.

His voice was all business when he cut in. "Yes. I'm on my way there right now. I'll let you know as soon as I find out what's going on."

"Thank you."

"Hang in there, okay? He'll be in good hands. It's a regional hospital, but it's top-notch. And they have a helicopter if he needs to go somewhere else."

I nodded and hung up before dialing my mom. Meanwhile, my car pulled up and I hopped in, grateful the app already told the driver where to take me.

"Honey, I thought you were playing in the game tonight?" Mom asked when she answered. "Your father's all set up in the den already, watching the pregame."

"Something's happened. Can you go to Aster Valley? Mikey's been in some kind of accident."

"Oh no, what kind of accident?" She called out to my father in the background, and within seconds, he was on the line. "Tiller? Where is he? We'll head there straightaway."

I blew out a breath of bittersweet relief. If only Mikey's own parents would react the same way. "Thank you. I needed to hear that. Thank you."

When I got off the phone with them, I tried Sam. There was no answer, so I left him a detailed voice message. I bolted out of the car with a shouted thanks to the driver and raced inside to discover Markus had worked his magic. I practically walked right onto a small jet, and within twenty minutes, we were hauling ass down the runway.

The flight seemed to take days, but when we finally landed, I was grateful to see it was at a little private airstrip just outside of Aster Valley. Gentry stood on the tarmac by the small terminal building in a familiar moss-green parka. As soon as he saw me step off the plane, he jogged out to greet me.

"He's okay," he called as soon as he was within shouting distance.

I almost stumbled over my feet in relief. Gent gave me a strong hug and told me again. "He's okay. Just a broken arm and some bumps and scrapes. Winter is with him right now. Let's go."

We hopped in his SUV and made our way through the dark night to the small, well-lit emergency room at Aster Valley Med. On the short drive, Gent explained that a drunk driver had careened off the road onto the sidewalk right where Truman was standing. Pim and

Mikey saw it coming and jumped forward to grab Truman out of the way. The car hit Pim and Mikey as they shielded Truman.

"Jesus, is Pim alright?"

Gent nodded. "Yeah, Bill's with him. Pim's bruised up from the fall, so they're keeping him overnight to keep an eye on him. Same with Mikey. Just as a precaution, though."

I blew out a breath and tried to relax now that I knew no one was in a life-or-death situation. But arriving there was still stressful. Was there anyone on earth who didn't get nervous in hospitals? Medical professionals, presumably. But the rest of us, especially those of us who had careers based on staying injury-free, had visceral reactions to the sights and sounds. I was certainly not immune. But never had I expected my next trip to a hospital to be for someone else—for Mikey.

Gent led me to his room and held the door for me.

Mikey was tiny in the bed. One side of his face was covered in bruises and scratches, and a purple cast covered his left arm and part of his hand.

His eyes moved to me when I let out an unexpected sound of relief. He was here. He was alive. He was talking.

"Tiller?" He sounded like he didn't believe it was really me. I advanced on him, trying to figure out how to grab him up and hold him tight without hurting him.

As I came closer, he realized it really was me. The sound he let out was almost feral, like a cry of pain and relief all mixed into one. He reached out his arms for me and burst into tears. Winter, who'd been holding his good hand, moved out of the way as I leaned in to wrap my arms around Mikey.

"Shh, I'm here. You're okay, you're okay," I repeated against his ear. His entire body shook against me, and he winced when he tried to move. I carefully let him go and moved my hands to cup his face, smoothing tears away with my thumbs the same way Mopellei had done for me earlier. "I love you."

Mikey's eyes widened comically in surprise. "Wh-what?"

The band finally loosened from around my chest. I had everything I needed right here. "I love you so much. I'm in love with you."

His gaze slid to the television on the wall, where I could see he had the game playing. "But..."

I gently angled him back to meet my eyes. "No buts. I don't care about the game... or your father. He can send me to the moon for all I care. I'll finish out the remainder of my contract and then reassess. With you."

He cried into my neck while Winter and Gent moved toward the door. I waved them back. "Stay," I said. "I want you to stay so I can thank you."

Winter smiled. "Your parents went down to grab some coffee. Why don't I go find them?"

My mom's voice carried from the doorway. "No need, dear. We're back." Mom and Dad bustled into the room with trays full of coffee cups.

Dad went around to the other side of the bed and reached out to squeeze Mikey's leg. "I thought you said you didn't need Tiller here? Said you'd be fine without him. I distinctly remember hearing you telling Winter to make sure Tiller stayed in Buffalo for the game. And now here you are acting like he's important or something."

I could tell he was teasing Mikey, and seeing my dad smile down at Mikey with affection made me want to cry like a baby. At no point had I thought my father would second-guess my decision to leave the game. My dad may have loved football, but he loved his family more.

Mikey scoffed and moved his arm as if to point. "Moose, he's important. Okay? I've been in love with your son for a long time. And you know that. I *told* you—" He winced and put his arm back down.

My heart went nuts at his confession, and I couldn't hold back a grin. When Mikey caught it, he smiled through the pain and rolled his eyes.

"Yes, you big dummy. I love you. Don't act so surprised."

"But I am. And I can be surprised and happy at the same time," I said.

His eyes turned soft. Maybe it was the pain meds, but I chose to believe it was love. "I love you," he said again.

I leaned over and kissed him carefully before pulling back and meeting his eyes. "I love you, too. And I don't like being apart."

He shook his head and then smiled. "Me neither. But I have a plan."

I had one, too, and I couldn't wait to tell him all about it.

24

MIKEY

I must have drifted off because when I woke up, the hospital room was much darker. Only a small light over a nearby sink was on, and Tiller sat in a recliner he'd pulled alongside the bed. He was dozing with his socked feet propped up on the edge of my bed.

My heart soared as I stared at him. His hair was messy, and his beard scruff darkened his jaws. At some point he'd removed his button-down dress shirt and suit pants and changed into a Riggers hoodie and matching track pants. I recognized his open gym bag on the floor nearby and realized he'd probably come straight from the stadium in Buffalo.

The television played silently on the wall, and familiar sports-casters talked each other's ears off as the day's sports scores crawled along the bottom of the screen. I didn't have my glasses on to read what they said, but I hoped for Tiller's sake the Riggers had won the game against the Bills.

Actually... fuck that. Now that I thought about it, I didn't really care. I was tired of caring about football. I wanted Tiller to be happy. That was all. If that meant the Riggers needed to defeat the Bills, then I hope they had. But if he didn't care, as he'd said earlier, then I didn't care either.

I needed to be honest with him, though. He needed to know what I'd done, how I'd stupidly gone behind his back and made a deal with the devil. His missing a game could have possibly been excused, but missing it to be with me? No way. My father was going to rain down punishment on all of us for that. Especially if he'd lost his precious game and his chance at the playoffs.

"You hurting, baby?" His voice was rough and grumbly from sleep. "Want me to call the nurse?"

He stretched and dropped his feet to the floor before reaching for my hand. His skin was warm, and his grip was gentle and familiar. My eyes smarted again. "I'm okay." I swallowed and took a breath. "I need to tell you something."

His body stiffened in his seat. I hoped like hell he wasn't going to hate me for admitting how weak I'd been.

"What is it?"

"It's about why I wasn't answering your calls and stuff. Why I left Houston without saying goodbye."

Tiller's face relaxed, and he leaned in closer. "I know what happened with your dad, sweetheart. I know about the threats."

His words surprised me. How on earth did he know what my dad had said? Had Coach threatened him, too?

"How?" I asked. "Did he say something to you?" If so, I was going to kill him even worse than I already planned.

"No. I think you accidentally texted Sam." He held up a hand. "And before you get mad at Sam for telling me, you need to know I was beside myself with worry I'd done or said something to run you off. I was in a really bad place. That's the only reason Sam finally caved and told me what he knew."

I reached for his hand and brought it to my mouth for a kiss. "I don't want you to be traded away."

"He's not going to trade me, Mikey. I'm the highest-rated wide receiver in the league. He needs me more than I need him, and we both know it. I wish you'd come to me about this."

Tiller studied me for a minute while I contemplated his words. "Mikey, are you worried about the cookbook? Because it's a good thing for the league in general. They're always looking for marketing opportunities like this. I don't think they're going to let your dad pull team support from the project. And if they do, you're still going to kick ass with it. You have so much support already from lots of people in professional sports in Houston. Even if the league and the team don't endorse it, the individuals can still provide quotes for the cover, right?"

I nodded, feeling a little clearer-headed than before. "No. The editor said they have contacts at the league and have talked to them already. I think it's fine."

Tiller's grin was huge. "See? That's great. Everything's going to be fine."

But it wasn't. Not really. Because after everything that had happened with my father, I didn't have any plans to go back to Houston anytime soon. I simply couldn't face him, and I honestly wanted nothing to do with the Riggers either. The team and the game had taken too much of my family's attention over the years, and I needed time to finally let myself process it.

I needed to mourn the loss of the father I'd never had but always wished I did.

I swallowed. "Did... did the team win in Buffalo?"

He ran his fingers through his hair. "Yeah. Thank god. Maybe the fallout of my absence will be a little better because of it. Brent and Mopellei came through with some great plays, and..."

As rude as it was, I let myself drift off while he told me about the game. I honestly didn't care. If Tiller didn't play in it, I no longer gave a shit about football. I cared about *him*, not the game, to the point I worried it might be a deal breaker between us.

Football was his life, his gift. It was my albatross. It was the thing that had taken my father from me my whole life and had almost taken Tiller from me, might *still* take Tiller from me.

His hand was warm on my forehead as he began to stroke my face and hair. "Sleep, baby."

But I couldn't. I knew tomorrow was going to bring a heapload of trouble. My father, Tiller's agent, and whatever other doses of reality I wasn't lucid enough to think of at the moment. I needed to find a way to let Tiller know I understood how important his job was and I'd do anything in my power not to stand in the way of it.

~

When I woke up again, Tiller was talking to the nurse about discharge instructions. They did the whole wheelchair routine, and Moose was out front waiting for us in Jill's minivan. The drive to the lodge was fairly easy, and when I entered the house, I felt the bittersweet realization this would be one of my last times "coming home" to it.

"They took the lodge off the market," I told Tiller. "I found out earlier this week." I'd texted him about the Civettis having a family emergency, but I hadn't explained about any of the rest of it.

"I know," he said, helping me down the hall with an arm around my back. I noticed the door to the locked bedroom wing on the far side of the entryway was open, and light flooded in from big windows looking out of the front of the house.

"Oh. That's nice. How'd you open that? Did Stacy come by?" I wondered if I'd have the energy to snoop once I took a nap.

"C'mere," Tiller murmured, steering me down the sunny hallway. We passed several bedrooms with sturdy four-poster beds and cozy furnishings. It gave me mixed feelings about losing out on the opportunity to live here and run it for the Civettis. But I had a plan.

"I found a place I want you to look at," I told Tiller, following him past a small wood-paneled office and into what looked like a large solarium at the end of the hallway. "It needs some work, but I think I can get Sam to come help."

I stopped in place and stared at the room we'd stepped into. It was completely made of glass and shaped in a large oval off the end of the house. I hadn't seen it from the outside because of the angle of the room and some overgrown trees in front of it.

"Holy fuck," I breathed, walking through the sun-filled space. It was the perfect breakfast room for my dream bed-and-breakfast. The room was empty except for a small conversational grouping of two love seats on either side of a coffee table, but I could picture it filled with a hodgepodge of dining tables surrounded by comfortable chairs.

"I thought this would make a good breakfast room," Tiller said, guiding me over to sit on one of the love seats.

"Yeah. It would. For sure. It's lovely."

Tiller sat next to me and reached for my good hand. "Can you picture it?"

I let out a short laugh. "Yeah, but it hurts, you know? It's hard to imagine someone else here. I've totally fallen in love with the place. That's selfish, I know. Besides, the place I found has an awesome screened-in porch. It's a little small, but—"

He cut me off. "Okay, don't be mad," he blurted. "Now I'm worried I did the wrong thing. Fuck." He looked out the wall of windows, down at the honeyed wooden floor, and back at me before taking a breath.

"What's happening?" I asked carefully, beginning to get an idea.

"I bought this place for us," he said before wincing.

"What place?"

"This place. Rockley Lodge. I bought it. Out from under the Civettis."

I stared at him. "You what?"

"Please don't be mad. Please. Am I a controlling asshole? Do you hate me for being heavy-handed?"

Lightness and laughter bubbled up in my chest. "You bought Rockley Lodge?"

He nodded. "Kinda? I mean. Yes. I did. I bought it. It's ours. Well... technically it's yours. In a trust for you. My attorney did it. Just in case you don't want me invol—"

"*Oh my god!*" I lurched at him and crashed my lips against him, throwing my arms around his neck and trying not to feel the pain of the stretch in my shoulder and upper arm.

Tiller's strong arms banded around my back and held me tight. I laughed against his mouth as his words continued to sink in.

"It's okay?" he asked, pulling back to meet my eyes.

"You're asking if it's okay that you bought us a multimillion-dollar dream home in our new favorite place? That you invested in our future together?"

His body sagged. "Well, when you put it like that…"

"Of course I want you involved. How can you think otherwise?"

Tiller leaned in and pressed a kiss against the edge of my lips. "I need you to know, no matter what happens, you running this inn is a sure thing. Even if you decided to leave me one day—please don't, by the way—this place would continue to be yours. It's not contingent on—"

I shut him up with a kiss. My eyes smarted with happy tears. "I can't believe it was you. You're the one who bought it."

He shrugged. "Honestly, part of it was selfish. If we own the inn, we can run it the way you want. And maybe that means we can hire someone else to manage it when we're in Houston?"

The way he asked it as a question made it clear he was floating the idea of splitting our time between Houston and Aster Valley based on the season. He quickly continued. "Only for a few more years until my contract is up. After that, we can move here full-time, but I'm obligated to stay right now. It doesn't mean you have to stay with me, but…" Tiller swallowed. "But I don't want to be apart from you."

"I don't want to be apart from you either. I was going to buy a little place for us where I could run my catering business in the off-season and we could still spend the season in Houston. It sounds like we had the same idea, only… I don't want to go back right away."

"Whatever you want is fine with me," he murmured, dropping a kiss against my temple. "Is it because of your dad?"

I turned my face into the familiar warmth of his neck. "My mom called to ask if I could water her plants while the family was in Galveston, I'd told her I was in the hospital in Colorado, and she'd said that was fine, she could ask Mrs. Nesbit, and she hoped I felt better soon. My father didn't get on the phone at all."

Tiller leaned back and pulled me into his chest. "Oh, baby. I'm so, so sorry. You deserve a better family than that."

I thought of Moose and Jill, who'd already made themselves at home in the lodge and had gone above and beyond making me feel loved and cared for. "Maybe I can have yours one day," I said softly.

I felt the huge grin against my head before the deep rumble of his voice hit me. "Only if one day is today. What's mine is yours. I hope you know that. This... this is it for me, Mikey. You and me. This place. Our dreams. Together."

My heart felt like I was going to overflow. "It's going to be amazing. I can't believe we own our very own lodge in Aster Valley."

"And, ah... and the ski resort."

I craned my neck to look up at him. "What do you mean?"

"The slopes. And the lifts. They were all part of the deal. So... congratulations? We are now the proud owners of Rockley Mountain and Aster Valley Ski Resort." He reached his arm out toward the pristine slopes that were barely visible from this angle.

I sat up and stared at him. "You had to buy a *ski resort* to get this place?" My voice sounded ten times higher than I'd intended.

"I didn't have to. But wanted to. I figured one day, when I retire, it'd be nice to have my very own place to snowboard. And I want to teach you to ski and bring our nieces and nephews here to learn, too. And between us and our new friends, I thought it would be a nice challenge for us in the next few years when we don't have to be in Houston. While you get this place up and running, I'll work on the ski resort. I thought we might make an attractive offer to Sam to come help us. What do you think? Want to bring the alpine industry back to Aster Valley?"

I thought of this gorgeous and cozy lodge, the impeccable commercial kitchen, the new friends who'd already welcomed us with open arms, and the old friend who'd jump into this with us in a heartbeat. I thought of being closer to Moose and Jill and having Steph and Mark's family in our lives. I thought of keeping the house in Houston and still being able to have Tiller's teammates over for dinner during the season.

I clapped a hand in front of my mouth to keep from squealing in excitement. Happy tears slid out of the edges of my eyes.

"Oh hell yes," I whispered. "So much."

Tiller's hands cupped my face, and the expression of love on his face overwhelmed me. "We're going to have an amazing life together, Michael Vining. You with me?"

I remembered the night we first got together in this house. The night we finally crossed the boundaries we'd tried to keep between us. "Mm-hm. Yeah. Yep. Yes. That," I said, teasing him with my silly babbled words from that night. "I would like that. Please. Yes, please."

EPILOGUE
TRUMAN - SIX MONTHS LATER

I watched Tiller throw bean bags toward a row of buckets while Mikey egged him on.

"Thankfully, you catch better than you throw," Mikey teased. "Your contract would be worth about a buck fifty if you were a quarterback instead of wide receiver."

Tiller shot him a look and resumed his laser focus on the festival game. I could tell the person manning the booth was less than impressed. Barney was already annoyed at having been suckered into running the bean bag toss booth in the first place, but dealing with the man Barney referred to as "Mister Moneybags" was probably pushing all of his buttons past the red zone.

I made a mental note to have a "headache" tonight. The last thing I needed was Barney Balderson pressuring me for personal intimacies when he was already in a mood. I wasn't the personal intimacies type on the best of days, but if Barney was in a certain funk, I'd learned early on to stay away.

"If you'd let me have a second helping of egg surprise for breakfast," Tiller complained, "I would have made the shot."

Mikey let out a bark of laughter and pinched Tiller's ass right as he let loose another bean bag. The missile sailed past Barney's head, nearly knocking his driving cap off.

"Mother of pearl!" Barney shouted in disgust.

Winter Waites walked up and handed me a raspberry slushy from one of the other booths. "What'd I miss? Mr. Balderson looks like he's about to blow a gasket."

I sighed and turned away. "Tiller and Mikey are so perfect for each other. Don't you think?"

Winter's forehead crinkled. "I do. They're very different, though. I know they spend a lot of effort making it work."

Gentry walked up and put a soft cotton hoodie over Winter's shoulders. "There. But if you need anything else out of the car, you're on your own. I had to pass the entire cheerleading squad on the way to *and* from, and every single one of them asked me to sign their phone cases. What even is that? I wish there was still such a thing as CDs."

Winter shrugged into the jacket before zipping it up and kissing his famous husband on the cheek. "I'd say I owed you one, but I had to help your uncle Doran do groin stretches last week. We're still so far away from being even, it's not even funny."

Gent let out a deep belly laugh and wrapped his arm around Winter's shoulders. "Point taken. Maybe I'll cook you dinner tonight to help make up for it."

Winter rubbed his stomach. "After all this fair food? No way. Besides, we're headed up to the lodge tomorrow night for Mikey's big cookbook party, remember? I'm fasting until then to make room for everything he's making."

Tiller botched his final bean bag before the two of them turned to join us. Barney shot me a look of stark disapproval. He didn't like it when I "consorted with the town neophytes." I didn't much care what he thought. Which, of course, made me feel guilty.

Barney was good to me, mostly. He kept the Stanner brothers off my back as much as he could, and when I did have an unfortunate run-in with one of them, it was nice having someone's shoulder to cry on.

Not that anyone knew what had happened back in December with the hit-and-run. No, that was a secret I'd carry to my grave. The last thing I wanted was to start something or bring undue attention to myself here in Aster Valley.

Mikey was obviously in a great mood. His cookbook had been finalized and was scheduled to launch at the beginning of football season. He'd received his first early copies in the mail, so we were all celebrating at the lodge so we could ooh and ahh over it. I couldn't wait. My personal favorite recipe of his from the book was the Tom Billing Power-Up Muffins, not because they tasted great, which they did, but because the name of the recipe made Tiller adorably jealous for some reason.

I lifted the slushy to my mouth and took a sip of the sweet, cool drink.

Mikey said, "Sam's plane lands tonight, so he'll be at the party tomorrow."

The blue drink went both down my throat and up my nose at the same time. I choked and sputtered and coughed. While everyone around me physically scrambled to help me not die, I mentally scrambled to come up with an excuse to bail on the party.

Sam Rigby was going to be there. The Sam whose dark stare penetrated my very soul. Or would have, if I'd ever actually made eye contact with him. The man scared the stuffing out of me.

He'd visited Tiller and Mikey once before. There'd been a snow-storm in early March, and I'd nearly buried myself in the drifts outside the shop when I'd finally finished work for the day. When I finally dug my Subaru out of the snow enough to attempt the drive home, I'd caught sight of a man on a ladder in front of the diner.

In a blizzard.

The stranger had worn well-worn jeans that hugged his... partic-ular body parts, just so. And a beaten-up leather jacket that had seemed similarly molded to his form. A black watch cap, black gloves, and black leather boots had been the only other thing he wore in deference to the weather as he fixed the letters on the sign. Someone had swapped them with letters from Bearwood Realty next door until the diner's sign had read Mucho Dinero instead of Mustache Diner.

I hadn't known who he was at the time, but when I'd asked Bill about it the following day, he'd told me it was Sam Rigby, the contractor who'd come from Houston to help Mikey and Tiller with some repairs at their new place.

After that, my eyes were like little radar arrays, constantly pinging the area in search of the leather-clad stranger with the nice... body parts. When I'd seen him eating at the diner one morning with Mikey and Tiller, I'd darned near hyperventilated in my attempt to get out of there before being seen.

It hadn't worked.

Mikey had tried to call me over to introduce me to their friend, but the scowly way the man had been peering at the diner menu had been enough to intimidate me right out the front door on fire-fueled feet.

No, thank you, sir. I'd had enough scary, biker-type guys around to last me a lifetime.

So there was no way in Hello Kitty I was going to a party where Sam Rigby was going to be.

"I have to wash my hair," I explained.

Everyone around me stopped talking and craned their necks in an effort to look at me like I was an ancient alien.

"Um..." I panic-shopped my brain for a more reasonable excuse. "I have to also... watch paint dry. And after that... I'm..."

I spotted Barney giving a small child a long-suffering sigh at the bean bag booth.

"I'm planning on giving Mr. Balderson my virginity!"

Finally, a believable excuse. I beamed my success at all of my friends. Until I caught Barney's oddly creepy wink from across the way and shuddered. Sometimes my mouth made promises my... particular body parts had no intention of keeping.

I sighed and turned back to Mikey. "Fine. I'll be there. What can I bring?"

Read Truman and Sam's story next. *Sweet as Honey,* the second book in the Aster Valley series, is available to order now.

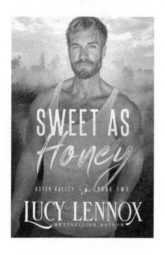

LETTER FROM LUCY

Dear Reader,

Thank you for reading *Right as Raine*.

In the next book, Truman can't avoid the gruff and standoffish Sam Rigby for long. But maybe the muscled stranger isn't as intimidating as Truman originally thought. Maybe he's exactly the protector Truman has dreamed of all along. *Sweet as Honey* comes out April 6, 2021. All Lucy Lennox novels can be read on their own so find a story that appeals to you and dive right in!

Please take a moment to write a review of this book on Amazon and Goodreads. Reviews can make all of the difference in helping a book show up in book searches.

Feel free to stop by www.LucyLennox.com and drop me a line or visit me on social media. To see inspiration photographs for all of my novels, visit my Pinterest boards.

Finally, I have a fantastic reader group on Facebook. Come join us for exclusive content, early cover reveals, hot pics, and a whole lotta fun. Lucy's Lair can be found here.

Happy reading!

Lucy

ABOUT THE AUTHOR

Lucy Lennox is a mother of three sarcastic kids. Born and raised in the southeast, she now resides outside of Atlanta finally putting good use to that English Lit degree.

Lucy enjoys naps, pizza, and procrastinating. She is married to someone who is better at math than romance but who makes her laugh every single day and is the best dancer in the history of ever.

She stays up way too late each night reading gay romance because it's simply the best thing ever.

For more information and to stay updated about future releases, please sign up for Lucy's author newsletter here.

Connect with Lucy on social media:
www.LucyLennox.com
Lucy@LucyLennox.com